The Trouble with Cowboys

ALSO BY VICTORIA JAMES

The Trouble with Cowboys

VICTORIA JAMES

Copyright © 2019 by Victoria James. All rights reserved, including the right to reproduce, distribute, or transmit in any form or by any means. For information regarding subsidiary rights, please contact the Publisher.

Entangled Publishing, LLC
2614 South Timberline Road
Suite 109
Fort Collins, CO 80525
Visit our website at www.entangledpublishing.com.

Amara is an imprint of Entangled Publishing, LLC.

Edited by Liz Pelletier
Cover design by Hang Le
Cover art by Cecilie_Arcurs/iStock
Paul Knightly/iStock
CampPhoto/iStock
Interior design by Heather Howland

Print ISBN 978-1-64063-541-8
ebook ISBN 978-1-64063-542-5

Manufactured in the United States of America

First Edition April 2019

AMARA

To Liz Pelletier: Thank you for believing in me six years ago and publishing my first book…and thank you for believing in me now and publishing the characters and the story of my heart.

To Louise Fury: Thank you for your guidance, your wisdom, and your encouragement.

CHAPTER ONE

*T*y Donnelly would rather be knee-deep in cow manure than back in his hometown of Wishing River, Montana.

He pulled his trusty Chevy into an empty parking spot outside Tilly's Diner, a long-standing town landmark, and sat still for a minute. Steady rain hammered against the roof of his truck and streamed down his windows as he peered out at the familiar sights of the town he hadn't seen in eight years. It was too early for stores and most businesses to be open—except Tilly's. Some things didn't change.

They probably still had the best coffee, the best breakfast, and the best gossip on Main Street.

He'd never been one for nostalgia, but it crept up his arm like a fast-moving spider, startling him. It was the damn town. It held too many memories, too many friends, too many secrets. He should just keep on going to the ranch and face everything he was hiding from. But after driving all night, he needed a coffee. Or maybe he needed an excuse to delay seeing his father. Even facing a diner full of gawking townspeople was more appealing than seeing his father.

Their final day together, his father's last words to him had changed his entire life, and he'd been running from them for eight years.

Hell. He ran his hand through his hair and glanced over at Tilly's again before putting on his cowboy hat and finally pushing his door open. Cold rain soaked him as he ran up the steps to the diner. He pulled the door open, and a blast of warmth and a good dose of reality greeted him as he stepped inside. His past slapped him in the face, a little too harshly for a guy going on no sleep. Flatware clanked against dishes, and the animated conversation dwindled to that of a whispering brook. He walked forward, sure to keep his head up but eye contact to a minimum in the packed diner.

Making his way around the round tables with their vinyl-backed chairs, he gave an occasional nod and tip of his hat but made sure not to stop. By the time he reached the long counter at the far end of the diner, he felt as though he'd walked through fire. He took a deep breath and held on to it for a moment as he recognized the man sitting at the counter. Dean Stanton. One of his former best friends—and now his father's doctor. He hadn't expected to see him this soon.

"Dean," he said, bracing his arms on the counter. Dean gave him a nod like he was a stranger. He hadn't seen him in eight years and hadn't had any contact until Dean had called, telling him his father had suffered a stroke. He could still hear the censure in his friend's voice. Dean had also made it pretty clear he was calling as his father's doctor, not as his old buddy. He looked the same—older, sure. Judging by his clean-shaven appearance and expensive-looking clothes, he seemed like he had his life together, too. Ty was the one still in faded jeans and an old cowboy hat.

He kept his eyes trained on the kitchen door and sure as hell hoped Tilly would come out of there soon, because he needed a coffee and then he needed to get the hell out of Dodge. When the door swung open a minute later, it wasn't Tilly. He didn't know who the waitress was. He may have been driving all night, his eyes sore and tired, but there was no stopping the instincts he was born with as he gazed appreciatively at the woman in front of him. Her honey-colored hair was pulled back in a ponytail, and she had familiar, large chocolate-colored eyes. She was wearing a T-shirt with *Tilly's* scrolled across the front, the shirt clinging to very nice curves. Her jeans were dark and showed off nicely rounded hips. When his eyes traveled back up her curvy length, her brown eyes were on his, and any of the warmth he'd detected was replaced by an unapologetic disdain.

"What can I get you?" she asked, now wiping the counter and not making eye contact with him.

"Large coffee to go?" He ignored the various glass-domed cake stands filled with muffins, doughnuts, and pies, even though he hadn't eaten in twelve hours. Tilly was known for the best and freshest baked goods for miles. He just wasn't in the mood for eating.

She didn't actually give him an answer, only sort of gave a nod. He noticed she glanced over at Dean before grabbing a white paper cup and pouring the coffee. She handed him the drink and a plastic lid. "That'll be a dollar and fifty cents. Cream and sugar are over there," she said, pointing to the far side of the counter.

He laid the correct change out in front of him. "How's Tilly?"

"Dead," she said, walking away with the carafe

of coffee in her hands. Damn. He hadn't expected that. He'd kinda assumed Tilly would always be here. He glanced over at the waitress again, studying her profile as she refilled Dean's cup. Hell. He knew her. Tilly's granddaughter. She'd always been at the diner with her grandmother. As a little kid and then later as a teenager. Now she'd turned into this gorgeous woman. It was well known that Tilly's daughter had saddled her with her baby and taken off. No one really knew much about her after that.

It was sad to hear Tilly was gone. She had always had a warm smile and a kind word for him. So maybe some things did change.

He put the lid on his steaming coffee and turned around, no need for cream or sugar. Of course, the entire damn restaurant was still staring at him like a lame cow being judged at the county fair.

Pushing open the front door with his palm, he jogged out to his truck, happy to be away from there. Now the last thing separating him from his past was the drive to his father's ranch. He pulled out of his parking spot and drove down Main Street, Wishing River.

Eight years and barely a thing had changed.

The old buildings still had that charm that beckoned tourists and artists, especially during the summer and fall. But this wasn't his home anymore; that much was clear.

He made the drive out to the ranch in record time, the need to get this over with encouraging him to drive faster. The winding country roads were virtually empty, and the rugged beauty of the land hit him—as a kid he'd sworn he'd never leave Montana. Wishing

River was nestled between the jagged peaks of the Bitterroot Mountains to the west and the Sapphire Mountains to the east. The valleys held the fall foliage like a secret prize from the other areas of Montana that couldn't boast the range of color they had here.

The rolling green hills, the towering trees, the pastures, the wide-open sky, they were as familiar to him as breathing. But something wasn't right.

Easing his foot off the gas, he slowed as the old three-rail wood fence bordering his family's sprawling ranch came into view. A couple of the posts were down, some in need of maintenance, but it was fall, and that's when all the maintenance usually happened around the ranch.

He pulled into the long gravel drive, dust and pebbles kicking up behind him, and he didn't bother avoiding the potholes, the mud splashing onto his already filthy truck. The pit in his stomach seemed to grow exponentially, knowing his mother wasn't at the door, knowing his father…was ill.

Once parked, he grabbed his keys and coffee and went to face his past.

His boots crunched against the gravel, and he took a deep breath. The red barn in the distance was just screaming for a coat of paint, and he couldn't make out any movement around there or the bunkhouse way in the distance, but he knew all the cowboys were out by now. He was the only one not working this time of morning.

The large, sprawling covered porch didn't have a single plant. The paint was chipping on the railing and spindles, and the shutters and windows looked like they hadn't been cleaned in years. His mother would have been mortified.

He rolled his shoulders as he stared at the faded red front door. He gave a knock and then walked inside. The smell of coffee greeted him as he did a quick survey from the front rug. The house was the same. Except it didn't have that welcoming, shiny clean feel from when his mother had been alive. Now it was obvious a bachelor lived here. The curtains weren't drawn, there was a fine layer of dust, and no fresh flowers.

"Is that you, Tyler?" Heavy footsteps approached, and he stood like a stranger in his childhood home.

"It is," he called out.

Mrs. Busby—one of his parents' close friends— appeared from the door to the living room. "Well, aren't you a sight for sore, sad eyes?"

He took off his hat and smiled. "Hi, Mrs. Busby."

Her hand was on her chest, and she gave him his first smile since coming home. "It's been a long time, child. I'm so happy you're here. I prayed for this, for you to return to Wishing River. You are just what your father needs. Better than any kind of medicine."

He swallowed down the lump in his throat, along with a hefty dose of guilt. He wasn't so sure he was going to do his father any good, but he was facing his responsibilities. His father was now his responsibility. All of it was. He owed it to him; despite everything, the man had raised him, and now it was his turn to take care of his old man.

"Well, I hope he agrees," he said, shoving his free hand into the front pocket of his jeans.

"Of course he does," Mrs. Busby replied, placing her hands on her hips. The older woman was almost exactly how he remembered her, maybe a little wider in what had already been ample hips.

"How's he doing?" he asked, feeling awkward in his childhood home.

She stepped out into the hallway, shutting the French door that led to the living room, where he assumed his father was sleeping. "He's stable. It could have been much, much worse. I'll let Dr. Stanton fill you in when he comes tonight for his daily visit."

Dr. Stanton—aka Dean. How the hell had his friend gone from troublemaker to doctor? But he'd always known Dean was going to do big things. He'd come from a long line of doctors and successful ranchers, and the guy had never strayed from his goals, no matter the amount of trouble they'd gotten themselves into as teens.

He stared down at his worn boots for a second as a wave of insecurity washed through him. "Dean comes every night?"

She nodded, her oversize gray curls standing still despite the motion. "Yes. On his way home from the office, he stops in and checks on your father."

Ty gave a nod. "You mentioned on the phone that you have a nurse who comes by?"

"Yes, yes. Two different nurses, one for morning and one for night. I usually drop by in the morning before church. But I'm only a phone call away, and if you need anything, you call me. We've rented a hospital bed for him so he can rest comfortably, and it helps with sitting up and such."

"Thank you," he said, following her into the kitchen when she motioned.

"You don't have to thank me. Your father and I go way back," she said. He knew they did. When Mrs. Busby's husband had been alive, the couple would often come over and have dinner or drinks with his parents. They had all been best friends. He could still remember hearing laughter into the late hours of the night. He hated thinking how things changed, how quickly time passed.

"I'd offer you coffee, but I see you already picked up a cup," she said, placing her empty mug into the dishwasher.

"It was a long night." He glanced in the direction of the living room, dreading having to go through with this but wanting to get it over with now. "Is he sleeping, or can I go see him?"

Walking forward, she placed a hand on his arm. "Of course you can. Now, don't expect him to be… like the man you remember. Martin is holding his own, and Dr. Stanton said he's very lucky that Lainey found him when she did, or it could have been much worse."

He cleared his throat. "Lainey?"

She angled her head. "You remember—Tilly's granddaughter?"

The image of the gorgeous blonde with the pissed-off gaze flashed across his mind. "Yeah. Right. Lainey. Where…did she find him?"

She shook her head and then did the sign of the cross, her dark-brown eyes filling with tears. "By the fence close to the road. I think he was trying to fix it. Apparently, he was unconscious when she found him, called the paramedics, and they coached her on what to do until they arrived. That sweet girl rode in the back of the ambulance with him and didn't leave his side." She sniffled and produced a handkerchief from those velour pants and blew her nose loudly.

Staring down at the top of her gray head, not capable of words yet, his mind flooded with questions and guilt and images of his father unconscious outside. Fixing the damn fence. There should be hired help for that. When he left eight years ago, there were thirty-five employees—any one of them could have done it. *He* should have done it. He should have been the one to help him, to be by his side in the ambulance. "He's in the living room?"

She nodded. "We did the best we could, finding a spot for him on the main floor. We figured that'd be the best place, since there's a door for privacy and it's close to the washroom. It's not perfect. Of course the house isn't exactly welcoming; I'm sorry for that. My arthritis is bad in the fall and winter, and we haven't really had time to get the place all spick-and-span."

"Don't worry," he said, wincing at the harshness in his voice. He tried to speak softly. "You've done more than enough. I can take it from here."

Her eyes softened, and she smiled at him with such sympathy and acceptance that she reminded him of his mother. She reached out and patted his arm again. "Oh my dear, we aren't going anywhere. You're going to need us. But I'm happy you're home to take the lead… And your father needs you, Tyler."

He swallowed hard against the emotion simmering inside. "Does he know I'm here?"

Her full cheeks reddened. "I…didn't know… I wanted to wait until you had arrived. I didn't say anything."

A pit formed in his stomach. She hadn't believed he'd come home. He gave her a nod. "That's fair enough. I understand. I, uh, I guess I should go see him," he said, looking toward the door.

She squeezed his arm. "Tyler, he's not the same man. He can't speak. He can't stand. He can't use his arms to eat or drink."

He was biting down hard on his back teeth. "Okay."

"The day nurse is Sheila; she's just on a call in the office. I always tell her to take a little break when I come and visit. She'll get him all washed up for the day. He's already had breakfast. Sheila stays until seven. That's when Lainey gets here. She usually stays for an hour, brings him dinner, until the night nurse, Michelle, comes in. Oh, and of course Dr. Stanton drops in after work, so anywhere between five and eight at night."

So the entire town was taking care of his father. Except him. He didn't bother asking why Lainey was bringing him dinner when he knew there was a cook in the bunkhouse for the men.

"I should probably get in there."

She nudged him forward. "I'll leave you two, then. You won't be on your own long. All our numbers are on the fridge in case of anything. I'm here if you need me, Tyler."

"Thank you," he said, forcing a smile. "I really appreciate what you've done."

She waved a hand. "Don't have to thank me — that's what friends are for. Now go on and say hi to your papa. I know seeing you will cheer him up."

Standing there, watching her gather her purse and keys, he desperately tried to figure out what the hell he was going to say to him. Eight years ago, his father had stood tall and proud. He'd been fit, the ranch keeping him active and strong. But the death of his wife had brought the man to his knees, and it had been the first time Ty had seen his father as something other than invincible—and then everything had unraveled after that. After his mother had died, he realized just how tenuous their relationship had been. But it wasn't until that last night, that last argument, that he realized why his father could let him go.

Tyler rolled his shoulders, braced himself, then slowly walked over to the living room door. Regardless of their argument, he owed his father. Tyler had always considered himself a pretty rational person, but the situation with his dad, his emotions about everything were irrational, and he didn't like that. He didn't like being at the mercy of his feelings.

He gave the door a knock and then opened it.

Nothing could have prepared him for seeing his father like this. He was lying in the hospital bed, his once-strong face now weathered and hanging loosely on one side. His eyes were closed. His hair had thinned out, the gray having given way to the white. He wasn't the man Ty knew. His father was strong. This man lying in the bed was broken.

He blinked, forcing the emotion away, not letting himself dwell on it, the passage of time, the stroke, the regrets.

Walking forward a little, he cleared his throat. "Hi, Dad," he said.

There was no indication he'd heard him. Ty walked around the bed slowly, noting the way all the old furniture had been piled up at the other end of the room. It was nothing like the living room he remembered. The plaid curtains his mother had painstakingly sewn were all closed up, hiding the large picture windows she'd loved. They had remodeled the house to his mother's liking, and she had made sure it was perfect at all times. It was nothing like the house of his childhood.

Taking a deep breath, he sat in the chair beside the bed. His gaze traveled from the disturbing image of his father sleeping to the slew of medication bottles on the nightstand. And the picture of his mother. He turned away quickly as emotion hit him in the gut.

He ran his sweaty palms down the front of his jeans and leaned back in the chair. His father's eyelids flickered but didn't open. Did his dad know he was here? Had he heard him? Heat washed over his body at the idea his father knew he was there and just didn't want to see him.

"Dad?"

His father's good hand moved slightly, and Ty stared at it as a wave of memories tumbled into his mind. He'd held that hand. As a child, he'd clung to it, hadn't given it a second thought. He'd reached for his father's hand so many times growing up, in the pastures, in the barns, when learning to ride a horse. It had always been powerful, rough, large, and Ty thought his father could save him from anything. The hand lying on top of the blanket wasn't a hand that could save him anymore. It was thin, without his tan, and with age spots and wrinkles.

He blinked past the pool of moisture in his eyes. Hell. This was hell. When had everything changed?

His childhood was over in a blink of an eye. The family of three that they had been no longer existed. He'd walked out on the man who had raised him, who had given him everything of himself, who had taught him all he needed to survive in the world. Their years together had meant nothing when the center of their world died. They hadn't been able to hold it together after she'd passed. They'd said harsh words to each other his last night at home.

They each blamed the other for her death.

But it was the last thing his father had said to him that had sent him packing, though, because the knife had been too deep.

Ty tried to breathe despite the heaviness in his chest. He cleared his throat and whispered his father's name, but it came out sounding more like a plea.

This time, his father's eyes did open. Faded blue ones, which he'd once thought so similar to his own, latched onto his. It was clear his father's mind hadn't been affected by the stroke, because the animosity shining in them took his breath away. Ty sat there, staring at his father, silently hoping for something—a softening, an indication that he was happy to see him.

"I, uh, came back as soon as I found out what happened. I'm going to stay as long as you need me. I'll help you get back on your feet, Dad." The words poured out of him, like when he was a kid and had done something wrong, how he'd always try and get out of whatever punishment was coming by making a million promises and speaking as fast as he could. His dad had never bought it.

He didn't question calling him "Dad" even though

he swore he'd never do it again. But that's what this man would always be to him, regardless of their argument, of the words that had been exchanged. He had raised him; he had loved him. He was the only father he loved.

Tyler held his breath, waiting for something from the man, just the tiniest sign that he had done the right thing by coming home.

Instead his father just shut his eyes, but not before he let him know, more powerfully than words could ever speak, that it didn't matter. None of it mattered. He didn't matter. His promises, his presence. It was all too late.

CHAPTER TWO

*L*ainey tucked a stray piece of hair back into her ponytail and stood at the door in the kitchen of the diner, waiting for Betty, her cook, to finish asking her questions about Tyler.

She loved Betty; she had been with the diner when her grandmother was still alive. If it hadn't been for her, she had no idea how she would have managed those first few months. Betty had guided her and picked up the slack when Lainey faltered.

Some mornings, that first year after Grandma Tilly had died, she would get dressed and come down to the dark diner, expecting Tilly to be in the kitchen, drinking coffee and prepping the food for the day ahead. She had never minded waking up before sunrise and sitting with her grandma at the island in the diner kitchen. Lainey would be perched on a stool, eating an egg and listening to her grandmother either dispense some words of wisdom or hum an old song under her breath.

She had never felt more alone than when Tilly died.

Lainey had started drinking coffee, mostly to try and reclaim that comforting warmth in the morning, to re-create the smells, the moments that she cherished. But coffee alone in the morning, in an empty, dark diner, only made her miss Tilly more.

She wiped the counter and turned back to Betty, who had a far-off expression on her face.

"I did manage to sneak a peek, and I swear it was

a young Martin Donnelly standing there," Betty said, pausing and taking a quick gulp of her coffee.

"I should probably get back out there," Lainey said, shooting her a smile. "I'll be sure to report all the gossip as it comes in."

"You do that, sweetie," she said, resuming her place behind the stove.

Lainey used the palm of her hand to swing the diner kitchen door open, trying to look nonchalant and not like the appearance of Tyler Donnelly meant anything to her or that she'd just been talking about him. It shouldn't. Who was the man to her, really? No one who mattered.

He was merely the older guy she'd fantasized about during her entire high school years. He was also the son of the man she'd grown to love like a father. She owed Ty's father so much, and she knew that her loyalty was to him—not the son who'd walked out on his father without a second thought. She also knew she had a biased opinion—on so many different levels. Not just because of Ty's father, but also because of her own past and her own decisions. She was loyal to a fault, and Ty obviously was not.

He'd gone away, lived out what must have been his dreams, and now he was back. The town had speculated for years what had happened to Tyler. He just got up and left one day without saying anything to anyone. No one knew where he'd been, what he'd been up to, or anything.

There was another reason she was worried about Ty being home, but she wasn't going to let herself worry about it yet. For all she knew, he might only be here for a little while and then be back on his way. There was no need to go worrying about something that might never happen. She had enough issues.

She approached Dean slowly, the stormy expression on his handsome face indicating that he'd been affected by Tyler as well. "Can I get you a refill, Dean?"

He glanced up at her, startled. If she'd been any other woman on the planet, having the attractive doctor sitting at her counter every morning would have been the highlight of her day. He was great—funny, polite, and charming. And he did absolutely nothing for her.

"No thanks, Lainey. I have to get going," Dean said, slowly standing. "I have a suspicion your day is going to be filled with gossip. I'm sure by now half the town knows Ty is back."

Lainey fingered the tie on her apron and tried to act nonchalant. "It's good he came, for Martin's sake. Better late than never," she said, watching his reaction.

Dean's face hardened. "Not this time," he said, obviously not ready to forgive his former best friend.

"Let's hope Martin will think differently. Maybe Tyler coming home is the push he needs to get better," she said, clearing their mugs and placing them in the rubber trough of dirty dishes behind the counter.

Dean shrugged. "Martin is—*was*—as tough as nails. Not exactly the forgiving type." He picked up his phone and tucked it in his jacket pocket. "Tyler will have his work cut out for him, though, if he actually intends on staying, between his dad and the condition of that ranch. Have a good day, Lainey."

She watched as he left the diner, thinking about Martin. He had always treated her so kindly. She didn't know what his relationship had been like with his son, but she couldn't imagine a father holding that much of a grudge over his only child.

The door swung open, and Mrs. Busby burst through, making a beeline for the "church table" in the front corner, perfect for people watching out the large window and people watching inside the diner. They were the loudest, funniest, and nosiest customers she had—all more than seventy, all widowed, and all best friends. They came in every morning right after church. Mrs. Busby hadn't been attending lately because she'd been busy taking care of Martin, but she was here this morning—because Tyler was home now.

Lainey made her way over to their table, bracing herself for the onslaught of questions she knew they'd be bubbling with.

"Isn't Tyler even more handsome now, Lainey?" Mrs. Busby said, sitting tall and proud as a peacock.

Lainey tried to fill up the coffee cups of all the ladies at the corner table without scalding anyone or revealing just how much she agreed with that statement.

"Is he really?" Mrs. Patterson said while adding three scoops of sugar into her cup. "What a shame we missed him. If Father Andy hadn't gone on and on this morning, maybe we would have caught a glimpse!"

Lainey glanced over at the door as the bells jingled and breathed a sigh of relief as her best friend,

Hope Roberts, walked—no, *marched*—through the door.

It was that perfect time of day, in between the morning breakfast rush and lunch, so she could actually take some time to chat with Hope.

"Well, enjoy your breakfast, ladies," she said, scooting over to the bar where Hope was already sitting.

"Why didn't you text me?" Hope hissed as soon as Lainey was within earshot.

"I had no time?" Lainey rolled her eyes with humor at her friend. Hope knew better than anyone that she hated gossiping. She filled up a large mug with coffee and handed it to her friend, then took her usual position behind the counter while Hope lifted one of the glass domes and plucked a pumpkin spice muffin from the stand. Her friend was dressed for work with her dark, glossy hair pulled back into a loose knot with a few pieces framing her pretty face.

"As if," Hope said, the jutting of her chin a clear indication she didn't buy her excuse at all. She pried the muffin top off and took a bite. "Details," she said while closing her eyes. "These are the best. Every September I wait for these babies to make it into the fall baking rotation."

"Don't turn me into a town gossip or I can start making carrot muffins instead," Lainey said while refilling her own bottomless mug. They had both agreed long ago that carrots and raisins should be banned ingredients from any baking.

Hope's green eyes snapped open. "So this means there are details to be shared!" She glanced over her shoulder at the church ladies' table then leaned forward and demanded in a not-so-quiet whisper, "All the details. Now. Who, what, where, when."

Lainey smiled and shook her head at her friend but moved a bit closer. "Ty Donnelly. Back in town. Swaggered into this diner. Approximately seven a.m. this morning."

Hope's eyes widened. "He came here first?"

"He seemed exhausted. Like he needed caffeine—which was what he bought. Nothing else. That was it."

"Not it. More details, or I'm going to have to go sit at the church table for the real scoop."

Lainey laughed, but it was replaced by slight guilt as she remembered telling him that Grandma Tilly was dead. It had been crass, but she'd been mad at him. Still was mad.

"Come on, Lainey. Did you serve him? I want more details, and I need to get to work."

"Okay, okay," she said, drumming her fingers against the countertop, not even attempting to pretend like she didn't know what her friend was talking about. "He's back, like back for sure. Mrs. Busby said he went home. But he's not the guy we remember."

Hope leaned forward, almost knocking her mug over. "Hotter?"

Lainey winced. "Epically hotter." She'd wanted to get Ty's face out of her head as soon as he'd left her diner. The young man who'd occupied almost all her silly teenage dreams had turned into a hard, hot, brooding man—one who was unfortunately even more physically attractive than the younger version. His blue eyes were as vivid as she remembered, but instead of sparkling with that carefree mischievousness of his youth, they were guarded, maybe wounded. What had already been a handsome face was now harder, leaner, the strong lines of his jaw accentuated with a day's worth of stubble. He was taller than she remembered, stronger, broader...badder.

"Wow," Hope said, setting down the remnants of her muffin.

"I know. But there's more. I had kind of expected him to be..." She paused, taking a sip of coffee, searching for the right words as she stared out the large window. Normally she loved the view of the historical buildings on Main Street. This was the time of morning that the shop owners started flipping their CLOSED signs to OPEN and sidewalk boards were placed outside. The town had undergone a minor rejuvenation as the Montana tourism industry became a thing. Little specialty shops had started popping up, and there was more funding for things like potted plants and shrubs on Main Street. This morning, though, she was too distracted to care that the cheese shop across the street just put out a sign advertising fresh cheese curds.

"Uh, you expected what?" Hope said, leaning over and draining the coffee carafe into her cup.

She turned her attention back to her friend. "Sorry, have you ever tried fresh cheese curds?"

Hope rolled her eyes. "You know you're sup-posed to stay away from dairy, Lainey."

"Details, details. Sometimes a little rumbling is justified."

"Can we please keep to the topic at hand? I need to go to work."

Lainey placed the empty carafe under the faucet and started brewing another pot. "I had expected Tyler to be a little more arrogant. Cold. I mean, he took off without telling anyone, and then he stayed away so long and without any contact. It took Dean weeks to get a hold of him."

"That's good he's not become some cold jerk, right?"

"Why?"

"Well, maybe he'll be able to help his father. Especially if he's staying for good."

"I doubt that. Martin hasn't talked about Tyler in a long time. Not a thing. I don't even know why Tyler left in the first place, but so much has happened, so many years have gone by."

"Did he leave a hint about where he's been, what he was doing all this time?" Hope asked.

Lainey shook her head and glanced around the diner, making sure no one was trying to get her attention or in need of a coffee refill before turning her gaze back to Hope. "Nope, but it's not like I stood around talking to him. For Martin's sake, I hope they can figure things out. I have no idea how he'll turn that place around, if that's what he's thinking. I'm sure he also has no idea who's running it—that will come as a blow for sure."

Hope just nodded. "So sad, what happened to Martin. I'm sure Tyler is filled with guilt."

"It doesn't help that his other friend barely said hi to him. Not that I was paying attention or anything."

Hope grabbed her purse and started fishing

through it. "Dean?"

"Yeah, who else?" she asked, picking up a dish towel and wiping the counter. It didn't really need it, but she couldn't sit still any longer. "I know how much it hurt Dean every time they had to downsize the ranch, and it wouldn't have happened if Tyler had just stuck around," she said, finding herself getting angry again.

"Yeah, well, not everything is as it seems," her friend said, placing her purse on the stool beside her. "There has to be a reason he left. Besides, as if Dean is in a position to judge anyone," Hope said, taking a sip of coffee.

The long-standing animosity between Dean and her BFF wasn't anything new to her. She had stopped trying to convince Hope that Dean was a good guy. Their history was too painful, and Hope had so much on her plate. She didn't think her best friend could ever go back to the person she was before.

"Well, he's been good to Martin. He drives out there every night. Not many doctors make house calls anymore, especially without charging."

Hope rolled her eyes. "He probably does it for the glory. That ego must need constant inflating. The handsome, dashing Dr. Stanton, racing around town in his BMW, saving lives."

Lainey choked on her coffee. "Hope...you know that's not the way he is."

Hope set her chin. "Nope, not really sure. That's what I see."

"What time is your first appointment, *Dr. Roberts*?" Lainey asked with a smile.

Hope let out a small laugh. "Nice try, but we're different kinds of doctors. I'm sure Dean wouldn't even think about referring to a naturopathic doctor as a real doctor."

Lainey cringed. That wasn't the reaction she'd wanted. "Well, you're a real doctor and your degree proves it. So does your thriving business."

"This is why we're friends," Hope said. She glanced up at the clock above the doorway. "I guess I should get going; my first appointment is in half an hour." Her friend stood up and grabbed her purse. "I have a full day, and then I'm taking Sadie back-to-school shopping. First grade is kind of a big deal," she said with a smile.

Lainey smiled back at her friend. "You're a good mama, Hope."

She paused and then returned the smile, even though Lainey could tell it was forced. "There are days where I think I'm a complete failure, but luckily I can still hide it from Sadie. She's young enough to think I'm the best single parent in the world."

Lainey placed two chocolate chip oatmeal cookies in a takeout bag and handed it to her friend, her heart squeezing in sympathy. She and Hope had been best friends since the tenth grade, and they'd been there for each other through the good times and all the heartache. Unfortunately for Hope, there had been too much of the latter in recent years. The death of Hope's husband three years ago had shattered her world.

Lainey forced those memories from her mind and smiled. "Give these to Sadie, along with a hug, and then let me know when I can come over this week to see all her new gear."

Hope nodded. "Will do. I'll text you later."

"You're great at what you do, Hope. Don't let Dean make you think otherwise. There's obviously a need for naturopaths or you wouldn't be so busy."

Hope smiled. "This is why we're *best* friends."

She laughed. "And the muffins. I'm glad you stopped by."

"Text me if anything interesting happens," Hope said with a wave as she left the diner.

Interesting? Really, the most interesting thing that had happened in a while was Tyler coming home. "And don't think I've forgotten about the fact that you promised you'd email that art school," she said, pointing a finger at her and then jogging out of the restaurant.

Lainey sighed, watching her friend go. She hadn't told Hope that she'd been having problems painting lately. She'd…hit a roadblock and she didn't know why. Since she'd started painting, she'd never stumbled, never wondered if there was a point. Now… she questioned all of it.

She'd been putting off her email to the school about her application. Her eighth application. Not because the school had rejected her, but because something always happened and she rescinded her app. Something always prevented her from leaving Wishing River. She was afraid of contacting them again. What if they flat-out told her to stop trying? Something like: *Lady, get your crap together and just face the fact that you'll never go to art school. You will be stuck running your grandmother's diner forever.*

She ignored that familiar, uncomfortable tightness in her chest whenever she thought about Italy. It wasn't that she didn't love the diner—she did. It was a town landmark. Even the old building, which she repeatedly cursed, was built in the 1800s and had so much charm and character that, despite the amount of money it cost to keep the place standing, she still adored it. But all those things, along with the complicated family she had, prevented her from studying abroad. Maybe the dream was foolish. Like, who in the town of Wishing River ever got to go to art school in Florence, Italy? It was a joke. Maybe the dream was a joke. Maybe *she* was a joke…

Tyler Donnelly had probably seen the world. Maybe Lainey was judging him harshly because he had gotten away; he'd done what she'd always dreamed of doing, except she hadn't.

She was happy, though. Yes, she was happy. She could still paint; she didn't need to make it her career. She could be content stockpiling her canvases in her second bedroom. This was home. Her dreams of being more, of being an artist, weren't out of the question forever.

She had her paintings. She had her customers, her friends. It should be enough.

She glanced over at the church ladies, all deep in conversation, and smiled wistfully. Their lives were more exciting than hers. She heard Martin's name mentioned, and her thoughts wandered to her friend. She hoped he wasn't too shaken up by his son's return. Tyler would probably be there when she brought Martin his dinner tonight, not that it mattered or anything; Tyler didn't matter at all. Tyler being there shouldn't change anything for her, and it certainly wouldn't keep her away. She owed Martin more than his son would hopefully ever know.

*L*ainey clutched the takeout container filled with Martin's dinner a little closer as the wind picked up. She knocked on the door and waited. She was slightly nervous about seeing Tyler again and didn't care to examine all the reasons why—just like she didn't care to examine why she'd taken the time to brush her hair or reapply some lip gloss before she got out of her car. Nope.

She shivered, and she doubted it had to do with the cold, damp air. The entire day at the diner had been filled with endless talk about Ty Donnelly coming home. Of course that meant that she couldn't get the image of Tyler out of her head all day, either. She had wanted to, of course. But with every cup of coffee she poured, she was either answering whether or not she'd actually seen him or she was listening in on patrons as they gossiped about Martin Donnelly's only son coming back home.

She knocked on the door again, this time a little louder, worried that the tray filled with shredded roast chicken, mashed sweet potatoes, and green beans wasn't cold. Usually the nurse had answered by now. She waited another minute and then rang the bell. A few seconds later, the door swung open. The man she'd been trying to convince herself wasn't really that handsome answered the door—and by just standing there in a T-shirt, jeans, stubble, and a scowl, confirmed that denial was futile.

To his credit, it appeared as though he was trying to soften his scowl. Slightly.

"Hi, um, I'm here with dinner for Martin," she said, lifting up the container.

He held open the door a little wider. "Come in. I should have called and told you that you don't have to do this anymore. I was just going to grab him some food from the canteen."

She stepped inside the warm house. There was no way she was going to stop coming here and helping his father. "Martin and I have an arrangement."

She could have sworn he straightened up and stood a little taller, which made her very aware of the fact that she only came up to his shoulders. "I don't think it makes sense for you to drive all the way out here when we have a cook for the ranch hands."

"Well, that's great for you. Go on over there and eat. As for your father, as I said, we have an arrangement. It was settled long before you arrived," she said, taking off her shoes.

His eyebrows rose. "What kind of arrangement?"

She held her breath, trying not to give anything away. Suddenly she was very aware of the fact that he might find out about the secret Martin had been keeping for her if he stuck around long enough. Not that she had anything to hide, but it was personal— between her and Martin—and she had no idea how Ty would react. "That I bring him dinner."

"He can't talk," he said flatly, his gaze unwavering. He seemed to take up the entire entry, and she resented his larger-than-life presence. She knew more about his father these last years than he did. She also knew how much his father had suffered without him.

"Before his stroke, he came into the diner every night for dinner. *Every* night. He's a friend in need, so I'm here to stay whether or not you like it."

He ran his hand over his jaw. "I didn't mean to imply that I'm not…grateful. It's very nice of you," he said, his voice softening along with his expression. "Why didn't he eat here?"

Maybe because he was depressed. Maybe because it was hard for him to eat with a bunch of men who were more loyal than his son. Maybe it was slowly killing him, having to eat without his family. She blinked back tears and kept her opinions to herself. "You'll have to ask him that. Can I go in now?"

He shut the door and gave a long sweep of his arm in the direction of the family room. She could have sworn she detected a touch of sarcasm in his eyes but didn't care enough to find out.

"Has Dean been by yet?"

His jaw clenched. "No."

"Okay, well, I'll help him with dinner, then," she said, walking past him. If these walls could talk. She had no idea how their reunion went today, but if Tyler's haggard appearance was any indication, she'd guess not too well.

Her heart squeezed when she saw Martin sitting slightly upright in his hospital bed, his eyes on the door. His frail face softened, his mouth attempted a smile that would have been easy a few weeks ago but was now a big effort. "Hi, Martin, I brought dinner. It's your favorite—roast chicken special at the diner," she said, sitting beside him. She was very aware of Tyler's presence in the doorway. He added a whole new vibe to the house. For Martin's sake, she hoped they could reconcile.

She opened the tray and started feeding him, just like Sheila had shown her. But he wouldn't take the food; he shut his mouth, his eyes going to the doorway. She frowned, glancing over at Tyler, and found herself blinking back tears as he tried to look nonchalant. But hurt had flashed across his face, and for a second, it was as though she had a glimpse of the real man. She turned back to Martin, who hadn't softened a bit.

"I, uh, I'm going to make myself something to eat," Tyler said, his features closed and hard again as he left the room. She hadn't really known what to expect, but that hadn't been it. She had made assumptions about Tyler for leaving. There was clearly more going on here than she was prepared for.

It was interesting that he wasn't going to eat with the ranch hands at the canteen. She wondered if he'd learned who his foreman was yet.

She glanced over at Martin and frowned. "Martin, come on, you know you have to eat or you'll never get your strength back."

He glanced at the doorway again and then back at the forkful of chicken she had, and he slowly opened his mouth. She waited patiently as he chewed, feeling obligated to assist in some kind of reconciliation. Holding on to whatever anger he had toward his son wasn't healthy.

"You must be so happy Tyler is back. What a wonderful surprise."

His eyes didn't reveal a thing, but she sensed "wonderful" wasn't exactly what he was thinking.

"I know you two have a lot to work out, but it will happen. The important thing is that he's here, that he can help you."

He closed his mouth and just stared at the forkful of food.

Sighing, she leaned forward. "Martin, you need him," she whispered. She didn't know the details of why Tyler had left, but she knew that Martin missed him and that on some level he blamed himself. It had happened shortly after Penny's death, and he never talked about it. But she knew that Martin had a big heart, and there was no way he would hold on to whatever anger he had now that Tyler was here.

"Come on, he came home. For you," she said, moving the fork a little closer.

He finally took the bite and began the laborious, slow chewing. Martin had been so kind to her and had shown her such generosity that it seemed so out of character for him to be so angry.

She jumped at the sound of clanking pots in the kitchen. Tyler was probably cooking. A stab of guilt hit her again. The man was obviously wiped, and now he had to cook dinner. She sat there in silence and helped Martin eat for the next ten minutes. By the time the food was finished, the aroma of bacon and frying eggs filled the house.

She stood and started cleaning up. Usually she made small talk with Martin, but he obviously wasn't up to it tonight. She gathered the tray and fork and heard the front door open.

"Hello," Dean called out.

"Well, I'm glad Dr. Stanton is here," she said, smiling at Martin.

He looked nonplussed.

She gathered the takeout containers and napkins as Dean and Tyler came into the room. They both had their arms folded across their chests and an almost identical wide-spread stance. She wondered if one of them was going to beat his fists against his chest. Her gaze went back and forth between the handsome men, one clean-cut and on top of his game, the other disheveled and irritable. Her heart shouldn't be squeezing for the latter. But it was.

"Hey, Lainey," Dean said, walking forward with an ease in this house that Tyler didn't have anymore. "Thanks for dropping off dinner at the office for me," he said, taking off his coat and draping it on the chair.

She smiled sheepishly, avoiding Tyler's gaze.

"No problem," she said, crossing the room. She really needed to leave. All the men in here seemed to take up all the available oxygen, and she needed out. "I'll see you tomorrow, Martin. It's pasta night," she added with a wink, knowing it was another favorite. His eyes didn't twinkle, though, and he turned away from her as she stood next to Tyler in the doorway.

"Um, I'll see you tomorrow, I guess," she said awkwardly, not really liking how she had to look way up at him.

"I'll walk you out," he said, surprising her. He moved aside so she could walk through the doorway into the kitchen. She caught a glimpse of perfectly fried bacon on a plate on the kitchen table. It was sad and lonely. She slipped on her shoes at the front door, regretting not bringing a jacket as the wind loudly hit the windows.

"Well, certainly feels like autumn," she said, hating awkward silence.

"Yeah," he said, opening the door for her and stepping out onto the covered porch. She automatically shivered as the damp air greeted her. She noticed he didn't even flinch. She was about to walk down the steps when he stopped her. "Lainey," he said gruffly.

She paused and waited.

"Thank you for taking care of him."

Her stomach dropped. She hadn't expected thanks, or the emotion that clung to his words. "We're friends."

He cleared his throat. "Mrs. Busby told me you're the one who found him."

She turned from him, from the vulnerability etched on his face as the memory of that day resurfaced. She tried not to think about that night, about her panic, the memories of Martin, and the way that it reminded her of losing her grandmother... "Yes. I'm glad I got here in time to call the paramedics."

"Thank you," he said, the thickness in his deep voice making tears sting her eyes. "Wait, let me get you a jacket," he said. She wanted him to be an ass. She wanted to despise him for leaving his father for so long, for not appreciating him. But the man in front of her didn't seem like the proud, carefree person she assumed he was. This man seemed unsure, maybe broken, and definitely guilty.

"No thanks," she said, taking a physical step back

from him, needing his face to recede into the shadows so his appeal would be a little more concealed. "I'll be fine," she said, pausing instead of walking down the front steps. She stared out into the darkened pastures, dimly lit by the moon, watching the way the wind kicked up leaves and sent them billowing into the darkness. The ranch at night always made her very aware of how alone she was, how small and insignificant compared to the land around her.

"Anyway, thanks again for coming here and bringing food for my father." He held her gaze for a beat, and she wondered how he managed to still seem so large against the vast terrain around him. "But you don't have to keep doing it. I'm here now. I can cook him dinner."

"You don't owe me thanks." She gave an awkward cough. He was really too tall and handsome for her to be standing this close. She could feel the warmth radiating from him. "I'm...happy you're back, for your father's sake."

He winced and stared in the direction of the barn. "I'm not sure he wants me here. But I'm here. For good."

Her stomach flipped over a few times. "Like, back in Wishing River for good?"

He gave her a nod. "Yeah. I'm going to resume my role at the ranch."

She pushed aside her own trepidation to be happy for Martin. She knew that this would have been his dream—for his son to take over the ranch. It had been in their family for generations. But Martin had started preparing himself for the fact that his son would never come back. "So much has changed," she said, not wanting to interfere but wanting to give him some kind of warning.

He shrugged. "That's okay. I'm ready to take it on and run the place."

If he'd been any other man, she might have reached out to touch his arm, to offer a bit of comfort to soften the blow of what she was going to tell him. But despite the glimpses of vulnerability, it was obvious this man didn't need her comfort.

"Maybe that was the case when you left. But a—a lot has happened in eight years. Dean warned your father that this ranch was killing him. He was too old to deal with the stress of it. It was either start selling off land and cattle or die. He resisted for a long time but finally started the process of downsizing." She didn't add that she almost thought that had been worse for him—that the loss of his lifelong dreams was what had really caused his stroke. Martin lived and breathed the ranch. She knew he'd dreamed of running it with Ty and then having his son eventually take it over. With no sign of Tyler coming home, the stroke had been the final straw for him.

She was pretty sure Tyler swore under his breath as he walked across the porch, staring east, toward the mountains, toward the wide-open pastures where cattle had once roamed. He was solitary and untouchable. But he belonged here—it was in him, in his eyes, in his voice, in his stature, he was every inch a rancher. And he was paintable. Damn.

"I should get going—it's a long drive back to town," she said awkwardly when he didn't say anything.

He turned around and gave her a nod. "You okay driving back?"

She stopped for a second, the question startling her. "I've been on my own a long time, Tyler. Nothing I can't handle," she said, running down the front steps and to her car before she let her imagination run away from her. It felt like forever since a man had been worried about her. Or maybe there had *never* been a man worried about her—even more pathetic.

The cold air chilled her, seeping to the bones, and she breathed a sigh of relief once she was in her car. She stared at the house, and her heart seemed to swell as she made eye contact with Tyler, who was still standing there. She pulled away, shivering, very aware of the man who was now back and going to change everything. She probably should have taken his jacket, but then again, that would have been like admitting some kind of truce. She couldn't do that. No matter how gorgeous he was or how wounded, she wasn't going to absolve him of his guilt. Only his father could do that.

She glanced over at the dimly lit bunkhouse and barns in the distance as she drove by. She only hoped that when Tyler discovered who was running his father's ranch tomorrow, he wouldn't take off, leaving his father heartbroken again.

CHAPTER THREE

𝒯yler walked back into the warm house after Lainey pulled away and shook off the dampness. Lainey…the woman who had clearly played a huge part in his father's life. He had no idea that his father had become close to Tilly's granddaughter. She wasn't the same girl…woman he remembered. Back then, he hadn't thought of her as a woman because she'd barely been out of her teens. Now there was no denying she was all woman. Gorgeous, even if it was clear she'd already judged him. Like this whole damn town.

But there was no denying his own physical response to her. He was a guy, and basically any guy on the planet would find her attractive. It was the other attributes he'd noticed that were a little more worrisome to him—like the fact that she had a sweetness to her that he wished he hadn't seen. The soft voice that she had used with his father, the encouraging and not patronizing smile she'd given his dad, hadn't gone unnoticed by Ty. They had a familiarity with each other that even he didn't have.

Nothing had prepared him for what he was facing here. His father. The ranch. Dean. Lainey. Hell, the entire damn town. So many parts of his dad's life he didn't know about anymore. He was going to have to piece it all together. And the ranch… His father had downsized?

He rubbed his chest absently as a tightness grew

there. He needed to find out how much had been sold. This was all because of him. His father's dream and legacy were dead because of him.

Dean appeared in the doorway, and Ty dragged his attention from the ruin he'd caused to the guy who'd once been his best friend. He needed some answers from him, regardless of what his current opinion of Ty was.

"All done?" he asked as Dean put his coat on.

"Yeah."

"How's he doing?"

"He's improving," Dean said, buttoning his coat and showing no signs of softening. "The speech therapist will be in tomorrow at nine. The next day will be physio at nine. I left all the contact information and some pamphlets on the kitchen table for you. He's stubborn, but he needs to start. He needs a goal."

Ty had a hell of a lot of reading to do. He knew nothing about strokes or physio. But he wasn't going to sit around being ignorant or asking Dean to explain everything to him. "Will all this eventually help?"

Dean shrugged and picked up his medical bag. "It should. It's hard to say how much of it is physical and how much is mental."

"Why wouldn't he want to get better?"

Dean's stare was steely. "Because he's got nothing to live for. He was ready to sell off the damn ranch because his son ditched him. He was a lonely old man with no one but Lainey watching out for him."

Tyler stood a little straighter, trying to not collapse

from the shame currently shrouding him. He refused to acknowledge the catch in his breath from the pain. Dean was right. But damn him for telling Ty to his face. "I don't need to hear this right now. Just tell me if he's going to ever get better."

Dean took a step closer, and Tyler shoved his hands in his front pockets. "Give him a reason to want to be here, Ty. Tell him you'll stay in Wishing River."

"I am here to stay. I already told him that."

Dean glanced away for a moment. "Maybe he doesn't believe you."

"Maybe he doesn't give a damn."

Dean opened the door. "Maybe. Can't say I disagree with him."

Tyler watched him walk out, the weight of everything pressing down hard. Hell, he had no idea what the point of any of this was. How could he help his father when it was clear the man didn't care if Tyler was here at all?

Money. He'd saved money. He'd had the foresight to stockpile, knowing he'd need some kind of peace offering if he ever came back. And the worst-case scenario had been that he'd have to start up his own ranch. First things first, though, he'd let his father know what he'd be contributing.

He walked into his dad's office, determined to find out what the hell was going on around here and if there was any way he could get the ranch up and running again. He stopped in the doorway and flicked on the lights. It was like this room had been frozen in time. The same family pictures in dark frames lined the wall behind his father's big desk. There were pictures of him and his mother in brass frames. Stacks of papers littered the large surface area. He could already see there was a pile of unopened mail. Hell, who needed sleep anyway?

He walked into the kitchen to brew a pot of coffee. The house was uncomfortably quiet, so he was glad the sound of brewing coffee seemed to make things less gloomy. Then he headed back into the office, coffee in hand, and settled in behind his father's old desk.

Three hours later, the night nurse, Michelle, gently knocked on the door. She was a pleasant woman, from what he could tell. She appeared to be in her mid fifties and seemed very efficient.

He gave her his attention, even though his mind was still on the mess of paperwork he was piecing together. "Everything okay?"

She nodded. "Yes, your father is settled for the night. Normally, I stay in the reclining chair in the room with him. Is that still okay with you?"

He forced a smile. "Of course. Just do what's best for you and him." He had no idea what to do with his father, so even though it seemed weird to have hired help while he was here, he didn't see any other option.

She smiled. "Great. I just didn't want to intrude."

He leaned forward, placing his forearms on the scattered papers. "Not at all. Can I ask you something?"

"Of course."

"How do you communicate with my father?"

"Oh, no one explained this?"

He shook his head, ignoring the wave of embarrassment that swam through him. No one had told him anything because no one liked him around here.

"Okay, no worries. It's quite simple once you get the hang of it. We use an AAC board that was given to us by the hospital. He can point at one of the pictures and let us know the basics."

He nodded slowly, digesting that piece of information. "Okay. So…can he not talk at all?"

She tilted her head and gave him a small smile. "He definitely has aphasia, so he has difficulty expressing himself. Dr. Stanton was telling me that he thinks part of the reason your father isn't speaking at all might be because he just doesn't want to, since his speech has been affected."

Pride. He ran a hand over his jaw, not knowing what to do with all this information being thrown at him. He hung his head for a moment. "So there's a chance he will regain his ability to speak."

She clasped her hands together. "Definitely. These are early days yet. He has a long way to go, but he is doing really well. I've very optimistic. Just knowing that you're home will go a long way."

He wasn't so sure about that. "Thank you."

"You're very welcome. I'll leave you to your work. I'm going to get settled for the night, but I'm on call and will help him with whatever he needs. I'll be here until seven a.m."

"Thanks."

She gave a small wave and left the room.

He turned his attention back to the stack of unpaid bills. He was going to have to deal with this. He just didn't have any of his father's banking information. It hit him then that he might need power of attorney over his father's finances. Tomorrow, he would ask his father about that and then find out what the procedures were for gaining access to the accounts.

He spent the next two hours trying to make sense of everything. In the morning, he'd go into town and speak with the bank and their lawyer. He was pretty sure his father still did everything in person with a shake of the hand. He was beginning to realize that his father hadn't been very diligent with record keeping, either.

He stood, stretching, his gaze going back to the picture he'd avoided all night. The picture of his mother, perched on his father's desk, was the only thing that wasn't filled with dust. It seemed as though it was polished and cared for. He shoved his hands in his pockets and turned away. If she'd been alive, none of this would have happened. His mother had had a way of making him and his father work things out. He rubbed the back of his neck and walked out of the office, needing fresh air.

Without thinking it through, he headed out of the house, knowing his father was cared for, and got into his truck. He turned on the wipers as rain started tumbling from the sky, and he pulled out of the driveway and onto the gravel roads that connected various parts of the vast ranch. He knew them like the back of his hand, even in the dark. He didn't think twice about where he was going, just knew this was long overdue, something he had to do.

He slowed the truck at the clearing and then parked. Fishing through the glove compartment and pulling out a flashlight, he grabbed his hat from the passenger seat. He took a deep breath before getting out. Stepping into a puddle, he cursed as he rounded the truck to the family cemetery, where three generations lay. He stopped abruptly as wind blew harshly around him, as though the weather had already judged and sentenced him.

He ignored it and just pulled his hat a little lower on his forehead and hunched his shoulders to shield him from the wind as he walked the cemetery. The trees towered and bowed ominously against the force of the wind. Slowing his pace, he pointed his flashlight when the tombstone that he hadn't seen in eight years came into view.

Placing his hands in his back pockets, he stood there like a kid again, hovering in the kitchen doorway with muddy boots and not knowing what to do. He blinked, and for a moment he could see her hands on her hips, a resigned sigh and a slight smile as she stared at him. Somehow, she'd never gotten tired of his antics, of his messiness, his scraped knees and broken bones. She'd always insisted they were one step away from the emergency room and could he please try to not give her a heart attack.

He didn't want to blink again because he didn't want the image of her to be gone. He hadn't let himself see her in years. He hadn't let himself picture her, because he wanted to see her again so badly. He wanted to hear her voice, he wanted to feel the softness of her hug, the smell of her lemon verbena perfume. He wanted her alive.

Nothing had prepared him for losing her. It hadn't been fair. She had deserved so much better. On her last day, she'd squeezed his hand with what little strength she had left, her voice long gone, and then slipped her engagement and wedding rings off her finger and placed them in the palm of his hand. Her eyes had been filled with tears and hope—the pain in them gone for those few seconds. He knew what she'd been hoping for, and standing here, he was reminded of that failure, too.

Maybe it was that moment, that moment when she slipped from their world and into the everlasting world she believed in so vehemently, that he realized how unfortunate his life had been. Not because he'd lost his mom. But because she had raised him with love and morals and kindness. She had raised him with so much. And then she'd left him, knowing exactly what he'd lost. What he'd never have again.

Because he never wanted to love anyone so much that the grief would seep into his bones and make him weak.

Rain started to thump harder against his hat. He blinked, and sure enough, he wasn't standing in the kitchen anymore, and his mother was gone. But as he walked toward the tombstone, he saw her again, heard her voice as he sat down, the cold, damp earth chilling him through his jeans. This time he was lying in bed, pretending to be sick so he didn't have to go to church. His mother would tug at his blue-and-white patchwork quilt, and her narrowed, knowing eyes would be on him. Most Sundays, she made him go. Some Sundays, she indulged him and let him stay home—but that was usually worse because when his dad got wind of it, he made him clean out the horse stalls. And while he was doing that, he'd end up miserably guilty at the thought of his mother attending church alone. His dad only went on the major holidays.

Her funeral was the last time he'd entered a church. He had never connected with it. Or maybe he associated it with her. Maybe going back there was too much of a reminder of her. He could still see her thin hand holding open the songbook, lifting it between them so he could see the lyrics. He never sang, though. But he'd loved the songs. And his mother's voice as she sang had been like a warm blanket on a stormy night. But now it all meant nothing to him. All that faith she'd had, what had it gotten her? A gruesome, painful death.

He took a deep breath and brushed off some of the wet leaves on the tombstone. "So I guess I'm back home," he said, feeling pretty stupid for talking out loud. "I know I've been gone a long time, and I know if you were here, you'd be pretty pissed at me. I did work hard, though; I wasn't bumming around." He ducked his head, knowing his mother would have also probably swatted his shoulder for using the word "pissed." He tried to tone down his language in case she was actually somehow listening to him. She was the type that if there was some way to listen, she'd find it when he was cussing just so she could reprimand him.

He swallowed. "Dad had a pretty bad stroke. I'm trying to help him out, to save the ranch. He's going to be okay." He cleared his throat and reminded himself to stay on track. "We aren't in a good place yet, Dad and me. He hasn't forgiven me for leaving, and I can't really blame him. I just want you to know that I won't abandon him, and I won't leave him again. I regret that I did that. I was running. We fell apart, Mom. Everything we were... Without you, we just couldn't figure each other out anymore, and...I blamed him. I blamed him for you dying, and he never forgave me for that."

He paused, not knowing if he'd be able to say the words that he'd kept inside for eight years. He didn't know if she'd want him to know her secret, since she'd never told him, even on those last days. Maybe one day he'd ask her, but not tonight. Tonight, she just needed to know that he was home and that he loved her.

The rain started coming down harder, and he knew it was time to go, time to ask for forgiveness.

"I know I didn't do the right thing or make you proud, but I'm starting over. I'll help him fix this place. I'll make it profitable. I'll get that house fixed up so it's like you remembered it. I'll keep the ranch alive." He stood, unable to move yet, to leave her here. "I don't know if I made it clear enough when I was growing up or at the end, but you were a good mother. The best." He backed away slowly, blinking rapidly. "I just... You should know that I miss you. Even though I didn't come here, I miss you every day. I'll...uh, see you again soon."

He walked back to his truck, finding it hard to breathe, wishing this had brought him solace. He'd hoped that maybe talking to her would help, would give him perspective, but it hadn't. Instead it reinforced how alone he was.

What he needed was some whiskey and then a warm bed.

He started his truck and drove back to the house, slowing as he passed the main barn and bunkhouse.

He had practically lived there during his childhood and teenage years. He'd loved hanging out with his father and the ranch hands. He knew their old foreman, Bill, must be long gone by now.

The last four years, he'd been working a ranch out in Wyoming because he'd missed ranching so much, and the rodeo circuit hadn't been his thing. But it wasn't the same. Nothing could replace working on his family ranch.

He wanted to go over there; to check on the horses; to ride out into the mountains, the pasture; to round up his cattle on his family ranch. He wanted all of it back, despite the censure he was sure to face. Cowboys were loyal, and he knew he'd be seen as a traitor. He didn't need it to be light out to know exactly what was out there. It was etched in his memory like a favorite painting.

Tomorrow morning, he'd go over there. He was going to saddle up. He was going to make his presence known. Martin Donnelly's son had come home, and he was going to save his father's ranch.

CHAPTER FOUR

Tyler stood in the doorway to the living room, watching his father sleep. Well, he assumed he was sleeping. The sun hadn't come up yet, but the glow from the kitchen gave him enough light to see that his father's eyelids twitched when Tyler moved across the room. Michelle was brewing coffee in the kitchen and making breakfast.

"Morning, Dad." He waited, not feeling so stupid today because this whole talk-with-no-response thing was becoming a little more normal. Though his father still hadn't acknowledged him. He cleared his throat loudly. "Just wanted to let you know that I'm going over to meet the men this morning. I'm going to let them know I'll be taking over the ranch."

He let that hang there, and sure enough, just as he suspected, his father opened his eyes. The man had been awake the whole damn time. Anger flashed in his eyes, but Ty held his ground. "Like I said last night, I'm back for good. I was going through the books, and there's a helluva lot of work to be done to get this place back on track. But I'm going to do it. I'm going to figure out where things went wrong and how to get it all back on track. I owe you. I've got money, and I know how to run this place."

His father shook his head in a stiff motion.

He knew the last thing his father would want was his help. Well, too bad. He owed his mother—that realization had hit him hard last night. It was time to man up and help his father.

"I'll let you know how the day goes." He put his hat on his head and walked out of the room, sensing his father's angry stare following him. He was in it for the long haul. It was going to take time, but he could pretend to be a patient man.

It was a ten-minute walk to the bunkhouse and canteen from the main house. The morning was chilly, and frost clung to the grass, but he knew by midday it'd warm up nicely. What he really wanted to do was saddle up and go for a long ride, but he knew he had to make his presence known before he did any of that. This was his ranch, and it smelled like home.

The cool, crisp air brought him right back to the autumns of his childhood. How many days had he spent sitting on a plodding horse trailing behind cows, heading for home? Sometimes a couple of hours; sometimes a couple of days. He knew the guys complained at the monotony of it, the cold that seemed to seep into your bones no matter how many layers you had on, but he loved it.

He took the gravel path, very aware that the ranch hands and foreman might not be anyone he knew. As soon as he opened the door to the canteen, the smells of bacon and eggs and coffee hit him. Deep voices and the clanking of dishes and forks wafted from the kitchen as he made his way down the corridor. He paused in the doorway, unhappy to only see half the number of men than he was used to seeing. He needed to push aside his guilt and be logical. He'd figured out last night that his father hadn't sold so much land that it would affect their operation. He just needed to rebuild slowly.

He stilled when a familiar figure caught his attention by the coffee station. Shock hit him as Cade turned around, made eye contact with him, and lifted his mug in greeting. The casual gesture was in complete contrast to the stiffness in his large frame and the hostility in his eyes. Hell, he worked here? He took in his other former best friend's appearance, reluctantly acknowledging that he was older, wiser, less like the idiot he remembered.

Tyler squared his shoulders and walked in, despite the cold greeting from his friend. This was his damn ranch, regardless of what his old friend thought of him. He sensed all eyes on him, and no one was talking anymore. He turned toward the tables. They were arranged the same. Long wooden farm tables with benches. There was no cook around, but maybe there wasn't a full-time one anymore, considering the amount of men here. Everyone had grown silent, and he knew he couldn't stand still and not say anything.

No point in beating around the bush. "Morning, everyone. For those of you who don't know me, I'm Martin's son, Tyler. I've returned home to help my father, and from now on, I'll be taking over the ranch and working alongside you."

No one said anything for a moment, but he made his way over to them, and they stood respectfully. He shook hands and got their names, repeating them back so he'd have a better chance of remembering. Back in the day, there had been thirty or so employees. Now there wasn't even a dozen.

As the men filed out, he caught snippets of their

conversation in hushed voices. They were surprised he'd come home. Everyone left except Cade.

He slowly turned to him. He was leaning against the counter, trying to appear casual, but Ty knew he was pissed.

"So what do you do here?" Tyler asked, folding his arms over his chest, really hating that Cade was just as hostile and judgmental as Dean.

"Foreman."

Shit. He rubbed his chin. "Funny."

Cade put his mug down and straightened up. "Just about as funny as you coming here thinking you're taking over this ranch. I've worked here for five years. Where the hell have you been, man?"

Tyler shrugged. "Making a living. Glad to see you and Dean have judged me."

"You don't know how lucky you had it, growing up here. Not all of us were born with a silver spoon in our mouths. You're an idiot for walking away from all this while I worked alongside your father, just like I was his son."

Tyler walked forward slowly, careful to keep his temper in check even though everything inside him was so tightly wound, the only way he'd be able to relieve some of the energy would be to smash his fist in Cade's smug face. "Well, you're not his son. You're on the payroll, so that makes you an employee. Looks like you'll be answering to me. I'm saddling up with you guys today. Get used to it. Apparently, there's a hell of a lot of work to do to bring this place back to what it used to be."

Cade swore under his breath and stormed out of the kitchen. Tyler had no problem keeping up with him, knowing that Cade was going to do his best to undermine his authority. Cade probably assumed he'd been sitting on his ass these last eight years. He had no idea that Tyler had worked the rodeo circuit but then settled on a ranch, honing his own skills, working his way up to foreman.

Well, everyone was in for a rude awakening.

*T*yler knew Cade was pissed off that he had taken the lead out there, moving the cattle out of rough terrain in the mountains. With colder weather settling in, it was a practice they always did. He didn't know if Cade was mad because he'd taken the lead or because he'd done it well and all the men had liked him.

It was just the two of them in the barn, the men gone in for supper. As much as he wanted to stay angry with his friend, he also knew he'd have to play things strategically. He needed the foreman on his side as he tried to bring the ranch back up to full operating capacity. Cade would know everything that had happened here—he knew the men. Tyler needed his expertise. "Well, I'd say that was a successful day."

Nothing but a snort was the reply.

He wasn't going to be personally insulted that his once best friend didn't even have the decency to speak to him. He watched as Cade started walking out of the barn. Hell. "What's your problem, Cade?"

Cade turned, leaning against the paddock gate, his cowboy hat pulled low over his eyes. "You're my problem, Tyler. You think you can just come back in here and act like you're king shit, the boss's son? I know better."

Everything inside him stilled. "What's that supposed to mean?"

"You don't belong here anymore."

He slowly walked forward, telling himself to keep his temper in check. "Why? You like it here? Running my ranch? You think you're going to take it over one day?"

Cade stood tall. "Well, that'd be fitting, wouldn't it? I'm surprised you had the nerve to show your sorry ass back here."

"Of course I was coming back. This is my ranch. My land. My home."

"You got a funny way of showing it."

"None of your damn business how I show it."

"I stood by your dad for five years. You didn't even call him."

"You don't know anything about our relationship, and don't make it sound like you were here just doing him favors. You're on a salary."

"What is it that bugs you? That I'm actually more deserving of this place or my relationship with your dad?"

Ty kept his jaw clenched shut, not knowing what it was. Maybe it was none of those things; maybe it was just the fact that his best friends had judged him so damn harshly, that they assumed the worst about him, just like his father had. "You'd like to think that, wouldn't you? That I'm just jealous. But no, I'm not, Cade, because judging by the books and how run down things are, my father might have been better off without you. You practically ran this place into the ground."

Cade swore at him and walked toward him, but stopped suddenly. Ty turned in the direction of his gaze to see Lainey standing in the barn door. Her hair was pulled back in a ponytail with wisps flying around her in the wind. Her brown eyes were gazing back and forth between them.

"Hi. Sorry to intrude, but Michelle told me you were out here, Tyler. I just came to let you know I brought dinner and, um, didn't want it to get cold," she said, making a point of glancing in his direction. He hadn't expected her to bring him anything.

"How you doing, Lainey?" Cade asked, all his anger gone and honey dripping from his lips as his mouth pulled back into a stupid grin.

Tyler leaned against the wall, taking in the dynamic here.

"Good," she said with a friendly smile.

Interesting. If he didn't know better, he'd say his former friend was very interested in her. Before he left, Cade shot Ty a glare that made it clear they weren't finished and then strode out of the barn.

Tyler turned to Lainey, who was watching him quietly. He could tell she was trying to figure him out. She must have gotten an earful about him. He had his own questions about her and her staunch determination to keep coming out here every night.

"I guess I'll go back inside. It's getting chilly," she said, folding her arms and shivering.

He nodded. "I'll walk with you. The weather is changing," he said, trying to be polite. It suddenly seemed like it mattered—her opinion of him. Or maybe he was just lonely out here, constantly under attack from everyone. They walked in silence, the wind picking up as dusk sank down over the pasture, sleek and cool.

"Michelle said your dad had a great day today. He made a lot of progress with the speech therapist Dean sent over."

Huh. No one had mentioned a thing. But then again, he hadn't gone inside since this morning, when he'd had his one-sided conversation with his father. He knew his dad was stubborn. He wouldn't even be surprised if he played that game for months. Maybe his dad had forgotten that Ty was just as stubborn.

His mother wouldn't have stood for any of this nonsense.

Growing up, she'd always gotten in between them and their arguments. Both as stubborn as mules, she'd say. He and his mother had rarely argued. She'd understood Ty. But his father had been so damn strict, his standards so high, that Ty had always fallen short of meeting them.

But then his mother had gotten sick. He and his father hadn't argued in front of her, but when she'd been admitted into the hospital, they'd exist in the same house without speaking to each other for days. When they did speak, it was some kind of disagreement over how her treatment was going or their opinion of the doctors. They never saw eye to eye.

And things had only gotten worse with his dad's final decision about his mom's care.

He didn't like thinking about it—their last argument. But he would. Whenever guilt would creep up on him, he'd replay his dad's last words to him.

"You must be hungry," Lainey said as they walked up the front porch steps.

Her soft voice pulled him from his useless thoughts and forced him into the present, reminding him he'd almost forgotten how to make polite conversation. "Yeah," he said, holding the door open for her. He was dreaming of a long, hot shower. The warmth from the kitchen flooded him.

"I'm going to head out after I finish cleaning up. Your dad ate. Dean hasn't been by yet, but he phoned to say he was running late. Michelle is sitting with your father now."

He took off his boots. "Would you mind staying for ten minutes? I need to discuss something with you, but I'm filthy and need a shower."

Her gaze quickly traveled the length of his body, and he could have sworn her cheeks turned pink. "Sure, I'll just finish cleaning up."

"Thanks," he said, walking to the main-floor washroom. He grabbed a change of clothes from his duffel bag and locked the bathroom door. He turned the taps on and let the shower run until it was almost scalding before stepping in.

As the water poured over him and he tried to scrub the dirt from off his body, he let the day play out in his mind. He was like a stranger in his own house, in his own town.

Five minutes later, he reluctantly got out of the shower and dressed quickly, knowing Lainey was waiting for him. He'd ask her about what he uncovered when he'd pored over the books last night.

He walked into the kitchen and tried not to appreciate how gorgeous Lainey was. She must have heard him come in because she turned around and gave him a smile. "Dinner's on the table."

Something inside him responded as he glanced at the table. A bowl of pasta and a plate of salad were laid out with a napkin and fork. He tried to speak, but the lump in his throat wouldn't let him. He cleared his throat. "Thank you. You didn't have to do that."

She shrugged. "No big deal. I brought food for your dad, too. You should eat it before it gets cold."

"Tell me how much I owe you."

"Nothing. It's on the house," she said, shooting him a smile. She reached for her jacket, and he knew he was going to have to bring it up before she left.

"There's something I want to ask you," he said, shoving his hands in his pockets.

She paused before picking up her purse. "Okay. Shoot."

"I know you mentioned you saw my father almost daily. I was going through his files, trying to make sense of everything and figure out the best way to take over from here, and I noticed he made a lot of omissions in his bookkeeping. Money being withdrawn without any records. That's really unlike him—my entire life he's been a stickler for detail. Do you know… Was my father showing signs of forgetfulness or confusion in the last few years?"

Her face went white, and she crossed her arms, but she never averted her gaze. Those dark eyes flickered with something as she shook her head. "He was as sharp as a whip."

Something didn't add up. "He didn't mention anything to you?"

"We didn't really talk business," she said, fidgeting with the back of the chair.

He wasn't born yesterday. She was shifting like someone who wasn't telling the entire truth. "Can you tell me again why you drive half an hour each way to bring him dinner?"

For a second, her chin wobbled, but she blinked a few times, and the tears turned to anger. She took a step toward him. "I already told you. Your father is a dear, dear friend to me, and I don't know where I'd be without him."

He didn't say anything for a moment as the image of Cade's expression when Lainey walked into the barn hit him. He wondered if there was something between the two of them or if she was somehow protecting him. "Okay, well, I'm just trying to make sense of everything. It seems like people are holding back, not exactly forthcoming with information."

Her knuckles turned white as she clutched the back of the chair. "Maybe because no one trusts you. While you were living your life, doing your thing, I was here, with your dad. And I guess without me you'd be without a father, since I was the one who was here and called for help and saved his life."

Well, shit. She gave as good as she got, and he had to admire her for it. He didn't like it, but he deserved it. Her arms were still crossed, and she was still glaring up at him, but there was no hint of tears now—instead her eyes were sparkling with anger. "You're right. I'm just trying to get a handle on what went down."

"Too little, too late," she said, flinging her purse

over her shoulder. "If you really gave a crap about any of this, you might have picked up a phone once in a while and called your father. You can't come back here and act like you care. I don't answer to you." She spun on her heel and was almost out the kitchen door when he called after her.

"We can talk about this later," he said, wanting that last word and irritated because everything she said was true. Or maybe he was more irritated that she might be protecting Cade somehow.

She shot him a glance over her shoulder that told him precisely her opinion about that. She shut the door, and he rolled his shoulders, trying to ease his tense muscles. Hell, this was not what he'd expected. His stomach rumbled, and he eyed the food on the table. Dammit. A part of him hoped it wasn't good.

Sadly, as he sat down and took the first bite, he realized it was the best damn food he'd eaten in a long time. He jabbed his fork into the pasta, very aware of how lonely it was in the kitchen suddenly. He hurried to finish the food, to leave this room. He needed to get a good night's sleep, because he was pretty sure he was onto something big that involved his former best friend and the missing money. Tomorrow, he would get to the bottom of it. No thinking about how lonely it felt in here without Lainey. He didn't welcome those thoughts. There would be no distractions for him, especially in the form of a woman with soulful brown eyes.

CHAPTER FIVE

The next night, Lainey stared at the bucket she'd placed in the diner's kitchen, watching the water drip from the ceiling at a rate that didn't warrant alarm but wasn't exactly comforting.

In fact, the entire leaky roof thing didn't come as a surprise at all. She'd had a problem with the roof since it had been redone six years ago. But the timing of this latest leak was dead-on; it was a reminder of what she'd done with the money Martin had loaned her…and what she hadn't told Ty.

It was fitting, really. The roof that had been fixed was now leaking again. His son was back in town and he needed the money, and of course she would give it back. It wasn't hers.

She should have told him the truth. Something had stopped her—his suspicion of her made her feel dirty, almost. Like he'd never believe that she was coming to visit and feed his father because he was very important to her. He'd twist it and think the worst of her—that she'd used Martin for the money. That would hurt. She didn't even fully understand the relationship she had with Martin… He had appeared in her life when she desperately needed someone…almost like a father.

She put her head down on the stainless steel island. She wasn't one to dwell on the past, and she rarely let herself think about it, but ever since Tyler came home, it was all she could think about. Especially since Tyler believed that there was money missing from his father's account. She had no idea Martin hadn't accounted for the loan and was completely blindsided when Tyler had mentioned it. Now it was all messed up, because if she told him the truth, she didn't think he'd believe her. She squeezed her eyes shut, letting the tears fall, knowing the diner was closed. Everyone had someone, and standing in the kitchen at the Donnellys last night had reminded her that no matter how close she and Martin had become, she wasn't family. He wasn't her father. She had no father. She had no real family anymore. This wasn't stuff she dwelled on, because her life was filled with people who cared about her. But every once in a while, it hit her; she was alone.

Grandma Tilly would have known what to do. Well, she probably would have never let Lainey accept any money from a man, especially not a cowboy. But then again, Grandma Tilly had never understood Lainey's dream to see the world, to go to art school, to be more than the girl who worked at the diner.

She opened her eyes and wiped them, her gaze immediately going to the envelope sticking out of her purse hanging on the hook by the kitchen door. It was for Tyler; it was a check for one thousand dollars—nine thousand dollars short. She'd drive over there tomorrow and give it to him. It was better than nothing. She would explain; she would tell him her repayment plan. She'd work double shifts and tell her part-timers that she needed the money. On slow nights, she could handle this place on her own.

She had phoned Mrs. Busby and told her she

wouldn't be able to get out there tonight. She felt guilty for ditching Martin, but she just didn't have it in her to see his son tonight. She'd been a fool.

So many years wasted here, doing nothing but running this diner, and what did she have to show for it? She'd put her art on hold, her dream on hold, for so long, and now it wouldn't happen. There was always one more repair to do, one more reason not to leave Wishing River. He'd seen the country; he'd lived for no one but himself for years. What had she done? She'd grown up in this diner, in the apartment above the diner. Everyone in town knew almost every detail of her life.

But she was a sham.

To the town, she was sweet, cheerful, dependable Lainey. The diner opened at seven every morning and closed at eight every night. She took Sundays off, just as Grandma Tilly had done. Sunday morning, she went to church, just like she'd always done. She poured coffee, she served diner food, and she asked people how their day was going. The only thing that had changed in the diner was that she'd added pumpkin-themed baking in the fall line-up. That was it. The one thing, the one dream she'd wanted for herself since she was old enough to clasp a crayon, was to be a real artist.

And that was the dream that was always dangling a little too far from her reach. Her grandmother, her mother, the leaky roof, the bills, they all had managed to keep her away from pursuing that dream. Or maybe it was her; that was the most frightening scenario. What if she'd been the one responsible for not pursuing her dreams? What if she'd let all those things keep her from leaving?

She stood, contemplating having a drink of Grandma Tilly's emergency whiskey.

$\mathcal{T}$yler stood on the front steps of Tilly's diner, his fingers clenched around the door handle, but didn't open it. The lights were off, just a faint glow from the kitchen and the streetlight illuminating Lainey as she wiped down the long counter. It was almost nine at night, and it struck him how long her days were. She ran the entire place, and he knew she wasn't close to thirty yet. She managed to bring his father supper every night, and she still had to come back and close up shop.

His throat tightened when he remembered how tactless he'd been when asking her about the money. Yes, she was like the others in that she had judged and sentenced him without ever really knowing him. But she'd also been there for his father when he wasn't. She'd been a friend. She'd saved his life. For that, he would be forever grateful. He could tell by the jerky motions and the deep frown on her forehead that she was angry.

He'd tossed and turned last night, plagued with guilt about implying that Lainey's motives for visiting his dad had been less than noble. He couldn't stop himself from driving to the diner to apologize tonight.

He knocked on the door, and she made eye contact with him, pausing. Then she scratched a corner of her cheek with her middle finger, and he couldn't tell whether she was intentionally flipping him off or not. It almost made him chuckle.

He knocked on the door again, and she placed her hands on her hips and frowned at him. He took the moment to appreciate her undeniable appeal. She had this mix of girl-next-door prettiness and sass that he suddenly found highly attractive. Although at the moment, with her stern frown, she reminded him of an elementary school teacher. And a rusty grin slipped across his face as he realized he was even more interested.

He pointed to the lock on the door.

She shook her head.

He nodded.

She shook her head again.

He nodded and knocked. Continuously. Relentlessly.

Maybe a minute passed before she finally whipped her dishcloth over her shoulder and marched across the dark diner. Two latches clicked, and then she swung the door open. He wasn't going to gloat with victory.

"I'm not feeding you," she said and then attempted to close the door in his face.

He held it open with his hand. "I'm not here for food. I'm here to apologize."

Some of the tension left her shoulders. "Oh."

"Can I come in?"

She actually took her time thinking about it. Finally, with a dramatic sweep of her arm, she opened the door all the way and stepped aside. He took off his hat and ran his hands through his hair.

She shrugged. "Now that you're here, I have some food you can bring... I couldn't get out there tonight."

He was taken aback and felt almost…bad because it was probably his fault she hadn't come to the ranch; he'd made her uncomfortable and had insulted her character. He cleared his throat. "You don't have to give us food. I told you last night, we don't expect that."

"No. I, uh, I want to. I like helping your father," she said, backing up a few steps. He didn't say anything for a moment, sensing again that there was something she wasn't saying. Or maybe he was just too paranoid. Maybe she was this lonely woman who had gotten close to his father and pitied him. This place, this diner, this was her entire life, and even though she belonged here, it also didn't seem right. She was too young for this.

No, not that. She didn't *fit* the diner. Like a pair of jeans two sizes too big.

He didn't say anything for a moment as her dark gaze searched his. She had intense eyes. They were one of her best assets. With just one look, they were able to convey hatred or happiness. Her other assets weren't really the kind she'd appreciate his thoughts on, even though they were very favorable thoughts.

"I'll be right back," she said, turning and walking toward the back.

"Wait. Don't," he said, waiting for her to turn around. "I'm sorry. I'm sorry I accused you of…I'm not sure what, but I was accusatory."

She raised one eyebrow. "You insinuated that I took advantage of your father."

He ran a hand over his jaw. "Right."

"Okay. Apology accepted. I'll go put together some food to take home."

"Wait," he said again. He didn't want the takeout food, and he didn't exactly want to leave yet. He didn't know why. Maybe he just didn't want to go home to that empty house with just a ghost of a father and all the memories and regrets. Or maybe there was something about Lainey that made him happy. She was a beautiful woman, so that could be it. But he knew that wasn't all it was. He'd seen beautiful women before, he'd been with beautiful women before, and he knew that it was more than that with *this* woman.

Lainey seemed like the kind of woman who could get under a man's skin. She was smart and sharp, but he detected that inside was a tender heart. That knowledge should send him running in the other direction. He shouldn't be around a tenderhearted woman. That wasn't what he needed. So then why the hell did it seem exactly like what he wanted right now?

"So I'm waiting, and so far all you're doing is staring at me like a television," she said.

He tried not to laugh. "Right." He thought quickly. He wanted an excuse to stay. "Can I buy you dinner?"

She threw up her hands. "I knew you were hungry; I called it the minute I spotted you standing there all forlorn, like some lost orphan in the doorway."

She had no idea—she couldn't know. He didn't say anything for a moment, trying to read her eyes. "Orphan?"

She waved a hand in front of him. "Sometimes you have a very tragic vibe about you. It will get you things you want," she muttered, palming the swinging door to the kitchen and walking through. He rolled his shoulders in an attempt to rid the sudden tension that had accumulated there.

"I can help you cook," he said, following her into the kitchen, counting on the fact that she wouldn't actually let him near the stove.

"Donnelly, I'm betting you can't cook anything other than bacon and eggs," she said over her shoulder. He cracked a smile and didn't bother denying it.

He stood at the large stainless steel island while she took out two dishes and went to one of the ovens, pulling out a tray of something. "You're lucky I haven't eaten yet. I have plenty," she said, placing the tray on the island.

"That looks amazing," he said, his mouth watering at the sight of the deep dish of mac 'n' cheese.

She placed two plates, cutlery, and napkins on the island. "Grandma Tilly's famous mac 'n' cheese recipe, plus salad, because, well, maybe it'll help unclog our arteries after all the cheese."

He smiled. "I'm willing to take my chances. If I remember correctly, Grandma Tilly made the best mac 'n' cheese for miles."

She paused and raised an eyebrow. "According to her, it was the best in the state."

He laughed. "She may have been right. This is way more than I expected. I would have been happy if you threw a loaf of bread at me," he said, taking a plate. "You go first."

"Well, you look like you could use some decent food," she said, placing a large helping of the rich and gooey pasta on his plate. Despite wanting to dive right in to his food, he waited for her to sit down and start eating before he picked up his fork. Unfortunately for his starving stomach, she didn't appear to be in a hurry. She eyed the stool, and he could see she was deciding if she wanted to sit beside him or not. Thankfully, a second later, she scooped some pasta onto her fork and started eating. He dug right in to what was still the best comfort dish he'd ever tasted. They ate in silence until all that was left was the salad.

"I think Grandma Tilly was right."

She smiled at him, a warm smile that made her eyes sparkle. "She never lacked confidence. Would you like a drink?"

"I don't suppose you have a beer?" he asked.

"Nope." She paused after a second and then stood and walked across the kitchen. She stood on a stepladder and pulled a bottle from the top shelf of the hutch at the far end of the space. She plunked it down in front of him with a *thud*.

"Grandma Tilly's emergency whiskey," she said, her full lips almost tilting upward into a smile.

He eyed the bottle. "Can't deny I'm surprised."

She shrugged and gave him two glasses. "It's only for extreme situations. Grandma Tilly advised not to make it a habit. Actually, her exact advice was, 'Say a prayer first, wait five minutes, and if you still need help, pour a glass…and continue as needed.'"

Laughing, he filled the two shot glasses. "She was wise. So I'm considered an extreme situation?"

She tilted her head. "A situation. Let's just say you're a situation."

He lifted his glass to hers. "Here's to Tilly. She was a great woman. I'm sorry she's gone, Lainey."

Her dark eyes glistened for a moment before she tilted her head back and downed the whiskey. He did the same.

"Thank you," she whispered, glancing away and then taking a forkful of food. "So…how are things going with your dad?"

"He hasn't acknowledged me yet. Cade isn't speaking to me; same goes for Dean. The books are really bad. When I left, that ranch had over eight hundred head of cattle—now they are at half. Half the staff, too. They haven't been operating in the black for three years. Dad's drained what he had left in his life savings," he said, wishing the burn from the whiskey could offer more of a distraction. She'd stopped eating, and he was embarrassed for dumping all that on her. He smiled to soften the news. "But you know what they say: can't rain all the time. How about you?"

Staring down at the table, she moved her lettuce around with her fork. "I had no idea it was that bad. I just assumed he was getting too old and, well, that he knew he didn't have anyone to pass the ranch to. I just… I wish he'd confided in me more."

He frowned at the sound of dripping and glanced over at the sink, but it was dry. "What's that dripping?"

She rolled her eyes and pointed to somewhere over his shoulder. "Just a stupid leak from the stupid roof I've already had repaired."

He turned and frowned when he spotted the bucket. He stood and walked over to the corner, his gaze focusing on the watermark on the ceiling. "How long has this been going on?"

"A day or so since we got a big downpour."

"But it's a new roof?"

She nodded. "Relatively. Six years, but it's been leaking since it was replaced."

"Isn't it under warranty?"

"Yes, a fifteen-year warranty! I've called them so many times. They send someone over and he claims to fix it, but it never really goes away."

He rubbed his hand over his jaw, not liking what he was hearing. She was getting taken advantage of. "Isn't there an apartment over the diner?"

She shook her head. "Not this part. The kitchen was an add-on, and it has a flat roof."

Flat roofs were notoriously bad. "What's the name of the roofer?" She gave him the name, and he made a mental note of it. "I'll see what I can do."

She waved a hand. "Don't worry about it."

They stared at each other across the kitchen. She was as closed off as he was in many ways, except she was younger, and it didn't seem right for her. She had her own secrets and, hell, they weren't his business.

Sometimes he hated himself for the decisions he'd made. He knew why he left, he knew at that time in his life he couldn't have stayed, but it didn't make it any easier. No one knew the real reason, the ultimate reason he couldn't stay. Even now, he felt like a sham. But it wasn't important what he felt like…it was important that he was here, that he was helping the man who'd raised him. He didn't need to convince anyone of what kind of a man he was.

People had already decided he wasn't a very good one, and maybe she'd made up her mind, too. It shouldn't matter to him. He had never needed anyone, and he wasn't about to start now.

"Are you finished with your dinner?" she asked, walking back to the table.

"Uh, yeah, thank you."

"No problem," she said and took the plates, put them in the large industrial sink, and started washing.

He joined her at the sink, not wanting to leave her with the mess. "Why don't I finish?" he said, reaching for the sponge she was using.

Of course, nothing with Lainey was that simple, it seemed, as she snatched the sponge away. "No need. You can leave. I'll lock up behind you."

He grabbed it. "No, I insist on at least washing up. You've fed me more than you needed to."

She tried to pry it out of his hand. "I've fed a lot of people in this town. I don't need you cleaning dishes."

He let go and tried to pretend he was a patient man. "Then I'll dry," he said. "Or I'll pay you."

"Fine. Ten bucks. Leave it on the counter beside the cash."

He let out an exasperated sigh and pulled a ten out of his pocket. "There," he said, slapping it on the ledge under the window. "But I'm still helping with the dishes." He snatched the sponge from her hand.

"Really rude, Donnelly. Fine. Don't miss any spots—I hate a poor job. I'll rinse," she said, moving over slightly so that she was in front of the empty side of the divided sink. She stood next to him, and he caught the faint scent of lilacs.

"Why are you doing dishes anyway? Can't you just load them in the dishwasher?"

"Thanks for the tip," she said, shooting him a look before pulling out the hose and rinsing the first plate.

He fought the urge to laugh as she scrubbed it

quickly and efficiently. "Well, why don't you?"

"Because there are only two plates. I'm not going to run the dishwasher for just two plates, and I hate starting a day with dirty dishes."

"All right, fair enough," he said, drying the first dish.

"Glad you approve," she said, turning and shooting him a teasing smile that seemed to punch him in the gut.

"You're spraying water on me," he said as water doused the sleeves of his shirt.

"The price just went up to twenty," she said and actually turned the hose in his direction.

Letting out a laugh, he grabbed the hose, wrestling it from her. She wouldn't give up and depressed the handle, a wash of water smacking him in the face.

He snatched the hose from her, and she backed away, her gorgeous mouth turned up in a smile. She held up her hands. "You wouldn't."

"You started it," he said, trying not to smile.

"It would end very badly for you if you did," she said, eyes narrowed. "Not very gentlemanly," she added, as though it might make a difference. The sparkle in her eyes, the smile on her face, transformed her and lured him in. Hell, what was he doing? He slowly lowered the hose back into the sink.

"Well, I can't ruin your perception of me," he said softly, hoping she couldn't hear in his voice that it actually mattered—what she thought of him actually mattered.

"I have no perception of you," she whispered.

He took a step closer. "You do. You think I'm an ass who ran out on my responsibilities, on my father." He didn't know why he was bringing this up. He told himself he didn't care about people's opinion of him, but maybe he did. Maybe he cared what Lainey thought of him.

She glanced away for a moment, then those gorgeous eyes landed on him, and emotion he couldn't quite decipher filled them. "I did judge you, and I'm sorry for that. Your father and I…became friends over the years. At first, he'd come into the diner every now and then. It was a really low point for me—my grandmother had just died, and I didn't want to talk to people. I didn't feel like hearing all their comments about how much they loved her, how much I was like her, how proud she'd be of me. I wanted to hide. I never wanted—"

He hung on every word, and when she stopped speaking abruptly, he waited. He wanted to know. What had happened to her, how she'd become so close to his father.

"So anyway, your father would sit in the corner table by the window, and he'd just stare outside. He seemed so lost, so sad, and I understood that. He never questioned me, never asked me a thousand questions, and I appreciated that. We had a sort of understanding. I wouldn't ask about you, and he wouldn't ask about my grandmother. But he always gave me a kind smile. That was all I needed. The years passed, and what had been once a week became every night. We both learned to get on with our lives and started talking more and more. He helped me out, especially with other things that happened…"

She turned from him quickly and started running the water again, grabbing the sponge as she picked up their glasses. He shut the water off and took the sponge from her hand, knowing she was avoiding him. She had opened up enough and was now shutting him out. "How did he help you?"

"This wasn't my dream. Running a diner in Wishing River was not on my top-ten list of careers."

"So why are you doing it?"

She shrugged. "Loyalty? Duty? Obligation?"

She said it without censure, but the differences between them clung in those words. He'd had none of those things. He'd left. He'd left the family ranch, and now it was almost all gone. He hadn't shown his father any loyalty. "Your grandmother's gone."

"I don't want to talk about this. You've been fed. You can get going," she said, picking up a dish towel and drying her hands.

For a few minutes, it was like he'd broken down some walls, like he was getting to know her, but it was clear she regretted telling him what she did. She'd revealed something he hadn't expected, though. He assumed she loved this place, but she'd been running it out of duty. She turned and started walking out of the kitchen.

He reached out to grab her wrist. "Hey."

Her eyes narrowed on him. "Hands off, cowboy," she said in a low voice.

Maybe it was the butcher block of knives, or maybe it was the slight tremble in her tilted-up chin, but he dropped her wrist immediately. His intention wasn't to scare her, just to stop her, or stop the hostility that was creeping into their conversation.

He was tired of being the bad guy. The cruel son who'd abandoned his father. He dropped his hand. "Fine. You can just go back to being judgmental. See you at the house tomorrow."

"Wait. I'm not judgmental."

"You've crucified me without a single question, right? Not everything is as it seems on the surface. You can go ahead and think everything is black and white and people should be perfect. Good luck with that."

Neither of them said anything for a moment, the tension in the room thick. He picked his hat up off the table and put it on. "Thanks for dinner," he said, walking out of the kitchen.

CHAPTER SIX

*L*ainey sat down at her favorite table at River's Saloon and pulled out her phone from her purse, just in case Hope texted to say she was running late. She leaned back in her chair and picked up one of the paper menus, even though she already knew she was going to have the Infamous River Burger and fries. Maybe extra fries, just because it was that kind of a night—no, it was that kind of week.

She had managed to avoid Tyler the rest of the week. Instead of waiting until later in the evening to go to the ranch, she made sure she was there by five because she knew Tyler would still be working. So far, her plan had worked.

But she was going to have to come up with the rest of the money she owed his father as soon as possible. The longer she waited, the worse she'd appear. The stress of all of it was making it almost impossible to paint anything, and she was going on her longest artistic dry spell ever. How would she ever be able to admit that she'd taken money from Martin to pursue a dream that had never even come true while he was losing his ranch and his savings? Saying she hadn't known just didn't seem adequate.

She toyed with the bowl of nuts on the table, slowly spinning it, wondering if she should tell Ty about her idea for his father's ranch. It would be a way for him to make extra money, and quite quickly. The only problem was if she started down that road, she'd be getting further involved with him and the ranch without telling him about the loan.

When had everything become so complicated? She wasn't a liar; she hadn't done anything wrong. Tyler was making everything complicated. He was turning out to be complex, and she was enjoying hanging out with him—too much.

Her gaze roamed the bar, trying to enjoy just sitting back and people watching for a while until her friend arrived. Maybe she'd find something paintable here. Maybe she'd get her mind off Ty and her money problems. Saturday nights at River's were pretty much a town tradition for the fifty-and-under crowd. There was always a live band, and once a month there was two hours of karaoke. The entire street was already filled with pickup trucks, and there wasn't a parking spot left. Drinks were cheap, and River's was one of the only places that still kept a running tab, payment required only once a month by locals.

The establishment had been here since the 1800s, the building probably as old as her diner. It had started as the Wishing River meeting hall and boarding house. It was a place where all were welcome, where ranchers met after branding, veteran groups met, Monday night football was watched, and where hunting buddies gathered.

The decor was classic Montana, with creaking old wood floors, and the smell was musky with hints of beer and pine. The ceilings were beamed, and there was antique taxidermy on the walls, along with old mining claim signs and black-and-white pictures of Wishing River.

"Sorry I'm late!" Hope said, looking frazzled as she flopped into the chair opposite her. She smoothed out her hair and took off her burgundy sweater coat to reveal a matching navy-and-burgundy-checked shirt. She was adorable, and Lainey noticed she'd even gone to the trouble of wearing lipstick. She wasn't going to bring it up, but she knew it was a big step for her friend. Hope hadn't bothered with her appearance in a long time, so Lainey took it as a good sign.

Lainey smiled at her friend. "No worries, I was just fantasizing about fries and Merlot."

Hope raised a brow. "Really? I thought you were going to say you were fantasizing about Tyler Donnelly."

Lainey sat back in her chair and tried to be a convincing liar. "Seriously? I'm not fifteen anymore."

"Have you ordered?" she said, leaning forward. "I'm going to need reinforcements before we get into good conversation. Don't think we're not coming back to the topic of Tyler."

Lainey shook her head. "No, but I'm basically planning on ordering a platter of grease and red wine to wash it down. Here comes Aiden." Aiden River's family had owned the saloon since it first started, and he treated Lainey and Hope like family whenever they came to the bar.

"Speaking of fantasies," Hope whispered, and they tried to keep a straight face as the handsome bartender and owner stopped at their table, giving them one of his infamous grins that produced a one-sided dimple. It was true that the two of them had declared Aiden one of the hottest men in Wishing

River, but that was before Hope had fallen for her own guy. Lainey was happy that Hope could even joke about fantasizing about a man again after what she'd been through. After her husband had died three years ago, she'd been left completely in shock, with a little girl to raise and a business to try and build. She and her husband, Brian, had been high school sweethearts, and he'd been a great guy and great father. These last few months were the first that Lainey could say her friend was really starting to come out of her shell again.

"Well, what can I get my two favorite women tonight?"

They both smiled up at Aiden's handsome face. He was gorgeous in a purely masculine, rough-and-tough kind of way that always drew female attention. The origins of the long scar on his cheek that was mostly covered by stubble had always remained a mystery—one that she and Hope had mused about on many a Saturday night.

"I'm having the River Burger and fries." She paused and smiled sheepishly. "Heavy on the fries."

He let out a short laugh, his green eyes twinkling. "You got it, Lainey. And am I getting you a glass of Merlot? A new case of imported just arrived for you two."

She nodded. "Definitely."

"I'm going to have the exact same thing," Hope said with a sigh.

He gave them a little salute and then left the table.

"So everything okay with Sadie?" she asked, noticing her friend kept checking her phone every few seconds.

Hope groaned. "Yeah, I guess. She has a cough, but I'm hoping it's nothing. It's just some days…" She paused and gazed up at the ceiling for a moment, and Lainey caught the wobble of her chin. "Some days I really, really miss Brian, and I worry about her not growing up with a dad, you know?"

Lainey's heart squeezed. "I can't even imagine, Hope. I just… I know that if there's anyone capable of raising that little girl alone and doing an amazing job, it's you. Sadie is so happy and bubbly and smart. Don't ever doubt you're enough. You are."

"I know you think that, but she asks about him. A lot. And now that she's in first grade, she's hearing about all these other kids and their dads, and I just want to make it all okay," she choked out.

"It will be," Lainey said, leaning forward. She didn't have kids; she'd never even had a serious boyfriend, so sometimes she felt like a fraud offering Hope reassurances. What did she know? Well, she did know that her BFF was strong and so devoted to Sadie.

They were both sniffling when a waitress brought their wine over. "Perfect timing," Hope said, taking a sip. "Here's to grandparents who enjoy babysitting," she said, raising her glass. "And to best friends who don't mind constant therapy sessions."

"Right. Like you haven't been there for me? This is why we eat burgers and fries. Life is hard—there's no point going through it depriving ourselves of good food."

They both raised their glasses. "One day, we really need to come here on karaoke night," Hope said, glancing over her shoulder at the podium.

Lainey put her wineglass down, horrified. "Excuse me?"

Hope nodded. "I think it'd be great."

"Since when?"

She shrugged, tucking a few strands of hair behind her ear. "Well, we could sing something."

She reached over to place her hand on Hope's forehead. Hope swatted it away. "Maybe some hot cowboy will get up there and sing," Hope said.

Lainey shook her head. Her poor friend. "That would never happen in a million years."

Hope shrugged with a smile. "If I ever get married again, the man has to be willing to stand up there and sing for me."

"Well, we all have our goals," Lainey said and grinned back at her, shocked that her friend even mentioned marriage again. It was a good sign. Despite the weird karaoke thing.

"All right, so tell me about Tyler," Hope said, twirling the stem of her wineglass.

"There's nothing to tell," she said, not really knowing why she was hedging. But there really wasn't.

"Let's just pretend you didn't say that and jump to the part where Tyler was at your diner a few nights ago after you closed?"

She paused with her wineglass halfway to her lips. "How did you know that?"

Hope's eyes sparkled with laughter. "I ran into Makenna from the Cheese Emporium, and she just happened to mention it."

Lainey leaned back in her chair and shook her head. "This town is way too small." She liked Makenna, and the three of them had all gone to high school together. "Nothing *happened*. Remember that loan that Martin gave me?"

Hope nodded.

"Tyler was going through the books and noticed there were withdrawals without any records."

"Did you tell him about the loan?"

Lainey shook her head slowly.

"Tell him. You have nothing to be ashamed of."

They both stopped talking as their mammoth plates filled with fries and a giant burger were delivered. "This is exactly what I needed," Hope said, grabbing a fry.

"Yeah," Lainey agreed, not even needing ketchup, since the freshly cut fries were so crispy and perfectly seasoned.

"Okay, so what are you going to do about the money?"

Lainey put down a fry with a sigh. "I have some of the money. I want to try and repay it before he figures it out."

"Don't you need that money for art school?"

"I'm not sure that's even on the table right now, Hope. There's too much happening, and it's not fair to hold on to that money when they really need it. I haven't even been able to paint—well, anything halfway decent—in months. I'm beginning to feel like a fake."

Hope put down her burger. "First off, you're not a fake. They wouldn't keep making exceptions for you if you were. Not going is not an option. I'll haul you over there myself if I have to. But for the record, I think you should just tell Ty the truth. Not telling him will only make you more stressed. How the heck are you going to pay him back, anyway?"

Lainey shook her head and reached for the wine. "More shifts. I'm going to do the downtime hours on my own."

"No offense, but that's not enough."

"I'm thinking of opening on Sundays. Maybe do an all-day brunch," she said, trying to pretend she was totally okay with working on her only day off.

Hope's eyes widened. "No, you can't do that. You'll burn out, Lainey. Then what? Tilly would wave a frying pan at you if she knew your plan. She never opened the place on Sundays."

"Yeah, well, she also never owed anyone ten thousand dollars."

"No. Tell Tyler exactly what happened. He'll understand. Do you have anything in savings?"

She put her head in her hands, her appetite suddenly gone. "A little. But not enough to pay him back."

"I have a couple thousand I could lend you," Hope said.

Lainey forced a smile for her best friend. "Thank you, but there is no way I'd take money from you. You need that—that's rainy-day money for you and Sadie. I'll be okay. I have some other ideas, too."

Hope gave her a long stare before picking up another fry.

"Oh, get this," she said, hoping to take Hope's mind off the money and her really bad plan. "So my roof started leaking again."

"Are you kidding me?"

"Wait, there's more. When Tyler was over, he asked about it, and I explained what happened. Well, the next morning, doesn't the owner of that roofing company show up? He went out to look at the roof for a while and then came back in and said he wasn't happy with the work his guys did. For now they'll do a little patch fix—he'll do it himself, he said. In the spring they are going to replace the entire flat roof over the kitchen. He gave it to me in writing."

Hope stopped chewing for a moment, her eyes growing wide. She waved a fry in front of Lainey's face. "Tyler did that?"

Lainey looked down at her half-eaten plate, knowing Hope was right. She didn't know how she felt about that. "He must have, right?"

Hope nodded. "Definitely."

Lainey sat back in her chair with her wine and crossed her leg over the other, just as Tyler walked through the door of the packed bar.

"He's here," she whispered, mortified that she sounded like she was in high school again. And even more mortified when her best friend almost fell out of her own chair in an effort to see Tyler.

"Oh man, Lainey, you weren't kidding about how he's changed," Hope whispered, not taking her eyes off him, her french fry hanging limply between her fingers.

Lainey swallowed a large gulp of wine. "I know," she croaked. Tyler was in extra-fine form tonight. He hadn't shaved, but he was wearing a blue-checked button-down shirt tucked into a pair of worn-in-all-the-right-places jeans. His dark cowboy hat was pulled low, but she could still see those sky-blue eyes from across the barn. Her gaze followed him as he approached the bar.

"I think you should go over there and talk to him,"

Hope whispered while dragging her french fry through an obscene amount of ketchup and not taking her eyes off Tyler.

Lainey frowned at her. "Why would I do that?"

"To thank him for the roof thing."

"But what if it was just a coincidence?"

Hope wiped her mouth and frowned at her. "Did the jerk roofer who refuses to ever repair that roof suddenly hear about the leaking roof, get a conscience, and then just come over?"

Lainey shook her head slowly. Doubtful.

"Well, then we both know it's not a coincidence," her friend said with a smug smile.

Lainey snuck a peek at Tyler again, but his back was to them, which she reluctantly noticed was also a good view. The man had no bad angles. "Oh no," she whispered, noticing some of the men near the pool tables.

"What now?"

"Cade and Dean are here," she said, nudging her head in their direction.

Hope turned in her chair. "Are they not on good terms yet?"

"I don't think so," she said, remembering the night at the house with Dean, and then when she'd walked to the barn to get them for dinner and it appeared as though Tyler and Cade had been about to get into it with each other. This wasn't her problem. She shouldn't be concerned. But she remembered the expression on Ty's face at his father's house, how lost, how sad he seemed.

"Well, I'm sure it'll be fine," Hope said, distracted as her phone vibrated on the table. She picked it up and sighed. "I need to get home. Sadie is crying and has a fever," she said, already standing. Lainey noticed how tired her friend suddenly seemed, tired way beyond her years.

Lainey grabbed her purse and stood up, ready to help out. "Want company? I can come with you."

Hope smiled. "You're the best, Lainey, but I'd hate for you to get whatever kind of plague she's picked up from school."

Lainey laughed. "Seriously, I don't mind. God knows what germs I'm exposed to every day at the diner."

Hope was shaking her head, her coat already on. "Don't worry about it. Besides, you have to take on a bunch of new shifts. We both have our issues. At least I got to eat all the fries and hear the latest Ty gossip."

Lainey reluctantly sat back down. She'd finish her dinner and then go home. "Yeah, but you didn't even have your wine," she said, pointing to the untouched glass.

"I had a sip. You can finish it off if you want. Are you going to be okay getting home? Maybe you can ask Tyler for a ride," she said with a mischievous smile as she glanced over her shoulder at the bar.

Lainey leaned back in her chair and crossed her arms. "Very funny. As if I'd ever do that. But don't worry. You go—I'll be fine. Text me tomorrow and let me know how Sadie's doing."

"Will do. Just do me a favor: Go and talk to that hot, lonely cowboy over at the bar," she said with a wink before walking away.

$\mathcal{T}$yler had walked into River's Saloon seeking a drink and some kind of perspective. What he got, not a minute into his old stomping ground, was a dose of his past in the form of his two former best friends glaring at him. He ignored their stupidity and went to sit his tired ass down on one of the old barstools.

He signaled to the bartender, who was busy helping some young women at the opposite end, and hauled himself onto a stool at the long counter. It was still wooden, with small dents and peanut shells littered across the top. River's was as much part of Wishing River as Tilly's Diner. When you needed to eat, you headed to Tilly's. When you needed to ease the wounds of life, you headed to River's.

Nothing in here had changed much, he was irrationally pleased to notice. There were still the dark, round tables with halfback chairs. Dark paneling on the walls. A few large flat-screen TVs were hung in different corners—so those were new. Pool tables at one end. The crappy podium on the other, where there was a young band playing some Sam Hunt songs while a few people danced on the dance floor. It was as though time stood still at River's.

"I heard you were back in town, but I needed to see it with my own eyes," Aiden River said, handing him a whiskey. He should have skipped the ice and gotten straight to the good stuff. "It's been a long time, man."

"Yeah, well, shit happens," he said, downing the

contents, not taking the comment personally. "Good to see you, Aiden. You running this place now?" Old Man River'd had a few heart attacks, and Ty assumed he was dead by now.

"Someone's got to keep it going," Aiden said with a rueful grin. "But welcome home," he said. Tyler appreciated the welcome, especially since he'd received so few of them. Aiden was a couple of years younger than him—more like in between his age and Lainey's, he figured. Lainey—why did his thoughts constantly wander to her?

"You look like you need another," Aiden said with a lift of his chin.

He needed a whole bottle since reentering Wishing River. "You're a smart man, but I think I'll pass for now."

Aiden let out a snort. "My instincts are finely honed to detect people's need for an emotional drink. How's your dad doing?"

He shrugged. "Holding his own. Recovery takes time, I'm told."

Tyler glanced over at Dean and Cade, who were at the pool table, their backs to him. Eight years ago, he'd have been right alongside them.

"You should go over and ask if they'll be BFFs with you again."

He stilled at the unmistakable voice—which was now filled with humor. Lainey. He turned in the direction of her voice and tried not to look startled by her appearance. She wasn't in her usual T-shirt and jeans—which he'd already decided she pulled off like no one else. Tonight, Lainey was dressed in a black figure-hugging sweater dress and tall black boots that almost went up to her knees. Her blond hair was long and wavy and fell over her shoulders. Her dark eyes seemed darker with the black dress, and her already-full lips seemed even more kissable with a glossy cranberry color. Hell.

"They aren't my 'BFFs'," he said, almost choking on the word.

She smiled mischievously, clearly pleased with her word choice. "Oh, come on. Everyone in town knows you guys were thick as thieves. You can't stay mad at them forever."

He shrugged. Actually, Lainey talking to him took away the sting of being rejected by his friends. "Things change. People change."

"Like you? I don't think you've changed all that much," she said.

He tightened his hand around the glass. "You didn't really know me before. I think when I left, you were still a kid."

She let out a *hmph* like she didn't really agree. "Eighteen is hardly a kid."

"Trust me. It's a kid."

"Well, I was running Tilly's by the time I was nineteen, so I couldn't have been a kid then."

He read the steel in her eyes. "You're right. You had to grow up fast."

"I should probably get going," she said, suddenly looking like she didn't want to be anywhere near him. Every time the conversation turned to her, she quickly changed it. Interesting. "But, um, I actually came over here with a purpose."

"Are you with friends?" he asked, wanting an excuse to keep the conversation going, to keep her here.

"I was, but Hope got called out on a medical emergency."

"Oh, is she a doctor?"

"Naturopath."

He vaguely remembered Hope—she had been at the diner a lot, hanging out with Lainey. "I didn't know naturopaths had medical emergencies."

She smiled. "Of course. But it wasn't that kind of a medical emergency. Her daughter isn't feeling well." She shuffled her feet nervously. "So, um, did you have anything to do with the fact that my roof got fixed?"

He tried to read her expression, because a part of him had worried she'd be insulted he'd stepped in on her behalf. "I did."

She pursed her lips. They were great lips. "Well, thank you. What did you do?"

He shrugged, not wanting to go into the finer details of how he'd gotten the roofer to go over. "I just told him to get over there and fix it."

She frowned at him. "There must have been more to it than that."

"Nope. He said he was happy to do it." True story. Of course, only after he'd hinted that he was checking up on the company's customer service, since he was considering re-roofing the ranch. "Everything should be fine now."

She gave him the side-eye. "I think I'll be going over to play pool with Dean and Cade."

"You're kidding me."

"Why don't you join me?"

He chuckled. "You don't need to try and set us up. This isn't kindergarten, Lainey."

She put her hands on her hips. "Of course not. As if I was trying to do that. So I'll just be going along, then. I'm sure one of them can give me a ride home," she said, leaving him with a small wave as she walked away. Hell if she didn't know him already.

He stood and followed her over to the pool table.

"Hi, Dean, hi, Cade," she said, shooting his ex-friends an extra-sweet smile, as though she weren't plotting anything.

They said hello but refused to make eye contact with him.

Lainey clasped her hands together and smiled at them, almost as though she were addressing school kids. "What a nice coincidence that we're all here tonight."

Dean and Cade gave him a nod, but then continued to play, completely ignoring him.

Lainey let out a theatrical sigh. "That's all you three have to say to one another after almost eight years? Hi and a couple of man nods. Seriously?"

They all shrugged and looked in different directions.

Lainey marched over to Dean and Cade and pulled their pool cues out of their hands. If this hadn't been about him, he might have laughed at the bossiness. "Why don't you ask Tyler what he's been doing all these years?"

Dean crossed his arms and gave him a deadpan stare. "So, Tyler, what have you been doing all these years since you left without a word?"

Lainey kicked him in the foot.

Ty tried not to smile. "Ranching for the last four years," he answered, rolling back on his heels, waiting for that to register.

"Ranching?" Lainey whispered.

He turned away from the disappointment in her eyes. Hell.

"So instead of staying and running your family ranch, you took off on your old man and went to help some other family ranch?" Cade said.

He crossed his arms, his gaze unwavering. "That's right."

"Why would you do that?" Lainey whispered.

"I needed to earn a living. Never mind. I didn't come over here to get questioned. See you later," he said, turning and walking away from them. He didn't want to get into a fight. Not with two guys who'd been like brothers to him, and definitely not in front of Lainey.

"So you're just too good? You don't need to answer to anyone? How 'bout you answer to the old man you almost killed?" Dean said.

He didn't think twice then. He crossed the room and had Dean pinned up against the wall faster than he could stop himself. "What the hell is your problem? When did you get so freaking judgmental? Last time I checked, you didn't have a clean record yourself."

"You pissed me off. You just took off; you didn't tell us. Nothing. Now you walk back in here, and we're supposed to give a shit?"

He slowly lowered his arm, his gaze not leaving Dean's. "No, you aren't. I never asked you to give a shit. I just never thought you'd be so damn judgmental. If I remember correctly, you guys both made your share of mistakes, and I never once turned my back on you." He glanced over at Cade, but it was Lainey, standing there, her face white, who made him regret losing his temper. He took a few steps back without saying a word, their censure loud enough, and walked away from his best friends one more time.

CHAPTER SEVEN

"This wasn't supposed to happen!" Lainey accused as she waved the pool cue at Dean and Cade after Ty stormed off.

Cade frowned. "Lainey, you need to be careful around Ty. He's got a lot of issues."

She gripped the smooth pool cue tightly. "I've been on my own a long time, Cade, and I know how to take care of myself. But you guys...tonight...you disappointed me. You didn't even give him a chance. You were friends for years."

"*He* left, Lainey. Not us," Dean said, his jaw tight and his eyes glittering.

She threw up her hands, letting the cue drop to the ground. "Fine. This is none of my business; I was just trying to do something nice. But Ty is back, and he's trying to do the right thing. At the very least, the three of you should try and have a real conversation," she said, backing up a step. How on earth had she gotten herself into this mess? Male relationships were an entirely different beast. None of them wanted to talk about their feelings, and all they did was throw accusations at one another.

"We'll try," Cade said, nudging Dean.

Dean didn't say anything.

"You should have a civil conversation where you're not hurling insults. Talk about your feelings, how he hurt you," she said.

Dean ran his hands down his face, letting out a groan.

Cade didn't look much better. "He didn't hurt our feelings. But I know you're trying to help, and that's really sweet of you… Just don't get too involved and wind up hurt."

"Well, I'll go and be a friend to Tyler," she said. "Hopefully you guys can remember what good friends you used to be and give him another chance." She hurried through the crowd, worried that Tyler was long gone by now.

Whipping open the door of the Saloon, her gaze scanned the area. He was already halfway down the parking lot. She ran after him, not sure why. Well, she did know why. She was a sucker for a tough man with a softer side. She got it. She got that he wasn't this arrogant, cold bastard she'd assumed he was. The hurt in his eyes as his former best friend told him he was still mad at him tore at her. She was responsible for that because she had forced the confrontation.

"Tyler!" she yelled. "Slow down. I'm wearing heels, and if I twist my ankle and can't work, you'll be waiting tables on Monday!"

He stopped short and turned around. She slowed her pace.

"Go back inside, Lainey," he snapped.

She ignored him. "I walked here when it was still light out. My ride left. You can have the privilege of driving me home, or I can just find my own way back. I have no problem walking in the dark," she said, catching up to him and giving his chest a pat, then continuing toward the road. She ignored how hard his chest had felt in that brief moment of contact. She couldn't actually believe she was doing this, but it must have been from a purely altruistic place, helping the tall, dark, brooding cowboy she'd crushed on her entire adolescence. Yes, that must be it.

He groaned and hung his head back. She may have also made out a muffled curse. "Get in the truck, Lainey."

She stopped. "I'd hate to put you out."

He didn't say anything as he unlocked her side of the truck and held open the door for her. Impressive.

"Thank you," she said as she got into the truck. "It's very nice of you to offer to drive me back."

He didn't say anything as he climbed into the driver's seat. A minute later, they were settled in his truck, and he pulled out of the gravel parking lot. She shivered a little, only partly due to the temperature.

"Cold?"

She nodded, and he reached and turned the heat on full blast then directed the vents at her. Shit. He was such a nice guy under all that bluster, and now a couple of glasses of wine were making him harder to resist.

"Did you say something?" he asked.

Clearing her throat, she sat up a little straighter. "Nope. Well, maybe. I think I may have said I'm sorry things didn't work out with your friends."

"Huh. 'Cause I could have sworn you said, 'Shit.'"

This was why she didn't need a man. "Clearly you're wrong. I'm pretty sure I said I was sorry things didn't work out with your friends. Also, after I said that, I was planning on saying that when you're trying to make up with your friends, you shouldn't slam one of them against a wall with your arm against his throat."

His profile was handsome, even though his jaw

was clenching and unclenching. It was a look that kind of suited him. It also seemed to accentuate the strong lines of his face. "Thanks for that advice; I'll be sure to keep it in mind next time I see them. But for the record, I wasn't trying to make up with them in the first place."

She tilted her head. "I disagree. I recognized the expression on your face. You're hurting," she said, her voice much softer. She suddenly didn't want to tease him anymore. She wanted to comfort him.

"I'm not five. They can't hurt my feelings."

"They can if they still mean something to you."

His jaw clenched again. "They mean nothing to me."

"Then why did you get so upset?"

"Lainey?"

She ignored the butterflies taking flight in her stomach at the sound of her name on his breath. "Yes?"

"When did you start talking this much?"

She sighed. "I don't talk a lot. I hardly talk. In fact, I think you talk more than I do."

"Then I'll try not to. I think we'll get along better if we don't speak." He winked at her to soften his words then focused back on the road.

"I find that highly insulting." She gave him a measured stare. "But I also know you're just trying to distract me so we don't have to talk about your feelings."

Running a hand through his already mussed-up hair, he pulled in front of the diner. The streets were deserted because everything in the downtown area was closed by this time of night. He turned to her, and she had to swallow nervously. He was mouth-watering up close. All hard lines, stubble, and wounded eyes. He was every dream she'd ever had about a man. And every nightmare.

"Why don't I walk you up?"

"Oh, that's okay. I'm used to going home on my own. Besides, I may have the urge to talk and talk. I'd hate to irritate you with all my chatter."

He let out a choked laugh. "Well, that doesn't sit well. It's late at night, and you have to go around the side. Come on. We'll try not to kill each other in the next few minutes."

"I'll try my best," she said, though killing him was the furthest thing from her thoughts at the moment. There was something about having Ty walk her up the dark stairwell to her apartment that made her feel cared for, safe. She'd been on her own so long that she'd forgotten what it was like to have someone beside her. He waited patiently while she found her keys and unlocked the door. She reached for the light switch on the lamp on the hall table, and suddenly his face was illuminated. It was a hard face to turn away from. The usual strong lines were softer, his eyes filled with something she wasn't used to seeing from him. The realization that she didn't want him to leave was disconcerting, and maybe it was the two glasses of wine she had, or maybe it was the sense of loss at the idea of him walking away that prompted her to invite him in.

"Do you want a drink or something?"

Surprise flickered across his eyes, and she held her breath waiting for his reply. "I, uh." He paused for a moment, and heat flooded her face. He was going to say no. What had she been thinking? Of course he wouldn't want to spend more time with her—he was trying to get rid of her. She was the woman who'd forced him to talk to his friends and had inadvertently almost started a barroom brawl. She wasn't equipped to handle Tyler Donnelly after hours.

"Sure," he said a moment later, walking in and shutting the door. Her apartment was small, which she liked, but he seemed to fill up the entire room, and her place felt even smaller than usual. His gaze was bouncing around from her cozy couch in the corner to her bookcase crammed with paperbacks to the granite bar leading into the kitchen. "I like your place," he said, following her into the kitchen that opened onto the living area.

"Thanks. It's where I grew up. I guess I've made it my own over the years, but it's convenient. At least I don't have to commute to work." She was scanning the sorry contents of her fridge, but there was nothing even remotely interesting to drink. Unsweetened almond milk and filtered water. She had no life, and her fridge was evidence of that. "So I think I kind of lied, because I have nothing other than coffee and water," she said, wincing with embarrassment.

"No emergency whiskey?" A corner of his mouth tilted upward, and her stomach flipped around a few times.

"All out… I've had a lot of emergencies lately," she said sheepishly.

He coughed, bringing his fist to his mouth, hiding a laugh no doubt.

She had to offer something. She'd never realized what an embarrassing person she was. What single person in her twenties only had almond milk and water? "I'm going to make some coffee. Do you want a cup?"

"What time is it? Isn't it late?"

She pulled the coffee canister forward and removed the lid. "It's nine thirty. Oh right, I forgot people over thirty can't drink coffee this late, right?"

His lips twitched, and his eyes sparkled. "I'll have a cup."

She was relieved that he seemed a little less tense than before. She smiled and started brewing the coffee as he walked around the small family room. She'd been so angry with him when he'd first come back, and she had made assumptions about him, but from that first meeting, she'd detected the hurt that was hiding beneath the tough surface. His last few moments in the diner when he'd told her that not everything was black and white—his voice had held such pain in it that she knew for sure something had happened to make him run. Tonight she'd witnessed it again, even though he'd chosen to lash out instead of really deal with the truth.

He glanced down the hall, and she panicked, not wanting him to see her art room. "Things going better at the ranch?" she asked, desperate to distract him.

He put his hands in his back pockets. "No. Not at all, but I think that's the new normal. I'm getting somewhere with the books, so that's good."

"I have an idea for your ranch," she blurted out, needing to break the intensity of his stare and needing to do something to help. Something that would ease her conscience. She hadn't planned on saying anything yet, because she hadn't really thought it through, but guilt was a strong motivator.

"Oh yeah?"

She pulled out her two favorite mugs from a local pottery shop and filled them both, scrambling to find the right words and to actually make a case for what she believed was a pretty good plan. She just needed to stay on track. She would pay him back—this guilt would go away when she came up with the money. "Do you take milk or sugar in your coffee?"

He shook his head. "Just black." Perfect. He was waiting for her, standing in front of the grouping of pictures she had along the mantel of her electric fireplace.

She handed him a mug, and her entire body tingled as his hand brushed hers. She was standing very close to him, and it was difficult to breathe or concentrate.

"Thanks," he said.

"Okay, sit down, and I'm going to get my laptop," she said, placing her mug on the coffee table and running to her bedroom.

A moment later, she joined him on the couch and opened her laptop, quickly pulling up the site she'd bookmarked.

"Here, read and then tell me what you think," she said, shoving her computer in front of him.

He gave her a look, letting her know with just his expression how skeptical he was of this idea. He didn't say anything for the next few minutes as he clicked his way through the site.

She watched his profile, but the man didn't reveal an ounce of emotion. "This is a guest ranch," he said finally.

"It is, but it's a working ranch, too. They rent out the cabins, and they give people a glimpse of what it's like to work on a real ranch. People are willing to pay a lot of money to be a cowboy or cowgirl for a week, or even just a weekend," she said, taking a sip of her coffee.

He made a small grunt as he clicked through different tabs on the screen. "They'd get in the way. I don't like the idea of a bunch of people hanging around and needing to be entertained. It'd take us away from a real day's work. And the liability. What if someone got hurt or an inexperienced rider fell off a horse?"

"There'd be waivers to sign, of course. Really, what you need to do is model yours after a typical week vacation at these other ranches. It doesn't have to be extravagant. In fact, people don't want it to be extravagant; they want to rough it out, like a cowboy."

He groaned and stretched his legs in front of him. "I don't like people, Lainey."

She choked on her coffee. "You could make an easy ten thousand a week. Can't you pretend to like people for ten thousand dollars?"

His jaw clenched as he snapped his head toward the screen again. "Are you kidding?"

"No joke. You wouldn't have to do it forever, either. Just until you get the ranch profitable again. It's a means to an end, really. How else are you going to make that kind of money for such little effort?"

He ran a hand over his jaw. "You make a really strong case."

She smiled, trying not to appear too smug, trying

not to get too excited in case he didn't go through with it.

"But I don't know. I'll have to think about it. I'm not sure what the men would say. Cade wouldn't like it, that's for sure."

"Well, would he like to work for a large, profitable ranch again? Besides, this is *your* family ranch. It's your responsibility to turn it around for your father," she said, hoping for a definitive yes.

"You want to present him with the idea?" he said, smiling. Little lines crinkled around the corners of his eyes.

"I can take some pictures of the ranch, of you guys on horseback." She wanted to add she should take a picture of him and Cade. They'd help boost sales for sure.

"Why are you looking at me like that?"

She tried not to squirm under his intense stare. "Well, I was thinking that maybe you could, uh, pose for some pictures."

He scowled. "Like a photo shoot? Nope. Not happening."

"Or Cade. Maybe on a horse, with his hat pulled low…"

"Fine, I'll do it." He turned his attention back to the computer screen, but it seemed like he was glaring at it now. She took that opportunity to study him. What had happened to her youth? she mused as she stared at Tyler's profile. There were gorgeous cowboys everywhere, and yet she'd been so busy working that she hadn't ever done anything remotely…fun. Tilly was partly to blame, maybe, with her dire warnings about avoiding cowboys and their charm.

She ignored the shiver that stole through her body as she noticed the smattering of hair along his forearm. Not too much, not too little. His forearm was also roped with muscle and tanned skin, and it flexed every time he pressed down on the trackpad.

"Do I have some kind of disease on my arm?"

Her gaze flew to his. Heat flooded her face. She had no idea he'd been watching her...watch him. She frantically came up with an excuse. "No, of course not. I just never noticed what a hairy person you are."

He turned away slowly, almost like he wanted to say something but thought better of it.

Phew. At least he'd bought the insult. She shoved her mug of coffee in her mouth, hoping the blush would go away.

"Seems to me like you have issues saying what you really think, Lainey," he said, a smile curling the corner of his mouth as he continued reading through the terms on the website. He leaned back into the cushions, and she realized that the man was actually much too cocky for her liking.

"That's what I was thinking. You're a hairy man. I'll make sure I don't get that in the pictures."

Laughing, he turned to her. She raised her eyebrows innocently and took a sip of her coffee then choked.

"That's what happens when you lie," he said, his blue eyes dancing.

Very charming. Too charming. Irresistible, really, she decided. That perfect smile was too perfect, too. "I'm not choking. And really, I was staring at your forearm. Relax. The fact that you're implying that

I've sexualized your forearm is really disturbing. It's a clear indication that your ego is entirely too large. I stand by my original statement of distracting, above-normal hairiness."

"Sure thing," he said, his smile not cracking.

"I think you need to get back to looking at those sites," she said, pointing her finger at the computer screen.

"Fine. But you need to keep your thoughts platonic."

She let out a choked cough. "Don't flatter yourself. I may have considered you somewhat attractive in my youth, but those days are long gone."

He stilled and then turned to her. Oh. *Oh*. Why had she just admitted that? And he was staring at her all funny, too, like that revelation actually meant something. She waved her hand around, accidentally sloshing coffee on her dress.

"I didn't know you had a crush on me when you were a teenager."

She held up her hand. "Oh, easy there, cowboy. I didn't say 'crush.' I said I thought you were somewhat attractive, and that in no way translates to a crush. I find lots of things attractive… Horses, cows…"

He rubbed a hand over his jaw, and something flickered across his eyes. "Sure, Lainey."

When five minutes passed with neither of them speaking, she had to admit to herself that he couldn't care less. It had seemed like they were flirting, but now he was just back to staring at the screen. She was reading too much into this. They were friends. He needed a friend. Another minute or two passed, and then he stood abruptly, placing the laptop on the coffee table.

"I'll think about this. Thank you for, uh, coming up with the idea."

She stood, too, trying to appear fine with the fact that he was ending their night and basically blowing her off. She watched him put his hat on and make his way to the front door, and it didn't seem right. None of it. His behavior, his abrupt departure.

"Why did you leave?" she blurted out.

His hand was on the doorknob, his back to her. She held her breath, not knowing if he'd bother answering or if he thought it was none of her business. But she wanted to know. She wanted to know that what everyone had said about him was wrong. She wanted him to prove to her that he had a heart, that his feelings ran as deep as she hoped they did.

He slowly turned, and his eyes were clouded, his mouth pulled into a tight line.

"It was complicated. If you're wanting me to prove that I'm a good guy, it's not going to happen. I am what I am, and I took off on my father for eight years. That's the whole story. I worked the rodeo circuit for a few years, then I worked my way up to foreman on a ranch in Wyoming. That's it."

Disappointment made it difficult for her to speak. She knew there was more, she could see it in his eyes, but it obviously wasn't something he wanted to share. That was fine. She had her own secrets, her own demons. She'd been foolish to think that their banter actually meant he was attracted to her.

She smiled brightly, trying to appear as though she wasn't hurt. "I wasn't wishing you'd prove anything. Why would I do that? Why would it matter to me? I was just being polite. Thanks for driving me home. Good night, Tyler."

His jaw clenched for a few moments, and she thought he was going to turn around and leave.

"I've wanted to tell you, from the beginning, how thankful I am that you are my father's friend. I know you have your issues with me, but I do…care for my father. You saved him, and I'm indebted to you."

Her stomach twisted painfully because she was the one indebted to him, and he had no idea. She swallowed hard, quelling the urge to tell him. It would end everything, and he would never trust her. She stared at the handsome, proud man in front of her and resisted the urge to reach out to him. She'd never seen anyone so hard and tough become vulnerable. "You aren't indebted to me, not at all. Martin and I are friends, and I'd do anything for my friends."

"Well, thanks," he said, the light in his eyes making her want to tell him everything.

She sighed, running a hand down her thigh. "He loves you. It wasn't an easy decision for him to start selling off land, and it took him a long time to actually go through with it. I'm sure you know land value went up big time out there, and I don't need to tell you how hard the ranching life is. He…didn't think you were coming back. Ever." She paused when he glanced away but continued speaking. "He got a very good offer from a motivated buyer, and the timing was right, you know? They wanted his cattle and a huge portion of his machinery. A lot of the ranch hands went to that farm as well, so your father didn't feel too guilty about laying off his boys."

He was nodding, one hand rubbing the back of his neck. "When was this?"

"Last year," she said.

He nodded but didn't say anything for a long while. "It must have gutted him."

A chill swept through her, and she folded her arms across her chest. "He didn't come to the diner for a week. I went up to see him and brought Mrs. Busby with me. He…was down. It was a lot to take. He missed your mom. He missed you." She didn't add that he hadn't actually said he missed his son, but she and Mrs. Busby knew. He would always stand in front of Ty's picture on the wall when he spoke about the ranch or how everything had changed. "After a while, he started coming back in again. He's not a man who stays down for long," she said, forcing a smile even though Ty's face was ashen.

"What about…the day you found him?"

She stared at the vulnerability in his gaze, and her stomach pitched, memories bringing tears to her eyes. "It was bad. It was right up there with one of the worst days of my life. I was worried about him. He hadn't shown up for dinner. I wanted to get out to see him because they were calling for freezing rain the next day, and I hate driving those roads when there's a storm. So anyway, I parked and was walking up to the house when I stopped. I don't know why I stopped, because there was no sound, nothing. But I stopped and turned in the direction of the red barn on the east end of the farm, and I made out…" She blinked back tears. "There was a lump on the ground in the distance."

He fisted his hands and shoved them into his front pockets.

She blinked back tears but didn't stop her story. He needed to know. He needed to feel. His father needed to become important to him again, and the best way to do that was for him to realize just how close he was to losing him forever.

"I dropped the container of food I was holding and ran. I couldn't exactly make out that it was him, but I knew in my gut. I ran as fast as I could, as fast as I ever have. I remember not being able to breathe properly, like the weight of my lungs was too much, that everything was too much. I was crying when I made out his form, his hat beside him on the ground. I thought he was dead." This time her voice did break, and she was unable to stop the tears as they rolled down her face.

"I'm sorry," he said roughly.

She took a deep breath, knowing this was her only chance to get it all out, hoping that maybe she could soften him toward his father. "He wasn't moving. I yelled his name, and then I turned him over slowly, and his face—"

Her voice cracked, and the loneliness that had followed her around in the years since her grandmother's death slowly receded as Tyler reached out and pulled her against him. She hadn't expected that. She had learned to never expect anything, least of all the sense of safety that came from being held. Her forehead rested against his hard chest, and she felt his chin sit softly against her head. One of his hands was slowly circling her back, and she took a deep breath.

She had lived in a world surrounded by people but had never fallen in love. She had never opened herself up to reveal what was really on the inside. It was one thing to have silly little fantasies about Ty, but it was another thing entirely to be held by him, to have him witness emotions that she kept tightly hidden. There hadn't been anyone around in so long to ever catch her when she fell.

"It should have been me," he said, his voice sounding like it had been drug along a gravel road.

"We can't go back," she whispered, holding onto him, not wanting to lose his strength. "I just held him while waiting for the ambulance, told him we all loved him. I told him you'd come home, Ty."

His hands tightened around her, and he pulled her closer, like he needed her, not the other way around. His lips brushed the top of her head.

"Thank you," he whispered, the roughness in his voice pulling her from the tormented memories of that day and into the reality of being held by him.

She was suddenly very aware of the strong heartbeat beneath the solid chest, the strength in the arms that were holding her, the clean, woodsy scent of the man who made her feel so many different emotions. She slowly pulled back, tilting her head up. Her breath caught in her throat as he gazed down at her. His eyes were dark and glittering with something that made it difficult for her to breathe normally. His large hands reached out to frame her face, and she felt the rough calluses beneath them; she felt the tenderness in his touch.

And then it was gone.

"I should get going," he said, his face closing up, almost like he regretted letting her see this side of him at all.

Maybe in her dreams he would have continued, he would have said how he wanted to be the one who was there for her. Maybe he would have leaned down and kissed her slowly, softly. Maybe he would have spent the night talking to her, holding her, laughing with her. Maybe he would have wanted more…than just her friendship.

But instead, he dropped his arms and put his hand on the doorknob. "Good night, Lainey."

She forced a smile. Her trademark Lainey-just-got-shafted smile. The Lainey-is-always-left-alone smile. That was okay. Her life was comfortable. There was no emotional baggage. There was no one to love and then lose. It wasn't like she wanted him to kiss her—that would be stupid. Getting involved with him would be suicide. He was clearly a man with a lot of baggage. She didn't need that.

Besides, Grandma Tilly had told her many stories about why she should never trust a cowboy. She needed to remember that—she also needed to remember she owed Ty ten grand and it would be better to keep her distance. She'd go and deliver dinner as usual, but she needed to avoid Tyler. It was a solid plan and maybe a week ago would have been doable…

Now, it seemed impossible.

CHAPTER EIGHT

*O*ne week later, Tyler had accepted the fact that Lainey had a pretty damn good idea. Not that he actually wanted to open up the ranch to guests, but he liked the idea of the money it could generate. They already had the cabins from the earlier days when their ranch was huge, and now they were just sitting there empty. Plus, they had the manpower, and they still had more than two hundred thousand acres. He spoke with his father's business accountant, and he supported the idea—several of her other clients were already doing the exact same thing to bolster their income.

He'd also decided he was going to live in one of the cabins. It was too awkward at the house. There was round-the-clock help, anyway. He needed some space from this mausoleum. All it did was make him remember his mother, and he'd worked so hard at trying to forget her.

It was also painful seeing his father…just lying there.

Of course, it didn't help that whenever he tried to talk to the man, he pretended he couldn't communicate. Well fine, then why should Ty just sit there begging him to acknowledge him every morning?

No, the cabin would be much better.

His first priority was making the place liveable. Then he could make it better. He needed running water, a functioning washroom, a fridge, a coffeemaker, and a microwave. There was a stone fireplace that was on the center wall of the one large room that would serve him well in the winter. He could easily fit two couches. Though that seemed kind of pointless, since he didn't have any friends. Still. A coffee table would be good, mainly so he could put his feet up on it after a long day, with a beer in his hand from the new fridge he had to buy. There was one bedroom, and he was mildly impressed by the window with the view of the mountains. He needed a bed, mattress, nightstand, lamp, and sheets and blankets. After checking out the washroom, he added towels and a shower curtain to that list. It was doable. It beat living in the house or at the bunkhouse where Cade was.

He just needed to convince his father that renting out the other cabins would be a good idea. Ty leaned forward in the chair beside his father's bed, pretty sure his dad was fake sleeping again. He'd been fake sleeping every time he'd walked in the room over the last two weeks. Well, there was one way to call him out on it.

"So I decided that in order to make some extra money and get the ranch profitable again, I'd renovate the old cabins at the base of the mountains and make them guest houses. Like, for people to take vacations." He paused when his father's eyelids flickered. Ty resisted the urge to smile. He waited for a few seconds, but when his father's eyes remained shut, he upped the ante. "Seems like it's a pretty popular thing. You know, people from the city wanting to see what it's like to be a cowboy. We can charge a few thousand a week. People will come out on cattle drives, sing 'Kumbaya' by the campfire, that kind of thing. It was Lainey's idea. Pretty brilliant. But then again, Lainey's pretty brilliant. Beautiful, too."

His father's eyes opened wide. "Alert and angry" would be the most accurate description of the glare. So it seemed his dad didn't like him noticing Lainey's attributes.

Lainey was a whole other issue he'd been grappling with all week.

The night at the bar and her apartment left him wanting... He didn't think he'd ever wanted to know more about any woman, even the ones he'd slept with. She'd also broken his heart a little bit, and he didn't know what to make of that. He was indebted to her. She had saved his father's life; she had been a friend to him when he was completely alone. But it hadn't been easy on her, and the more he thought about it, the guiltier he became. She had been through a hell of a lot in her young life, and he was in part to blame for that. It should have been him who found his father.

He had also realized just how close she and his father had become. The softness in her voice when talking about him made it clear that he was very dear to her. He could understand why his father would be drawn to Lainey—she was sweet and she listened and she was good. He'd never really been on the receiving end of any of that warmth. He didn't begrudge Lainey and the relationship she had with his father, and on some level he was happy for her. She'd grown up so alone and had never known two parents.

As much as he'd understood her pain that night,

there was much more. She'd felt good in his arms…
like she belonged there, like she fit him. It had been
natural for him to comfort her, to hold her, when
he'd never had those desires before.

She had managed to avoid him all week by faith-
fully dropping off dinner while he was still working.
He'd made it easy for her by eating with the men at
the canteen. Well, he'd enjoyed making it easier for
her and harder on Cade. Working day in and day out
with his former best friend was aggravating to say
the least, but they'd managed to keep it civil. There
was no time, anyway, to get into their problems.

But he should have thanked her for thinking of
the idea for the ranch. She didn't have to do that.

He stared at his father, wondering if he was ever
going to crack and have a decent conversation with
him again. "You think it's a good idea?" he asked,
leaning back in his chair, knowing damn well his dad
would hate it.

His father's mouth actually drew into somewhat
of a perfect semblance of a frown. Well, at least he
was getting a reaction. It was the most he'd had from
his dad in a week.

"I wasn't too crazy about the idea of having a
bunch of strangers wandering around the place, but
I did some research with Lainey, and it seems to be
a growing industry. We wouldn't have to invest too
much money up front, and I've got that covered
so you don't need to worry about it. I could work
on those cabins now that things are slower around
here. But if we rented out each one, we could make
supplemental income of around ten thousand a
week before expenses."

His dad gave an awkward shift of his head. A clear no.

"You know, this just means more work for me, not you. Those cabins aren't in great shape." It wasn't that he was afraid of hard work—hell, he'd grown up on a ranch with a dad who was more like a drill sergeant than a father. Then when he'd left town, he'd had to work twice as hard to earn a decent living. But now he'd just added this to his plate, plus he was already working long hours on the family ranch again, plus trying to make some sense of the books, and to top it all off, he was now stuck renovating three cabins in his "spare" time.

His father just continued to frown at him.

Ty straightened up in his chair, unwilling to bend on this. "We have no choice. I took down the listing, and we're not selling off any more land. Not an option."

His father's eyes flashed with fury, and his good hand clenched into a fist.

"I'm home. This is my ranch, too, and you're not just going to get rid of it. This is my heritage. Granddad's legacy. I'm going to turn this thing around. Once we're in the black again, we won't have to keep renting it out. I don't want to take this from you; I want to work it with you—when you're better."

His father shook his head again. Tyler took a deep breath in an attempt to keep his temper in check. He was trying. He was trying to reach out to him, to show him he wanted to start a life here again with him, to give it another chance, and he was being rejected.

He stood. "I've saved some money the last few years. I already deposited it into the ranch account. It'll cover the cost of the renovation for sure."

His dad squeezed his eyes shut, his fist now turning white.

"Hey, stop making my patient angry."

Shit. Tyler turned toward Dean, who was now walking through the living room like he owned the damn place—or worse, like he cared more for his dad than Tyler did. "I'm not trying to make him angry. I'm actually sharing the news of how I'm going to turn the ranch around. It's supposed to make him happy."

Dean stood in front of him and glanced back and forth between the two of them. "Well, don't overload him with stuff. He's supposed to be resting and recovering, not dealing with ranch business. Or, here's an idea: Maybe he doesn't trust you."

Tyler gritted his teeth. "Thanks. That's exactly what he needs to hear right now," he said, unable to contain his sarcasm. "It's really great you're able to put aside your personal differences with me in order to help your patient."

Tyler walked away from both of them, the uncomfortable sensation that he was still a stranger, still an outcast, making him want to run again.

Instead he walked out onto the porch, the desire to see Lainey taking him by surprise. It wasn't closing time. He could go there, get a good meal... Hell, he just wanted to see her. He braced his hands against the cold railing and took a deep breath, staring out at the mountains, even though they were barely visible in the darkness. He knew they were there. He'd memorized them. He'd see them at night, in his dreams, all those years he'd been away.

This place was in his blood. But it wasn't the same, and maybe that was part of the reason he'd run. He knew after his mother was gone it would never be the same—it *could* never be the same. She was the glue.

He stopped thinking about her with that. He didn't want to think about the secrets she'd kept, the other life she'd had. He preferred to think of the woman he did know, the one running the diner, the one he wanted to see at the end of a long day.

$\mathcal{T}$yler took a sip of the piping-hot coffee and tried not to turn on the barstool inside Tilly's. He'd spent a helluva lot of time on these stools as a teenager. He glanced around the diner, careful not to really linger on any one person in case they took it as an invitation to talk to him. Not that he was the most popular guy in town at the moment—far from it. He knew everyone was loyal to his father, and he was fine with that. He didn't have to prove himself to anyone.

Lainey walked past him with her coffeepot and set it back down on the warming burner.

Except her. Maybe he had something to prove to her. He didn't know why, but the quiet hurt in her dark eyes bothered him. It shouldn't, because Lainey was supposed to just be an acquaintance. Nothing had happened between them, despite their time together. Nothing *could* happen.

Yes, she was gorgeous, but that didn't matter, because she didn't seem to like him that much, and he had no time for anything except getting the ranch profitable again. Getting his father better and then repairing the ranch was all he had time for. Not only were women not on the agenda right now—women like Lainey weren't on any agenda in the past, present, or future. Women like Lainey were right for either one of his former best friends—men who had their shit together and wanted the whole package deal. He owed her his gratitude, and that was it. Anything more and he'd be screwing up her life.

He frowned as he tore his eyes away from Lainey's perfect profile and forced himself to stare into his cup. He didn't like thinking of Lainey with either of his best friends. Fine. So not them. Maybe... Hell, this was a useless line of thinking, because for all he knew, Lainey already had a boyfriend. That was probably the case. There was no way a woman like that wouldn't be attached to someone. She probably had tons of boyfriends. But she had been alone at a bar on Saturday night and had invited him in. So maybe she *was* alone.

"Are you getting something to eat or just drinking coffee until closing time?" she finally asked. She'd been avoiding him and hadn't even served him when he'd walked in an hour ago. She'd had her part-timer, Sally, bring him his coffee. He was now on his third refill.

He pushed the cup away slightly. "Well, would *you* serve me if I ordered food?"

She crossed her arms, leaned a hip against the counter, and eyed him with the wisdom of a much older woman. "Of course. It's not like I was avoiding you or anything."

He knew she was lying. She was avoiding him because she'd shown him her vulnerable side, and he'd reached out and comforted her. "Well, then if that's the case, I'll have whatever the special is tonight."

"Sure. Oh, and you picked a great night to come in. Father Andy is always in on a Wednesday."

His face must have gone white, because she actually smiled at him—at his discomfort. "Father Andy is still in Wishing River?"

She nodded, her smile widening even more. Dammit if her smile wasn't the nicest one he'd seen in…hell, he didn't know how long. "I'm sure he remembers you. Maybe he could even set up some kind of penance thing, like on a daily basis you could use the church—"

"You're very funny, Lainey," he said, cutting her off.

She raised her eyebrows innocently, a hand flying to her chest. "I don't know what you're talking about."

"I want to be talking about food," he lied.

"Well, I'll see if I can help you," she said before walking back into the kitchen.

The jingling on the front door of the restaurant made him turn, and his stomach dropped as Father Andy walked in. The man had barely aged—except for the thinning of his hair. Tyler and his father had never really been ones to be…enthusiastic about going to church. He had no idea if his father went after he left. He hadn't gone back to church after his mother's funeral; it wasn't a place that he wanted to see again. He'd always liked Father Andy, though. He'd been the type of priest who'd been approachable and friendly and great with youths. But he knew the other side of the man, too, the side that had brought his mother so much comfort in her last days. He'd shown her compassion and wisdom and faith. He'd held her hand, he'd read to her from his weathered bible, and he'd prayed with her.

At the time, Tyler had almost been angry when he'd seen that. He'd always left the room. What was the point of any of it? What was the point in believing in a God that was going to let you die too soon? Sitting around and praying was useless when they all could have been coming up with another way to save his mom. But no one had listened to him—they had all just let her die.

Father Andy made eye contact with him from across the diner. His palms were sweaty as he stood and raised a hand in greeting, not knowing what the priest was going to do. He held his breath and then suddenly, Father Andy was in front of him, taking his hand, pumping it, clasping it with his other one.

"It is good to see you, son. Welcome home," he said. Deep lines appeared on either side of his mouth as he smiled at him, and his dark eyes shone with a happiness no one had given him since coming back to Wishing River. There wasn't a speck of judgment in the man's gaze, and relief flooded him. He hadn't realized how much the censure had been getting to him.

"Father, it's good to see you," Ty said, clearing his throat.

"Your dad must be so happy to have you home.

A prayer answered," he said.

Ty had never witnessed his father pray. Well, once. At the end. He'd heard him, loud and clear. But never before and never since. Certainly not for him to come home. "I guess."

"Well, it's good to see you. I'm going to go sit and have my dinner now," he said, clasping Ty's shoulder. "I hope I see you on Sunday."

He didn't wait for Ty's reply, just smiled at him and went to the table in the far corner and sat down. Lainey followed the priest, and Ty watched as she smiled and laughed with Father Andy. She'd already brought him his dinner and a cup of coffee. There were so many regulars here—because of her. Sure, people had been coming to Tilly's forever, and there had always been regulars, but there was something different about the place now that Lainey was running it. There was a warmth about her that people picked up. She smiled as though she hadn't seen a person in years, and she listened as though she really gave a shit about someone's day.

Tilly had been nice and chatty, but there had been a harder edge to her that Lainey didn't have.

He caught Lainey saying something to Father Andy about not attending on Sunday, but couldn't make out the reason or the priest's reply. He shouldn't care so much.

"So I guess you still have some food in the kitchen, then?" Tyler called out as Lainey walked back behind the counter.

She pursed her lips, gave him a stare that had him rethinking her warmth, and then walked into the kitchen. She came back out a few minutes later with a plate filled with roast beef, mashed potatoes, and roasted broccoli, with two biscuits on the side. He almost died from the smell.

"Here. I guess I can't have a cowboy starve in my diner."

"Uh-huh. Or maybe it's because there's a priest in here, and you're afraid of what he'll think of you."

He had the pleasure of watching her cheeks go red as she glared at him. He laughed softly but dug into the plate of food, just in case she decided to remove his plate.

"I have nothing to hide," she said, crossing her arms.

He scooped up some potatoes on his fork. "Really, 'cause I think you might."

Her face went red. "What is that supposed to mean?"

He swallowed the smooth-as-silk potatoes and kept his eyes on Lainey, noticing her reaction seemed a little dramatic for his teasing. "I just meant that I heard you saying you won't make it to church on Sunday. Big plans Saturday night?"

She drummed her fingers along the counter. "I always have big plans on Saturday nights. That's not the issue. I decided to open up for brunch on Sundays, that's all."

He put his fork down. "Why would you do that?"

"Just a business decision. Your dad seems a little better. His color is coming back, and he's been using his good arm again to eat. Dean was saying that he started physio and speech therapy?"

He nodded, deciding not to press her on why she was opening on Sundays and the fact that she'd made an obvious attempt at changing the subject. It wasn't his business if she wanted to open on Sundays. "Yeah.

It's been going well. They give me an update after every session. So far, he's been meeting their targets for improvement. Hasn't spoken a word when I'm around, though."

She gave him a small smile, sympathy flooding her brown eyes. "He will. Give him time."

"I guess two weeks isn't long enough to erase eight years," he said, hating that he'd blurted that out. He had no idea why he actually had the urge to talk and…share. He never did that. But when she'd asked him at her apartment why he'd left, he'd taken the coward's way out. He didn't want to get involved with Lainey because it was too complicated. He was attracted to her, but he knew some kind of cheap hook-up wasn't possible. He didn't want that with her. Hell.

"No, maybe it's not. But what matters is that you came back. Not everyone gets a second chance. Not everyone gets a parent to start over with. Don't give up on him." She gave him a pointed stare before she walked over to check on the last few customers.

He knew he couldn't give up on his father. He glanced over at her and wondered about her mother, if she had a relationship with her. If he remembered right, her mom had run off when she was only six. Hell, for all their differences, they had a few things in common.

After a while, everyone—including Father Andy—had left, and he was the only one still in the diner. She flipped the sign to CLOSED, and suddenly everything became personal. Tyler stood up, grabbing his plate and coffee mug and bringing them into the kitchen, fully intending on leaving right away so they weren't alone together. He would never be able to give Lainey what she deserved, and he needed to remind himself of that.

And in the back of his mind, he was prepared for the possibility of his father never forgiving him. It had occurred to Ty that once his father recovered enough to take part in some ranching again, he might kick Ty out. And then what?

Ty would have to leave Wishing River for good. He'd already damaged enough people in his hometown. As she walked over to him, he decided he wasn't going to add her to the list.

"*T*ime to stop avoiding going home?" Lainey asked when Tyler walked into the diner kitchen. She had been surprised to see him tonight—surprised and inexplicably pleased.

He gave her a half smile and brought his dishes and cup to the sink, standing beside her. She tried not to let herself get all flustered like a teenager with him standing so close to her in the empty diner. "Nope. Thanks to you, actually, I no longer need to live there."

She turned, frowning up at him. "What? I never said to not live there."

"Well, I'm living on the property. I'm turning one of those old cabins into my own."

"Oh," she said, turning back to the dishes in the sink. Before she could argue, he took the rinsed dish and started drying. "Well, that's good."

"And I have to thank you. I'm going to move

forward with your plan."

She turned slowly. "You're kidding!"

He frowned. "Why?"

She turned back to the sink, placing her hands in the soapy water while she talked. "Well, I didn't actually think you'd do it! This is *great*. Did you tell your dad?"

"He's not exactly a fan of the idea, but he doesn't really have a choice."

"I have some thoughts for advertising, and I have a good friend who can put together a website for you. Something simple, just to get going," she said.

"Lainey…"

"Don't say no. I owe this to your dad. Really. Let me help." She knew he wasn't the type of man to readily accept help, but if she made it sound like she needed to do this for his father, then maybe he would let her.

"I don't know. That doesn't sit right." He rubbed the back of his neck. "How about I give you a commission?"

"What do you mean?" She handed him the last dish, careful not to let her fingers brush his.

"Like a finder's fee. For each booking you get, I'll give you a percentage."

Lainey didn't say anything for a minute. That would totally help her reach her goal to pay him back, especially considering how much they were going to charge. Between the Sunday hours at the diner, the commission from the guest ranch bookings, her evening solo shifts, and the little bit of cash she had, she might be able to pay him back before he discovered the loan his father had given her. She cleared her throat and turned off the tap. "Okay, I'll take you up on your offer. Thank you."

He was leaning against the sink now, all hard lines and masculinity. This would probably be a good time to walk across the kitchen and tidy up the island. She expected him to leave, but he stood there, watching her.

"So how are things with Dean and Cade?" she asked, hating the silence.

He made a grunt that didn't seem very promising. "I guess you could say we are managing to be civil."

"That's good," she said, sounding a little too chipper to be completely natural. Ugh.

"Sure. I'm going to head out. Thanks for dinner," he said, pushing himself from the counter and walking across the kitchen. He paused at the door and ran his hand through his hair. "I'm sorry about the night at your apartment."

"For what?"

"I just ran out on you. I'm sorry."

She shrugged. "Oh, no you didn't. I didn't notice." She had, of course, noticed.

"Well, thanks again for dinner," he said, turning to leave.

"Do you regret leaving?" Lainey asked, the words slipping out before she could stop them. It was what she'd always wanted to know. Tyler leaving hadn't ever sat well with her. As a teenager, she'd had her silly notions about him. She'd always imagined he'd grow up into this responsible, gorgeous cowboy. She'd believed he'd been filled with honor and principles, but then he'd walked out on his grieving father and hadn't looked back for almost a decade.

Her grandmother's words about cowboys would echo ominously every now and then. *Don't trust them, Lainey. They'll charm you…*

Especially now, when Tyler was standing there all wounded and irresistible. He was demonstrating all those qualities she'd imagined so many years ago. It was highly unfortunate for her. He ran a hand through his already-disheveled hair and then stared up at the ceiling for a moment. The fact that she took that opportunity to check the man out without his knowing was a tad unsettling. Then there was the even more disturbing fact that she wanted to walk up to him and have him wrap his arms around her and hold her close and show her that he could be the man she thought he was. Wow, clearly she needed to get out more.

He cleared his throat, and she snapped her gaze up to his again. "We argued a lot toward the end of my mother's life."

"Well, that's understandable with the stress of everything," she said softly.

His jaw clenched. "It was beyond that. I…I didn't agree with the choices he was making for her. I knew they weren't going to be able to save her. I forced her oncologist to admit it instead of just giving us false hope. One more round of chemo, one new drug. Their cure was killing her. We had tried it their way for two years, and it wasn't helping."

Wrapping her arms around her waist, she tried to hold back the shudder that coursed through her body. She hadn't expected this was what he was going to say. She hadn't expected to be bombarded by compassion for him or the fact that she knew so

painfully what he was talking about. The pain that
shone from his blue eyes told her this still hurt. She
wanted to walk up to him and offer him some kind
of solace, but she couldn't do that. They weren't
friends, and he wouldn't welcome it. "I'm sorry," she
whispered, not knowing if he was going to continue.

He gave a small shrug. "We argued. Outside so
my mother wouldn't hear. But our relationship was
rapidly falling apart. I begged him to try something
else. I begged him to go to the city and see a
naturopathic doctor who specializes in cancer—
even just as a supplemental treatment to what they
were doing. The way I viewed it was, her oncologist
couldn't cure her, so why not? At that point, what
did we have to lose? Try anything. She was so damn
weak, and it was killing us to see her like that."

Her nails were digging into her skin as she
listened to him, as the emotion in his voice touched
her, dragging out her old feelings for him. Tyler
wasn't without a heart. Maybe Tyler had had too
much heart and he couldn't stay.

He blinked a few times, and then the sheen in
his eyes was gone and he was back to being all
hard man. "My father refused, he blindly trusted
her oncologist, and in that last month, we didn't
speak a word to each other. We just sat uselessly
by and watched her die, and when it was over, I
blamed him. My last night at the ranch, my father
had too much to drink, and we got into it. He told
me to get the hell out of his house. He said I was a
disappointment of a son. I was soft and weak, and he
said that was why I was blaming him. I'd had enough
because I still blamed him for her death. There

were…other things said. Stuff that just pushed me over the edge and made me never want to see him again. I packed my bag, took…a memento that my mother had given me, and left."

He said it so matter-of-factly. But he appeared alone and stoic—and wounded.

She realized how quiet it was now in the room, how close to him she was standing.

"I'm sorry," she said. If he had been anyone else, she would have reached out to hug him. Or she would have offered her hand. Or a shoulder to cry on. But this was Tyler, the man who had occupied so many of her girlhood fantasies…and now he was the man who was affecting her just as much as he had when she was a teenager. She wanted to ease his pain. The moment she realized that, she took a step back.

He grabbed her hand, and she stopped breathing. The look in his eyes was more intense than she was prepared for. The touch of his strong hand gently clasping hers, a silent plea that she'd never expected, was more than she was willing to process.

"Lainey," he said in a gruff, tender voice that seemed to touch and light every defenseless place inside her body. She pulled her hand free, lurched backward, and bumped into the stainless steel island. A bunch of mixing bowls fell to the ground, their crash almost deafening in the quiet room.

"I think I need to, um, close up the restaurant for the night. You should probably get going," she said, turning her back to him. She was a coward. Tension pulled her muscles until they were taut. She couldn't even turn to see his expression. There was no movement or noise. But a few seconds later, the sound of his boots walking across the empty diner made her breathe a sigh of relief. Maybe regret.

She squeezed her eyes shut and replayed what he'd told her. The image of him, so vulnerable as he spoke about his father, tormented her. She hadn't been a good friend. A good friend would have comforted. But then, she and Ty weren't friends. They weren't…anything.

But he was alone.

She stopped thinking and ran. She ran to the front of the restaurant and whipped open the front door, not sure if he was around at all. The street was deserted, and the wind had picked up. She scanned the street for his truck, and her heart stopped for a moment as she spotted his large figure walking toward the lone pickup down the street. *Go, Lainey. Just call his name. Do what you'd never do and take a chance for once in your life.*

"Tyler!" She yelled his name without thinking twice.

He paused and then turned around, and she forgot how to breathe. She didn't know if he was going to get into his truck and drive away or…

He walked toward her, like a man on a mission, like a man who needed something, like a man who needed her, like a man who wanted her. She stood there, not caring about her warnings about cowboys, not caring about anything except the man who was staring at her as though she were a beacon, a siren. He stopped when he was an inch from her, and she gazed up at him, at his mussed-up hair; the perfect, hard features; the stubble; the eyes that were filled with pain…and hunger. "Lainey," he whispered and then raised his hands and cupped her face.

Maybe it was that moment, that half second before she knew what it was like to have Ty Donnelly kiss her, that she would remember forever. But then when his warm mouth finally took hers, she knew that no, it was the second his lips touched hers that she would remember forever. She grabbed onto his biceps because she didn't know what else to do, because nothing had ever prepared her for this. There was no prep course for Ty. He kissed her as though she were the most important person in the world. He kissed her until she couldn't think at all. She wasn't cold because the minute she let go of his arms, he'd wrapped her up against him and all she felt was the hot, hard man against her.

The sound of a car approaching in the distance finally pulled her from the spell of Ty, and they slowly came apart. He still had one hand on the side of her face and was looking at her as though he was seeing her for the first time. The hunger in his eyes was still there, along with something else. "You should probably go inside before you get cold," he said, his voice gruff.

She swallowed with difficulty, and she couldn't make herself turn away. She made the mistake of staring at his mouth again and then up to his eyes.

He pulled back a step, dropping his arm. "Why did you come back out here?"

She smoothed her hair and forced herself to concentrate, to be careful about the words that came out of her mouth. "I, um, I was going to ask if you wanted to bring some leftovers home."

He blinked. And then a slow, satisfied, smug male grin broke out on his face. It really should be outlawed that a man that handsome could look even better. "Is that right?"

She nodded rapidly and crossed her arms. "Obviously."

His eyes traveled the length of her body, and when they met hers again, she knew from the stark appreciation and hunger staring back at her that she hadn't fooled him a bit. "I think you're lying."

"I don't lie, Donnelly," she said, poking him in the stomach.

He actually threw back his head and laughed.

"I need to go in. It's freezing out here," she said, backing up into the door, away from his appeal. She should run, really.

He gave her a nod. "It's probably a good idea." With that, he turned around and jogged toward his pickup.

Fumbling up the steps of the diner, she realized that she had lied. Again. To the man she was falling for.

CHAPTER NINE

*L*ainey jumped, almost dropping her prized dish of just-out-of-the-oven homemade lasagna as thunder boomed outside. She needed to focus or she was going to burn herself. Even the bubbling, gooey, comfort-food-at-its-best dish wasn't worth that. *Probably* not. But she'd had trouble focusing all week, thanks to the epic, movie-worthy kiss with Tyler. Then there was the fact that she was turning into a liar.

As if that wasn't enough to deal with, she'd also received a message from her school—and it wasn't good. Tonight's food was an ode to a lost dream. Her obsession with all things Italian would have to come to an end very soon. But she wasn't going to dwell on that. This meal was all about gorging on comfort food. Life was really crazy lately, and she wasn't used to crazy...she was used to mundane, boring, predictable.

But the kissing-Tyler-in-the-middle-of-the-street moment—it was a moment that didn't happen to Lainey Sullivan. Lainey Sullivan's moments were all about not getting what she wanted. That moment had been about getting the thing—*the person*—she really wanted. But she was fooling herself, because she didn't "have" him. Tyler wasn't a guy to claim, she could tell. He was a guy who'd break her heart, just like Grandma Tilly had warned her. He was a charming, noncommittal cowboy—the worst kind.

He was way out of her league; he'd lived a life that she never had. Her entire life was growing up in this place. The diner, the town, was her frame of reference. If she had a man like Tyler, she wouldn't even know what to do with him. She barely even knew how to have a conversation with him—which was alarming, really, since she talked to people all day. She didn't consider herself a shy person, yet… She groaned out loud.

She should have just left him alone and not asked about why he'd left. That had been mistake numero uno because it had endeared him to her. She'd proven to herself that she'd been right about him. She turned off the diner's kitchen lights and marched to her favorite table—the church ladies' table. They really had picked the perfect spot—the view of the quaint downtown was next to none and also offered prime viewing of the diner. She placed her dish of lasagna on the center of the table.

It was long past closing. She'd turned off the outdoor lights as well—the town did not need to witness her scarfing down an entire pan of cheese-laden lasagna. God forbid Hope caught her eating all this dairy—she'd really have a field day. She stared at the table, her hands on her hips, and realized she needed a drink. She knew exactly what this meal and this day called for—one of her highly prized bottles of San Pellegrino sparkling water she kept in the back. Not that they were so expensive, but they were still a luxury beverage. She had started buying them the first time she'd had to postpone her scholarship to art school in Italy. It had seemed like a good idea to remind herself of the country she wanted to visit…sort of like a promise that she'd get there someday.

She ran across the room and plucked one of the large bottles out of the case in the refrigerator in the kitchen and paused, wondering if she should use a glass or drink straight from the bottle. She glanced over at her giant dish—not plate—and thought that drinking straight from the bottle might just be stooping to a new level of sad. She grabbed a glass and marched back to her corner table. It was perfect. She loved watching the falling rain, illuminated by the streetlights. Because the lights were off, any passersby wouldn't be able to see her.

She poured herself a large glass and sat down with a satisfied sigh. She examined the magnificent display in front of her and picked up a fork. She was impressed with the almost-perfect ratio of homemade sauce to mozzarella to noodles. She almost moaned out loud as the rich, gooey, and oh-so-comforting lasagna filled her mouth. At least there was no one here to witness this sad act of gluttony. If this was the closest she got to Italy, then so be it.

She grabbed her phone and pulled up her email again so she could read and eat at the same time.

The banging on the window right beside her almost made her fall out of her chair. She stopped breathing when she noticed Tyler standing there with a wide grin on his face. Heat flooded her body at the realization that he'd just spotted her sitting alone in the dark with a giant pan of lasagna. Maybe she could hide under the table. But as she sat there, unable to decide how she was going to save face, she grappled with the other emotion that was bubbling inside her—the one where she was really happy he was here.

He motioned to the front door, and she grabbed a napkin from one of the stainless steel dispensers on the table and wiped her mouth furiously as she ran to unlock the door. Her happiness immediately vanished as he opened his perfect mouth.

"You missed a glob of sauce," he said, pointing to her shirt.

Heat infused her face as she followed the direction of his gaze, which was on the stain on her breast. She frantically wiped it. "Thanks. So, um, what can I do for you?" she asked, crossing her arms over her sorry display.

She ignored the heat in his gaze and tried not to give away that the attraction was very mutual. As though having a hot cowboy in her dark diner was something that happened to her every Friday night. He took his hat off, water dripping on the front mat, and ran his hands through his hair, scuffing it up slightly. She had no idea why this action should make her stomach suddenly start flip-flopping. She knew it had nothing to do with the pasta and cheese.

"So, uh, you serving up some of that, whatever it was you were gorging on?"

She raised her chin, trying to fool him into thinking she was dignified when she was so very far from the definition of the word. "I don't know what you're talking about. I wasn't gorging."

He walked by her, toward her food-orgy table.

"I was just experimenting with a new recipe and obviously I was planning on…sharing," she said, holding her breath, hoping he'd buy it. Of course, he didn't. Instead he turned around and then back again, the twinkle in his eyes sending a warmth through her body, even though he was making fun of her.

"I don't see anyone here."

She swallowed her laugh at his teasing. "You're here. You do have an uncanny ability to know when there's food available," she said, desperate to turn the tables.

"Because it's a diner?"

"Were you planning on eating some of that lasagna, Donnelly?" she asked, smiling.

His lips twitched, and she could tell it was taking everything he had not to burst out laughing. "I'd hate to impose," he drawled, not sounding the least bit sorry.

She finally laughed. "Fine. Sit down."

He sat and eyed the dish. "So, what have you got here?"

She sighed, resigned to the fact that there was no getting rid of him, and sat. "Made-from-scratch lasagna, right down to the noodles. Fresh sauce. Authentic mozzarella that Makenna had brought in for me from the cheese shop."

"Wow. Honestly, I didn't even really care—it smelled so good and I'm so hungry. But your explanation was highly entertaining."

"I'm glad you find me so entertaining."

"Well, entertaining among other things. I know you looked pretty sad in the window just now," he said, leaning forward.

Her heart swelled unexpectedly at the concern in his voice. She quickly averted her gaze, uncomfortable with sharing her feelings or the real reason she was sad. She reached for a fork from the table beside them that she'd already set for the next day and handed it to him. "Here, I give you food and water, and we don't discuss anything remotely personal."

"Works for me," he said, filling her glass up to the brim.

"Seriously?"

He shrugged. "I can drink out of the bottle, then. Almost half each. Although I'm not sure what this water is."

"It's imported mineral water. It's really good for you," she said, pleased with her explanation. Better than the truth.

He took a sip and shrugged. "Tastes like soda water."

She picked up her fork, choosing not to take issue because they were running out of time before the mozzarella solidified. "Okay, just a few things I need to point out before we get started. This half"—she paused and drew an invisible line with her fork—"is mine. You can't cross that line because I really hate saliva sharing through food."

She stabbed her fork into the huge mound in front of them and ignored his choked laugh. She was relieved when he managed to get an even bigger forkful in his mouth. He paused after swallowing it down. "I think this is the best thing I've ever eaten in my entire life."

She nodded wisely. "Agreed. But you shouldn't stop to talk; we are dangerously close to having this get cold, and then the mozzarella will thicken and be gross."

"Message received," he said, stabbing his fork into

the noodles three times. She was pleased to see there was no judgment here with the copious forkfuls of decadent pasta.

They ate in silence for ten minutes, but then she started to slow down, sadly eyeing the remains on her side of the platter. It was too much. Too rich. She couldn't go on.

His side was almost polished off, and he showed no signs of retreat. She picked up her glass and leaned back in her chair, watching the rain fall instead of the hot, hungry cowboy in front of her.

A few minutes later, he was wiping his mouth and standing. "I think I need more water to wash this down."

She sat up a little straighter and smiled. "Oh, you mean more imported soda water?"

He gave her a lopsided grin. "Yeah."

"In the back of the fridge."

He laughed. "Okay. Be right back."

She turned away from him because she found herself checking out the way his worn jeans fit him. She had been around cowboys her entire life, growing up in rural Montana. While she'd always found them to have an innate sort of appeal, no one had ever made her this nervous, that giddy kind of nervous that Ty did.

He was back a moment later, his long strides taking him across the diner until he sat back down across from her and refilled her glass. "Thanks for that dinner."

She ignored how cozy it was to be here with him. "You're welcome."

"Do you do this often?"

She didn't know what he was referring to. The emotional eating? The sitting in the dark? The homemade lasagna? "Do what often?"

"You know, sit in the window of your diner with the lights turned off and creepily stare at people?"

She choked on her water and sat up straight, coughing. When she was finished, she swallowed her embarrassment and answered him. "I'm not creepy."

"I didn't say *you* were creepy. It's a little weird to be sitting in the dark and peering out at the street, though."

"No, it's not. I wasn't spying on people," she said with a huff. Not entirely the truth, but whatever. People watching was a secret pleasure, but still, the way he made it sound, she was basically a stalker.

He shrugged and took another sip of water. "Fine, fine. So what were you doing, then?"

"I was sitting down to some comfort food after a long, hard day. I wanted to watch the rain and hear the storm without dealing with people. If I were to keep the lights on, then people would inevitably knock on the door and ask if I was open." She tried not to let any emotion into her voice as she spoke, but she was reminded of just how crappy her day was. She took another long drink of water, wishing it were wine.

"What happened, sweetheart?"

Oh dear. It must have been the carb-loading that was lulling her into this state of warmth and happiness. She could handle Ty teasing her—in fact, that was almost preferred to this. Him teasing her was actually perfect, because he made her so embarrassed that she could ignore his appeal much easier.

But this? His deep voice touching her insides, softly landing on her like a warm blanket? This she could not handle without major effort on her part.

"Lainey, what's wrong?" he asked, his voice gruff. He leaned forward, bracing his elbows on the table, his blue eyes filled with concern. For her.

Tears actually pricked the backs of her eyes. It had been a long time since someone had showed this much concern for her. Well, that wasn't true. She did have people who cared for her—Hope, Martin, Betty—but male concern. That…that had never happened, because she hadn't let anyone close. Ever. She never bothered her friends with her dreams about her art. Hope knew she hated talking about it, and she was busy with her own life and trying to keep everything together. Ty's father knew, but again she minimized it. She was always fine. Dependable Lainey. She opened the diner; she closed the diner. All day long, six—now seven—days a week, everyone could depend on her to greet them with a smile. And she did a good job at faking she was okay.

Now Ty was here, and he was concerned, and she couldn't tell him about the loan. What if he assumed the worst? What if he thought she'd been using his father for money? That would crush her. No, she needed to work hard and pay off that debt. At least if she had the money in hand when she told him, it wouldn't look so bad.

She waved her hand in front of her face. "It's nothing. Really. Just a long day."

His gaze was steady and knowing—so much so that she turned to stare out the window. "So you get to ask me things and I don't get to ask you anything?"

Twirling the stem of her glass a few times on the table, she tried to come up with an answer. He was right. She didn't do sharing well; it was awkward and intimate.

She told Hope everything, but they'd been friends for so long that it felt natural. Her grandmother knew so much about her, and sometimes she wondered if she was destined to be the same: alone, with the diner patrons as her family. Tilly had kept to herself, and as much as she'd loved Lainey, they'd never really had that close affection she witnessed in other families. That was okay. Lainey knew that her grandmother had done her very best.

There was not one day that Lainey had felt like a burden to her, even though she knew that's what she'd been. When her mother had walked out on her and her responsibilities, Tilly had already been in her sixties—she hadn't wanted to raise a baby. But that's what she'd done, and she'd given Lainey the very best of herself. But they never sat around talking about feelings. She had known that Lainey wanted to be an artist, and even though she hadn't come right out and discouraged her, she'd made it clear that it was better to just be grateful for the certainty of the diner. Of course, her grandmother had said that because she was trying to protect Lainey, so they just didn't talk about it.

They rarely discussed Lainey's mother. Her grandmother had never asked her how she felt about her. They had never discussed the pain of being discarded, like she wasn't worth it, like she wasn't worth the sacrifice of changing her life to accommodate a baby. She hadn't been important enough for her mother to change.

"Lainey?" Tyler said, ducking his head slightly to make eye contact with her.

She raised her gaze from her glass, startled. She hadn't contemplated any of that stuff in so long, but sitting here across from him made her realize just how much she didn't know. She didn't know how to be in a relationship, how to open up to anyone. "Sorry, just a busy week. I, um, should probably turn in."

"Hey," he said gently. "Seriously, what's wrong, sweetheart?"

The backs of her eyes burned. She was so silly, but the endearment coming off his lips so easily, in that deep voice, made her believe she was…special. Maybe he'd said "sweetheart" a hundred times to different women, but sitting here with his gaze fixed on hers and filled with concern made her think she was the only woman he'd ever said that to. She forced a small smile. "Just some work stuff that came up."

"Is the roof leaking again?"

She shook her head. She didn't want him to go, but it was hard to let him in. She'd thought that she loved her private time here, in the dark, but having him fill the emptiness had made her very aware of how empty her life was.

It wasn't that anyone would do, though. She'd had guys ask her out, she'd spent time with different men, but she'd never had a connection, never wanted to lean on someone. Ty was big and strong and so capable. It was nice being around him. Even though they had their differences, conversation with him was actually easy. "Do you want some pie?" she asked, hoping he wouldn't see through her desperate attempt at steering the conversation away from herself.

He glanced over at the dessert stands, and she wondered if he knew. And if he did, what he'd do about it.

Lightning stole through the diner, followed by a loud crack of thunder a few seconds later, and then all the lights on Main Street went black. They were engulfed in darkness. Ty pulled out his phone, and a small ribbon of light from its flashlight gave them enough light to see each other.

"Some storm. Bet it knocked down a tree or something," he said, walking over to the window.

"You should probably go home and check on the ranch," she said in a desperate attempt to get him to leave before he remembered what they were talking about.

"That sounds pretty convenient, Lainey. I'll just run out the door and forget I ever saw you scarfing down lasagna by yourself on a Friday night because you're hiding from life."

She threw her hands in the air. "Fine! Between the two of us, I'm the one with issues."

He let out a muffled laugh. "I never said I didn't have issues. Why don't we light some candles and sit down and continue our conversation."

She placed her hands on the back of the chair. "Well, if we do that, then anyone who passes by is going to see us and think we're having some kind of romantic dinner, and then by morning the entire town will think we're together."

"Oh yeah, and I hope it wouldn't be the same person who drove by and saw us kissing in the middle of the road," he said, laughter in his deep voice.

Heat engulfed her face, and she was glad the lights were off. "Clearly you have no issues with people talking about you. I, for one, hate it."

"Fine. Let's go up to your apartment, light some candles, and wait out the storm. While we're doing that, you can tell me what's bothering you."

Her stomach flip-flopped, and she clutched the back of her chair. He said things so matter-of-factly. *Go up to your apartment and light some candles.* Well sure, for him it wasn't a big deal. How many times had he been invited upstairs? Maybe daily. "Fine. If you need a place to stay until it's safe for you to drive home, then you are welcome to hang out at my place," she said, smiling directly at him.

He walked over to her, close enough that she could make out all his features in the dim light from his phone. She liked how his lips twitched when he was torn between being irritated and laughing with her. "Lainey?"

She didn't bother hiding her satisfied smile as she looked up at him. "Yes?"

"You know perfectly well that I'm not afraid to drive through some rain."

"It's okay, Ty," she managed to choke out with her laugh.

"Do you want to lead the way?" he asked, staring at her.

"Oh, right." She started walking and then stopped. "Should I bring the pie?"

"What kind?"

"Apple?"

"Definitely."

"Okay, point the light in the pie direction," she said, handing him her phone as well. Once the pie had been secured, she led the way to the back hallway with the private staircase up to her place.

She slowly climbed the stairs, careful not to fall flat on her face and into the pie. Who would have guessed that she would be hosting Tyler in her apartment for the second time this month? Who would have also predicted that they'd shared the most amazing kiss in her lifetime? Of course, that had its own implications, because what if they never kissed again? What then? What if that was her one shot, and then no other man would compare?

As they walked up the stairs in silence, she promised herself that she would kiss him again.

CHAPTER TEN

*T*yler didn't consider himself to be a stupid man. Going up to a dark apartment with a woman who he couldn't get his mind off of, a woman he shouldn't get involved with, probably wasn't the brightest move. He wanted Lainey. Badly. He hadn't been able to get the night they'd kissed out of his mind; the way she'd run out into the street, the way she'd called his name, and then what she'd tasted like, what she'd felt like in his arms.

The more time he spent with her, the more he realized that beneath that tough act she'd put on, she was actually quite vulnerable. He also realized that the woman never spoke about herself. She carefully maneuvered the conversation away every time. Regardless, though, besides their obvious physical attraction, he liked her company. For the first time in his life, it was easy to talk to someone. And he liked hearing what she had to say. He liked the softness in her voice, the way her eyes laughed when she was trying to purposefully irritate him. He had even been touched by her trying to get Cade and Dean to talk to him.

He wanted her friendship as much as he wanted her as a lover, and that was something he'd never experienced.

He held the door open for her once she unlocked it. He should walk away, because being in her small apartment with no lights was just asking for trouble.

But what kind of person would just leave Lainey alone in the dark? She deserved more than that. He remembered the sadness on her face when he'd been on the sidewalk, before he'd knocked on the door... it had gutted him. Not that he'd let on, because he knew she would have clammed right up. She'd looked as though someone had died and there was no one there for her, no rock, no shoulder to cry on. He knew what that was like, to go through grief alone, but it wasn't right for her. He was an ass, he'd made his choices, but Lainey wasn't like him. She was strong, but she was so damn sweet.

"How about I slice the pie?" she asked, pulling two plates down from one of the overhead cupboards.

Following her into the small kitchen, he pushed aside his thoughts, not wanting her to know how he felt. He was kind of wishing they had Tilly's emergency whiskey. "Good idea."

She lit a candle that was on the counter, and the room was filled with the scent of cinnamon. In the dim light, he could make out her fine features, and he wanted nothing more than to pull her close and kiss her again. But she turned away as she sliced the pie.

She held out a plate with pie and a fork on the side. "Thanks, this looks great," he said as they walked into the small family room.

"Sure."

"So are you planning on telling me what happened today?" he asked once they were settled on the couch. He caught the faint smell of lilacs again, and he remembered them from the night he'd kissed her.

"I think my plan was to get you drunk enough on food that you'd forget to ask, and also, I was planning on emotionally eating instead of speaking," she said.

He chuckled. "Nice try, but no matter how good the food, I'm not going to forget."

She put down her plate of pie. "Yeah, and I don't think I can eat any more," she said.

He picked up his plate. "I've never been one to refuse apple pie. So I'll start eating, and you can start talking."

"It's really not a big deal. A long time ago, I got it in my head that I wanted to be an artist. But blah, blah, blah, life got in the way, and that's that."

He put his plate of pie down. "Uh, blah, blah, blah?"

She waved a hand. "No biggie. I had a scholarship to my dream art school in Italy. It was a full scholarship, all expenses paid."

He was shocked. Not because he didn't think she was capable of receiving a full scholarship but because she never went. The Italy part was a big surprise, though. He'd always pictured her here. But Europe...Italy? The lasagna. The Italian water. He stared at her, realizing there was this entire other layer to Lainey, and she obviously didn't share that with many people. He was trying to figure her out. It actually seemed like she had issues talking to him. Hell, he'd have bet out of the two of them, he was the one who had problems sharing. She looked like she was torn between choking and leaving.

"I didn't know you were an artist," he said, picking up his plate.

She gave him a wobbly smile. "It's not something I really talk about. Not really diner conversation."

Right, because she was Tilly's granddaughter. She ran the diner. She made everyone else feel special, she listened to their problems, she soothed their souls with home-cooked meals and sweet smiles. He cleared his throat. "What happened?"

She shrugged and stared out the window. "The first time? My grandmother got sick. I couldn't leave."

"I'm sorry," he said.

"I promised her I'd find a way to keep the restaurant going. My mom came back for the funeral, and I'd hoped that maybe she'd want to take it over, you know, be responsible or something. But no, she said she couldn't handle the emotional baggage and that she hated the diner and waiting on people. Her boyfriend needed her."

He didn't want his pity to show on his face because she'd take it the wrong way, but damn had their lives been different. Lainey's mother had ditched her repeatedly for her boyfriends. But Lainey had stuck around, had managed to keep going. "So you stayed."

She shrugged. "I called the school, and they were really great about it. They understood my situation and said they'd defer my scholarship until the next year."

"They must have really believed in your talent," he said.

She smiled at him, but it was a sad smile, her eyes not sparkling and her mouth wobbling. "I worked so hard that year. I mean, I'd grown up in this diner with my grandmother, but I didn't realize until that year just how much I relied on her. The ordering of food, the part-time help, the cooking, the books, the cleaning, all of it. I quickly had to learn it. I was a basket case that year. I missed my grandmother so much, but I had to just keep going. I had promised her." She stopped speaking and clasped her hands together in her lap. "I made that promise without realizing what exactly I was getting into. But I was nineteen, and I didn't know anything else. Plus, I owed her. I owed her everything. She raised me when my own mother didn't want me."

The weight of her words kicked him in the chest. He understood but was unable to put it into words, because it was stuff he'd never admitted to himself, either. But he got her loyalty. He admired it.

"I kept telling myself all I had to do was get through the year and then leave it in Betty's capable hands. She'd be able to handle the part-time girls, and I would check in. My program was only two years, and I could come home in the summer."

"Sounds like that was a good plan."

She nodded and pulled her knees up, resting her chin on top. "It was. But, um, then my mother walked through the door—she'd been diagnosed with lung cancer."

He swore under his breath. He already knew where this was going. Lainey had stayed behind to nurse the mother who had never given a crap about her.

"The doctors told her it was terminal, and she only had maybe a few months."

"Lainey," he said.

She waved a hand and scooted a little farther away. She hated the sympathy, he knew. She hated showing him this softer side. He knew what it was like to be strong and never break down. There was this fear that the moment you did, the moment you let the real emotion out, you'd lose your grasp on reality, on your control over your life.

"I'm sorry," he said, his throat tightening.

"I was so angry," she whispered, her eyes filling with tears, the hurt in them gutting him. "I mean, she wasn't here when she was well, but she was here when she needed me? She knew I wouldn't just walk away from her. It wasn't good. Our relationship that year. I mean, most people find a way to come together in a tragedy, but I felt used. So used. All her boyfriends, where were they? She had spent her whole life with different guys—searching for 'the one,' she'd say, but not one of them cared enough to even call.

"But she walked into the diner like I owed her. That first week, I didn't make a decision. I wanted to just pick up and leave this reality behind, like she'd done her entire life. How was she my responsibility? I owed her *nothing*."

She stood up abruptly and walked over to the window.

"You didn't owe her a thing. Still, you stayed, didn't you?"

Her back was to him, but she nodded. "I called the school. Again. I even emailed them a copy of her doctor's report because I didn't want them to think I was lying. Because it sounded so stupid, right? Like, how can this actually happen to someone?" She spun around, and her tears were gone, replaced by a wry smile.

"What did they say?"

"They sympathized with my situation. They said they'd hold my spot for next year, but they couldn't hold that scholarship anymore."

He winced. "I'm sorry."

"That was probably the worst year of my life. I was bitter and angry with my mother. But I had to spend day in and day out with her. I helped her. I took her to the doctor, to the hospital. I helped her when she was sick and couldn't care for herself, knowing she would never have done the same for me. I did everything for her. All the while, do you know I think she was the one who was bitterer? She was here with me, in the town she hated. It's like she finally realized that all her men, all her years of putting her love life ahead of her family, had rendered her empty. But instead of trying to repair our relationship, she was nothing but mean."

"Lainey…" he said, his voice trailing off because he didn't know what to say to her.

She shook her head. "She died a year later. We had talked about funeral arrangements and all that stuff. She hadn't expected anyone would show, and I kind of thought she was right. But, um." Her voice broke, and tears spilled from her eyes. "Everyone came. The entire town, practically."

He cleared his throat. "They came for you. They came to show you how much you mean to them."

She nodded, wiping the tears from her face. "They had been more of a family to me than she ever had."

"What happened with the art school?"

She sighed and shrugged. "Without a full scholarship, how was I going to afford to go there? The

travel expenses alone were huge. The year after my
mother died, I just poured myself into this place. I
made this apartment my own, I painted in all my
free time, and I worked double shifts instead of
paying for part-time staff, thinking that maybe I
could slowly start squirreling away money, but it
was impossible. I was left with so many medical
bills from my mother's last year that anything extra
I had went to paying those."

"You're amazing. Holding onto everything,
paying everything, working so hard. Like, what, you
were twenty at the time?"

She shook her head and avoided his gaze. "I…
made some mistakes. I did my best, though, and I
had no choice. I wasn't going to let my grandmother's
place just fold. It had been her pride and joy. And the
town needed Tilly's. I mean, those people who walk
in every day—they are my family. They tell me about
their lives, they come in on a bad day and they come
in on a good day. Tilly's is a landmark."

"You're right. I have so many memories of this
place growing up."

"So I gave up my dream of going. Then they
contacted me to let me know about a new program
for older students—an accelerated one-year diploma.
It was meant for people who already had careers but
wanted to pursue their dream of art."

"And?"

"The money. I couldn't swing it. But, um, that's
when I really got to know your father. Your dad had
been coming in regularly, and bit by bit, we formed
this relationship. He wasn't much of a talker at first,
and that was fine with me, because that was not a

time in my life that I could give much to others. I just wanted to serve food and fill up coffee cups. But eventually, after the dinner crowd would leave, he'd linger over his coffee and we'd start talking."

He didn't want to think of his father sitting by himself every night at a diner. He'd probably been so damn lonely. And Lainey had such a big heart; she'd worked away at him.

"I told him about the art school. He was actually so genuinely interested that I couldn't wait to talk to him every day. I was just as lonely as he was. Hope wasn't living here at the time, and I just wanted someone to talk to."

"So you brought in your work?"

She smiled. "I brought in a few pieces, and he loved them. He said he didn't know much about art but that he could tell I was very talented."

He smiled at her. His father had never shown any interest in art, but he knew he must have cared a lot about Lainey.

"After a while, I realized I was never meant to go. I was meant to be here. I'm George Bailey from *It's a Wonderful Life*, essentially. I had always wanted to leave Wishing River, but it's my home. These are my people. I don't need a dream Italian art school to paint."

"Lainey," he said, his voice hoarse. "It's never too late."

"Actually, I think it's finally too late," she said, grabbing her phone and opening her email. She cleared her throat. "Dear Ms. Sullivan, we regret to inform you that we can no longer extend your admission status. Should you wish to pursue the

Art Intensive, you must do so through the regular admission channels." She stared at her phone.

He leaned forward and gently took the phone from her hand and put it on the table. "That's not a no. That's a 'chin up and get it done.'"

"The deadline is only a few weeks away. I would need to paint something new. I haven't painted a real…anything in more than a year. I've done bits of things, half-completed pieces. I can't find a subject, sketch, paint, and then put together a portfolio!"

"If you want it badly enough, you will."

"I think I regret sharing my lasagna with you," she said, crossing her arms.

He chuckled. "Seriously."

"I don't see a point anymore."

"Then why did you contact them? If you had no intention of going, then why bother reaching out to them at all?"

She put her head in her hands and groaned. "I don't know. It's kind of like a safety net. Like the dream isn't lost if I can still access it. It didn't seem so far. Now…it's far."

"Hey, you can't think like that. You know you want it. You know you're talented. You should go. You should do everything you can to get there," he said.

"I don't know. I don't know what I want. I mean really, can I leave this place for a year?"

He shrugged. "Of course you can. Betty runs that kitchen anyway. You do some hiring now. Part-time with them becoming full-time while you're gone."

She nodded. "We don't have to keep talking about this. How's your dad?"

"You're changing the subject."

"I don't want to talk about me all night. I'm worried about him. I'm worried about the ranch. I think you're doing the right thing, trying to rebuild it for him even if he doesn't know it yet. He couldn't handle it dying. I think he regretted selling off land, letting his dream die. That ranch was everything for him—it was your mother; it was you. It was in his blood. I want you to rebuild. I want you to turn it profitable. I want him to know all his work, all those years, wasn't for nothing. And most of all, Ty, I want him to know how much you love him, that he's not alone."

He hung his head for a moment, hating the choices he'd made. Lainey had stayed out of duty. The irony was not lost on him. Her entire life, she'd dreamed of leaving this place and couldn't. His entire life, he'd dreamed of staying, of building a life here, and he'd been the one to leave, to see the world. He owed all of them. He owed Lainey. She needed to go to that school. And he owed his father. For all the years he'd been away and left him alone, he owed the man.

If they could form some kind of new relationship, then fine, but if it was too late, he'd have to accept that. At the very least, he could put in the work, the time, and rebuild. He knew he had it in him. He knew how to do it.

He resisted the urge to reach out and touch her. Instead he searched for the words he knew she deserved to hear. "You know I'll never be able to thank you enough for what you did for him. Not just the day you found him, but for being his friend when

I was gone."

She smiled softly. "He sort of became the father I never had. Maybe he felt like I was the daughter he never had. Stupid. Silly, I know." She shrugged, her cheeks turning pink.

"Not stupid or silly. I'm sure he feels the same way. Never give up on your dreams, Lainey. You're young. You can still go to Italy."

She gave a little laugh that was years beyond her age. "I think maybe some night classes at a community college will be fine for me. I haven't given up my painting. I still do it. I've toyed with the idea of getting it into some galleries. Maybe in the summer, when things slow down a bit."

They stared at each other, and she could tell that they both knew what she was doing. Excuses. The dream was fading, and she was just lying to herself to save face. He didn't know anything about art or galleries or art schools, but he knew what it was like to see hope die. When he left Wishing River eight years ago, he felt like everything had died.

"I know what it's like to lose a dream, Lainey, to tell yourself you didn't really want it that badly. Even though my dad and I weren't that close, I always thought I'd work alongside him. When that didn't happen, a part of me died. I searched for different ways, I worked different ranches, I rodeoed, but nothing took the place of my dream. None of it was good enough. It was always second best."

She swiped at a tear. "Well, you're back now, and you have a second shot."

But *she* didn't. She'd never have the cash to leave her business behind and take off for Italy. They both knew it as they stared at each other. "Yeah. Maybe you will, too," he said, even though he didn't see how.

"Were there any places you wanted to stay in and start over?" she asked, coming back to sit beside him.

He stretched out. "There were. I kept telling myself I could work as a manager at a ranch for the rest of my life and be happy. I was lying to myself, though. There's something about your own ranch, working for your family, for your future family, that you just don't get by working at someone else's ranch." He stopped abruptly as he thought of Cade. If his former best friend hadn't been such an ass, he would have felt sorry for him, knowing that he'd never have that option.

"Did you, um." She cleared her throat. "Have any relationships while you were gone?"

"Relationships?"

She nodded, rolling her lips inward. "You know, women? Girlfriends."

He didn't want her asking him that, because he knew where this was leading, where they were leading if he didn't stop things, but he didn't want to hurt her, either. "Well, no one really memorable. No one who meant anything."

They stared at each other for a moment, and he stood. The table lamp suddenly turned on and he was relieved the power was back. He needed to break off whatever it was that was happening between them. If he and his father couldn't come to terms, he'd leave Wishing River again. He didn't need women in his life right now. Not a woman like Lainey, anyway. She was someone who deserved a man who would be the real deal. A man who could offer her everything she needed. A man who could heal her wounds, who could be her rock, who could give her her dreams.

He read the vulnerability in her eyes, the longing, and knew he should turn away. He should just walk out of here and stop sharing any personal stories or asking about her.

"What about you? All these years running the diner, I'm sure you've been on the receiving end of a lot of good pickup lines," he said, placing his hands in his front pockets. He promised himself this was the last question. No more. Lainey's dating life was none of his business.

She smiled. "Yeah, I've witnessed a few good ones. But no, there's been no one special. Holding out for a hero, I guess," she said, her cheeks flaming now.

A hero. Ha. Well, that was something he definitely wasn't. It was a good reminder. He cleared his throat and broke her stare, broke the tension, broke the momentum of the conversation. "Well, you deserve a hero. I'd, uh, better get going," he said, turning to leave and then pausing. From where he was standing, he could see inside one of the bedrooms. It was filled with canvases and an easel. "Do you paint in there?"

She nodded and waved a hand. "It's just a mess of a room. Nothing worth seeing. After my mother died, I decided I didn't want any of the furniture anymore, so I donated it and cleared out the room. I needed to make it into something new."

"Can I see?" He was asking as a friend. A friend getting to know another friend. Or maybe he was just being nice because she seemed so alone. It gutted him to think of her in this small space, all alone, in the middle of the night. She was too good for that kind of a life.

"Oh, it's not like a real studio or anything. It's really messy, too. I don't usually let anyone in there," she said, quickly walking to stand in front of the hall that led to the bedrooms.

He held up his hands. "I won't judge. I'm the perfect person to let in. I'm a slob, and I have no experience with art, so you don't have to worry about me critiquing you."

She gave a wobbly half smile. "Okay, fine. Come with me."

He followed her into the room, and when she flicked on the light, the space came alive with colorful paintings. He stood in the center, his gaze going from picture to picture. He didn't know how long he stood there, overwhelmed.

It was like he was suddenly enveloped in Lainey's life. The paintings were landscapes, mostly. Familiar landscapes. It was all Montana. Mountains. Farms. Barns. Old houses. They were all…he didn't know what. They all had heart; they all had warmth. They were all Lainey. It was like the woman he was getting to know had come alive in the canvases in front of him. She was beautiful.

"Well, I'm getting tired now. It's been a long night," she said.

He turned sharply to her, hearing the insecurity in her voice. He realized he must have been standing there for a long time without saying anything. "This is amazing. More than I would have expected. Why don't you get these into a gallery or something?"

Her mouth opened slightly, and her eyes shone with emotion, like his words meant something. "There aren't many around here, and—"

"You can't just leave them in here. Don't be afraid of getting out there and taking a chance."

She cringed. "I guess I don't feel like a professional. I haven't had formal training."

"Sell them in your diner."

Her face went white. "The diner?"

He shrugged. "I don't know anything about art, but I know this is the kind of stuff people would hang in their homes. And you should go to a gallery, too. Hell, who cares if they reject you? You keep trying. You could make some money on the side from all this. The school, the art…don't give up."

She crossed her arms and turned to her paintings. He could tell she was actually considering it, and he swore he caught a spark of something in her eyes.

He followed her gaze. Remorse choked him as he recognized his ranch, the old wooden-post fence leading up to the main house. It was his ranch, but through Lainey's eyes. It was desolate in her painting. It wasn't the ranch he'd grown up on, not the one filled with laughter, with tears, with *life*. The grasses were swaying in the breeze, some wildflowers moving in the grass, horses grazed in the distance, yet there was no life.

He cleared his throat past the emotion that clogged it. "You're very talented. Even I can see it. Each one of these tells a story." He knew the story of his ranch. He'd left a home that had once been a place filled with life and love, and he had destroyed it.

"Thank you," she said softly. He turned to her and knew what she was thinking, knew she was reading him. But he wasn't a guy who confided in people or leaned on others. He didn't like anyone really knowing who he was. Right now, he felt like *he* was on exhibit, like he was choking on his past—the one he'd failed to fully acknowledge.

"I gotta go," he said and headed to the exit, stopping in the doorway, gripping the doorjamb tightly. "You shouldn't give up on your dream. I have an early start tomorrow. I'm fixing up the cabins."

He left the apartment and got back in his truck, finding it hard to breathe normally.

He didn't know what the hell was happening to him. He was dispensing life advice to Lainey, when his own life was a mess. He was looking at art. He was feeling…things that made him uncomfortable.

He hadn't needed anyone since his mother died.

He'd been fine on his own.

He glanced up at Lainey's apartment, wondering why the hell that wasn't enough anymore.

Hell.

CHAPTER ELEVEN

*A*lmost a week later, Lainey still didn't know what to make of her evening with Ty.

It had seemed like everything was going well—she'd opened up about her mother and her dreams, and he'd been so kind in his responses. But something had happened when he saw her paintings. No, it was the painting of his house that had changed everything.

His face had closed up, and he'd left abruptly. She hadn't anticipated that. It's not that she'd expected him to profess his undying love for her or anything, or, um, maybe even just show some interest. But they had connected—or so she believed. Maybe that's why he'd left. Tyler didn't open up easily, and when he'd revealed the softer side of himself, he'd run.

Really, she should be happy nothing had happened; it was far less complicated like this. Just because they'd shared that one epic, straight-out-of-the-movies kiss in the middle of the road didn't mean there was actually something going on between them. They were so wrong for each other. Anyone could see that. He was…not the kind of guy who'd be happy with someone like her. He was a loner, wasn't a man after commitment. He wouldn't want to settle down and be a family man.

Talking about her art scholarship had made the old wounds resurface, though. She'd gotten over her bitterness toward her mother years ago, but hearing her story spoken out loud made her realize just how much she'd missed out on. As much as Ty believed that she could pursue her dreams, she knew it was empty talk. They both knew she was chained to this place.

She gazed out onto the streetscape of Wishing River, with its quaint shops and history, and knew in her heart this was her home, but she still wished for more. She'd been so lonely here, surrounded by so many people who cared for her, yet alone.

It was still dark out, and she longed for Grandma Tilly to be in the kitchen, to share her coffee with her this morning. She wouldn't have been impressed with Lainey spending any time with Ty, because he was a cowboy who had already proved he could leave once, and she probably would have warned that the man was entirely too handsome, too smooth, and too much of a loner to be trusted. She would have also been upset that Lainey had opened on a Sunday. If she were being honest, she was wiped; that one day of rest had been more important than she realized. But she had to do this. She wasn't a liar, and even a lie of omission was a lie. She knew Ty wasn't the type of guy to take that lightly.

The aroma of coffee filled her senses, and as soon as the last drops finished brewing, the kitchen door opened.

"Morning, dear," Betty said, popping her head in.

"Hi, Betty. Perfect timing. I'll get you a coffee," she said, pouring Betty's coffee into a mug that said TOO HOT TO HANDLE and adding the usual three spoonfuls of sugar and splash of cream.

"Thank you, dear," she said, turning on the gas and tying her apron.

"Did you have a good weekend with your grandkids?" she asked, gathering extra napkins to refill the dispensers on the tables.

"I did, but of course it was too short. Ah, well, it was good, though. Precious babies—they don't stay children for long, you know?"

She smiled. "You're right," she said, thinking of little Sadie. It seemed like just yesterday Hope was calling her to say she was pregnant. Now Sadie was in first grade.

"Lainey, dear, you seem worn out," Betty said with a frown.

Lainey forced a chipper smile. "Oh, I'm fine. Just haven't had my coffee yet."

"You know Tilly would have threatened me with her frying pan if she knew I let you open up on a Sunday," she said, taking eggs out of the fridge.

Lainey glanced down at her watch, quickly changing the subject. "I'd better get to work. I'll be fine—don't worry," she said, walking out to the entrance of the diner.

Lainey unlocked the front door and then poured herself a large mug of coffee. She kept her own mugs under the counter where the cash was. The diner mugs were too small for her coffee consumption levels, and she also liked the personal little messages her mugs had, like Wake up and Be Awesome or Work Hard and Do Good Things or But First, Coffee.

She was glad when the first customers of the day walked in, because it meant Betty couldn't question her and she wouldn't have to dwell on what happened with Ty over the weekend. Pretty soon the diner had filled up with the usual suspects, and she found herself trying to hear if there was any gossip about the Donnellys. The morning flew by without anything eventful.

By the time afternoon came around, she was ready for more coffee. She loved this time of day—the afternoon-lunch crowd was long gone, and the slower dinner crowd hadn't started yet.

This was when she usually got caught up on deliveries or placed new orders. Or, like today, did secret projects.

She stared at the box filled with her paintings on canvas. It had seemed like a great idea when Ty had suggested she hang them up around the diner and put a price on them. And the thought of making some extra cash on the side was a huge motivator. But now, standing here, the prospect of displaying her work for the entire opinionated town to see was another thing. And what would they say about the prices? She had an idea of what she wanted to charge after going through some online galleries and shops that stocked and showcased local artists. She'd been shocked at the prices. She wasn't going to charge that much, but still. She painted because she had to. It was in her. It had always been her escape from the real world. Even though she painted sights and buildings from around Wishing River, it was her own interpretation of them.

She'd conjure up a thousand stories about an abandoned old house, imagining the people who had lived there at one time. Or the empty field with wildflowers—how many cowboys had ridden through it over the years? Or the old dirt road that had seen stage coaches in the nineteenth century?

But would people think they were worth paying for?

A twinge of nausea hit her, and she clutched the edge of the counter. She was about to bare her soul to the entire town. She took a slow, deep breath, willing her stomach to calm down. It was time to move forward. Wasn't putting them up around the diner better than having them stashed in a box in her closet or leaning against the wall in her "studio"?

She drank her coffee and stood behind the counter, trying to get up the nerve to just do it. She'd promised herself when she was finished with her mug that she would hang them up. She drank extra slowly and watched the occasional person walk by. But minutes passed, and her coffee was nearing the end.

You can do this, Lainey.

She marched into the kitchen and smiled at Betty, who was taking her break at the kitchen island and doing a bingo scratch card, her turquoise reading glasses perched on the tip of her nose. "Betty, remember how I do some painting in my free time?"

"Yes, dear," she said, scratching the card enthusiastically.

Lainey reached down and lifted the large box she'd tucked away in the far corner of the kitchen this morning. "Well, I've decided to hang them around the diner and see if anyone is interested in purchasing them."

That got Betty's attention. She sat up straight

and took her glasses off. Lainey held her breath as her stomach started tying itself into knots again. "I think that's a fine idea, dear. Why not make some extra money? It's good for young people to have ambition—and older people like me, too—do you know why?"

Lainey shook her head and waited.

"I'm saving up for a cruise. Maybe by the end of the year, between my bingo and my extra Sunday shifts, we'll have enough for a cruise for two!"

Lainey blinked back tears but forced a smile. It wouldn't be enough. Betty working extra Sundays probably wouldn't be enough. And her bingo cards, the ones she only ever won five or ten dollars on... She wanted to cry for her and wished she could pay Betty more, but they were all barely scraping by. Betty's weathered face was glowing with possibility, and Lainey knew it right down to her bones that she was making the right decision to move forward with her art. She needed to try. She needed to put herself out there, to pay back that debt, and then start building a more secure future for herself. And she had to take a chance. Maybe one day, she'd even have enough to help Betty get on that cruise. "I think that's a great goal, Betty," she said, walking to the front of the diner, more determined than before.

A wave of nostalgia hit her as she picked up her first painting—it was the old red barn a few miles away from downtown. The day she'd taken the picture had been shortly after her mother had come back to town, and the enormity of what Lainey was going to have to deal with had suffocated her. Bundling herself up and leaving behind the apartment she was suddenly forced to share with her mother, she'd trudged through the freshly fallen snow, camera dangling around her neck, and followed the winding dirt road that hugged the banks of the Wishing River shoreline. The river had frozen over, and the freshly fallen snow was pristine and pure and glistening under the bright sunshine. She had walked, the cold air making the weight in her chest even heavier as she toyed with the idea of what it would be like to just keep going, to leave Wishing River and be free.

But then that red barn appeared around the bend and she stopped walking. It called to her, its bright-red paint a beacon, a sign. She snapped her pictures through blurred vision. How many storms had that barn weathered; how much life had it seen inside its walls? Yet it stood there, proudly and as strong as it had been since the day it had been built.

Lainey gripped the sides of the painting, knowing she was a different person than the lost girl who had painted it. She was stronger now. She shook off the memory and pulled her hammer out of her back pocket and then picked a nail from her box. She knew exactly where she was going to put this one: right on top of the ledge where rows of teapots had sat for decades. The shelf was dustier than expected, but if she leaned the picture just so, she didn't even need to use a nail. She backed up a few steps to see if it was straight. It was perfect. She was almost shocked that it seemed like it belonged. She plucked one of the little folded cards she'd made with the name of the painting and the price and placed it right beside the picture. There. One painting hung, nine more to go.

In the next half hour, she worked quickly to display them all around the diner, trying to finish before any customers walked in. She didn't want to have to answer any questions. She'd rather just display them all and then hope people noticed on their own. Betty poked her head out of the kitchen every five minutes and gave her either a thumbs-up or an enthusiastic clap.

After she'd hung the last one—in the little corridor on the way to the bathroom—the front door chimes rang. She breathed a sigh of relief. She'd done it.

She made her way out to the front to see Hope and her daughter sitting at the counter. "Hi, guys! This is a nice surprise," she said, giving Sadie a big hug.

"Uh, hello? I think the nice surprise is your gorgeous artwork hanging on the walls!" Hope said, beaming.

Sadie nodded vehemently.

Lainey smiled at her and Hope. "Thanks, guys, I was nervous, but they're all up there…just waiting for the entire town to see them…"

"I had no idea you were going to do this. Good for you. Hang in there. I think today will be the toughest, but tomorrow will be easier. The nerves will wear off, especially when they start selling. Be confident—you are very talented," Hope said.

Heat filled Lainey's cheeks. She'd never been great with receiving praise, even though she really appreciated it at the moment. "Thanks. Now enough about me. Sadie, I have a hunch you need a treat."

Sadie nodded, grinning.

"And coffee for me," Hope said.

"All right, Sadie, you pick whichever dessert

you'd like," Lainey said as she poured Hope a cup of coffee from her personal mug stash.

"I think I want a brownie," she said, licking her lips.

Lainey laughed. "You have good taste. I'll give you this if you promise to tell me all about school." She took the dome off the brownie display and used the tongs to place one on a plate. "Shhh, don't tell your mom, but I picked the biggest one."

Sadie slapped her hands across her mouth and tried to hide her very loud giggle. "Sure, Auntie Lainey, but first let me take a bite."

Lainey tried not to laugh as Sadie managed to cram half the brownie in her little mouth. She quickly handed her a glass of water when it appeared she was having trouble swallowing. Hope patted her on the back. "Small bites, sweetie."

Sadie nodded, swallowing. "First grade is all right."

Lainey tried not to laugh at Sadie's word choice. "Only 'all right'?"

She shrugged. "Sometimes I don't have anyone to play with at recess."

"That happens. Don't be afraid to just walk up to someone and ask them to play. Some kids are just shy. You might think they aren't going to be a friend now, but as they get more comfortable at school, who knows, you might become best friends," Lainey said, hoping she was giving good advice.

Sadie nodded like she agreed.

"Your paintings really look great. They transform the whole place," Hope said, wandering around the diner.

Sadie nodded. "My favorite is the barn."

Lainey smiled at her. "Mine, too."

They all glanced over as the chimes on the front door interrupted them. Dean walked in, handsome in a checked button-down shirt and dark jeans. "Hi, ladies," he said.

"Hi, Dr. Stanton!" Sadie said, clearly excited to see him and oblivious to her mother's change of demeanor.

Dean broke out into a big grin. "Please tell me you saved me a brownie."

She shook her head. "I ate them all!"

They all laughed, but Hope's smile seemed a little forced. Dean and Hope had never seen eye to eye, but when her husband had gotten sick, she knew Hope had blamed him for his death. In a lot of ways, she felt that Hope had misjudged Dean. Dean was a great doctor, but also a very nice person. As much as she loved her friend, she knew she was wrong.

"Well, we should probably get going," Hope said, walking back over to the counter.

"Mommy, I want to stay and color," Sadie said. She cleverly dumped the cup of crayons Lainey had placed in front of her.

Hope sighed and offered another one of those tight smiles. "Sure, just a few minutes, then."

Lainey turned to Dean, who also had an odd expression on his face. "What can I get you?"

"Just a coffee and brownie. To go, please."

"You got it," she said, quickly getting his order together. "Busy day?" she asked, anything to break the tension in the space. Really, she hoped other customers would walk through the door to end this painful situation.

"Uh, yes, but not too busy to notice this place seems a little different." The shock in Dean's voice made her almost knock over the coffee she'd just poured him. He was slowly turning on the swivel barstool, obviously taking in the paintings.

She rubbed her sweaty hands on the front of her apron. "Yeah, I figured I'd…change things up a bit in here," she said, trying to sound nonchalant.

"Auntie Lainey is an artist," Sadie said, filling in the missing pieces.

"I can see that. These are amazing, Lainey," he said, his eyes filled with sincerity.

"Thank you," she said, trying again to take the compliment professionally. She slid the coffee across the counter.

"Thanks. I really needed a little afternoon pick-me-up," he said with a grin, placing a five dollar bill on the counter.

"Mommy says sugar is really bad for us," Sadie said while coloring a picture of Elsa. "She said it's fake energy."

Dean glanced over at Hope. "Well, I'm sure a little sugar here and there won't kill anyone."

"Mommy also says that sugar can cause all sorts of problems, from diabetes to cancer to—"

"Sadie, why don't you finish up your coloring? I'm sure Dr. Stanton knows all the bad things sugar does. He can just prescribe pharmaceuticals to fix the problem."

Lainey coughed while keeping her eyes on Dean. His jaw was clenching and unclenching, and his green eyes glittered. This was definitely not their first conversation about such things. But she didn't think

Hope was being fair to Dean. It wasn't his fault that her husband had died. Dean had done everything. But she knew Hope still couldn't think about it rationally. Maybe she'd never get over it, over the loss, over the fear. Her life hadn't gone as she'd planned, and there were so many days that she had so much on her plate, running her practice and being a single parent.

"Thanks, Lainey. I'm going to go enjoy my brownie and coffee. Oh, can you pass the sugar for the coffee?" he asked, his voice as smooth as maple syrup. Lainey had to stifle her smile because she knew that he never added anything to his coffee; he always drank it black.

Hope had turned her back to the entire conversation and was pretending to study one of Lainey's paintings.

"That's lots of sugar!" Sadie giggled.

Dean smiled and placed the plastic lid on the paper cup. "It sure is. You enjoy that brownie. Goodbye, ladies."

Lainey watched him leave and tried not to smile as he took a sip of his coffee outside and spit it out. Poor Dean.

A family walked through, and another couple, and then pretty soon Lainey was busy handing out menus as Hope and Sadie waved goodbye.

She managed the tables efficiently, and Betty performed as usual in the kitchen. As seven o'clock neared, though, she started having those butterflies in her stomach at the thought of seeing Ty again tonight when she drove Martin's dinner over. She'd managed to avoid him the whole week. It had been too busy to leave by five, which meant he'd definitely be in from working the ranch. A slight shiver stole through her.

She also kinda liked seeing Tyler when he was all sweaty and tired at the end of the day, as insane as that sounded. He put in long hours at the ranch, and she knew he was working himself to the bone, trying to prove to his father that he could save the place. She hoped he was right. But no matter how tired he was, how drawn his handsome face was, he always smiled at her. That was the reason for the butterflies in her stomach. That smile. The light in his blue eyes as he looked at her. From the first day she met him, she thought he was the most handsome cowboy in Wishing River. When she'd been a teenager, she'd always made sure she waited on his table. He'd been polite and friendly. He'd had no idea that she'd been secretly planning their wedding.

"Oh dear, oh dear," Betty said, coming out of the kitchen.

"What is it? Everything okay?" she asked, concerned by the deep frown on Betty's face.

"My husband might have the flu. Lainey, do you mind if I leave?"

"Of course not. You go," she said, ushering Betty back into the kitchen and helping her with her coat and purse. "Don't worry about me. The dinner crowd is gone."

"Oh, but I know you were going to Martin's ranch tonight," Betty said, pausing at the back door.

She waved her hand. "Don't worry about that. I'll just give the nurse a call and tell her to get something from the canteen. No one will starve over there," she said, opening the door that led to the back parking lot and gesturing for Betty to leave. "Go take care of your husband."

Betty nodded finally and then plodded off. Lainey locked the back door and dialed the nurse's number, then left a message.

She sighed and took in the messy kitchen before her. There would be no seeing Tyler tonight. It was probably for the best.

She quickly cleaned the space, hoping the more she did now, the less she'd have to do later, especially if she only had one or two customers. Maybe she could actually have an early night. She could use that time to research some local galleries like Tyler had suggested…or maybe she'd try painting again. She had come up with a new subject idea, and she hoped that if she was right, it might be just the inspiration she needed to get back on track with her art.

Today hadn't been a total bust; most people seemed as though they liked her artwork. She knew they weren't just going to go flying off the shelves, but no one dismissed them. She'd even heard people talking about the familiar sights she'd captured. Then again, there had been the more…amusing comments that she'd shrugged off. All in all, Hope had been right—today was the hardest. Tomorrow, she knew she wouldn't be as apprehensive about her paintings on the wall.

There wasn't another customer for the next half hour and she used that time to clean the kitchen. She was straightening out a painting when a group of cowboys walked in. Great. So much for an early night.

"Hi, gentlemen, have a seat anywhere you like,"

she said, waiting with a stack of menus.

She bristled as one of the guys checked her out, his gaze wandering up and down her body slowly. She hated being made to feel uncomfortable, especially in her own diner. She chose to ignore it, to stand a little straighter with her head held high, and handed out the menus. Thankfully, the rest of the men were polite enough.

"I'll give you a few minutes to read over the menu," she said, walking back to the bar.

"I don't suppose you're on the menu," the creepy one said with a smug smile.

She resisted the urge to roll her eyes or tell him to leave. Instead, she ignored his comment and walked back into the kitchen. She gave them a few minutes while she made sure everything was prepped.

She came back out and almost stopped dead in her tracks at the sight of Tyler sitting at the table with the other cowboys.

*T*y barely had time to register Lainey had her artwork displayed around the diner before his rodeo buddies waved him over to their table. His chest tightened at how big a deal this must be for her. Her art transformed the diner. He would definitely be bringing this up with her later.

But for now, he sat down and stared across the table at his old buddies. It wasn't like they were his best friends or anything, but they had gotten him through some rough times. When they messaged him earlier and said they were passing through town, he'd agreed to meet up. Tilly's wouldn't have been his place of choice, considering.

He'd been trying to stay away from Lainey, and he sensed she was doing the same, since she was never around when he finished his day at the ranch.

"So, how is it being back on your old man's ranch?" Luke asked.

Ty shrugged and glanced in the direction of the kitchen. Lainey hadn't spotted him yet. He knew she was the only one working tonight because she'd left a voicemail for Michelle. "It's all right. I wasn't exactly welcomed with open arms, but I wasn't expecting to be anyway."

"Least you got a place to call home," Rick said. Out of the three friends, he and Rick had never been that close. Sure, Rick had had it rough growing up, but he'd never trusted the guy. He had a jaded view of the world and people, and Ty knew enough about life to know that those kinds of people were the ones to drag you down.

"You guys order yet?" Ty asked, staring down at the menu, suddenly uncomfortable around them. They reminded him of the person he used to be when he left town eight years ago. He didn't like that guy anymore. He'd grown up, maybe, while they were still living that carefree life. As much as he knew he wasn't a marrying man, the idea of never having anyone to come home to didn't exactly seem right, either.

"Not yet," Cain said. He had always been closest to Cain. He was a guy who had come from nothing, but he had principles. He worked hard, kept to himself, and stayed out of trouble.

"No. A hot blonde with a great rack will be back in a sec to take our order," Rick said.

Blood thundered in his ears, and he narrowed his eyes. "Don't talk about her like that."

"Relax," Rick drawled. "She's a sweet surprise."

Tyler wondered at what point in this conversation it would be socially acceptable to plant his fist in Rick's stupid jaw. While he was contemplating that, Lainey walked out with her notepad and pen. When she made eye contact with him, relief flickered across her gaze, though he was pretty sure she'd deny it if he asked her later. The more he thought about this scenario, though, the more he didn't like it. Here she was at night, alone, in her diner. Who knows what kind of asswipes could come through here? Sure, Wishing River was a safe place, but all it took was one person. He was going to have to talk to her about this. Later. Right now, he needed to make sure his old acquaintances behaved.

"Hi. So what can I get you guys?" she said, turning from him.

Everyone placed their orders, and he kept his gaze trained on Rick as he did the same. When she closed her notepad and walked back to the kitchen, he breathed a sigh of relief.

But he didn't like the idea of her serving him in front of these guys, and his stomach was in knots anyway. He wanted them to leave. He wanted nothing to do with his old life. The sooner they left town, the better. "So how long are you here for?" he asked, trying not to appear like he wanted all of them gone. Really, he had nothing against Cain, but his friend wasn't here by himself. He didn't want this part of his life mingling with Lainey. It didn't feel right.

"Just passing through," Luke said, leaning back in his chair.

"We knew you lived around here, so we figured we'd stop by. I think I actually missed your sorry-ass face," Cain said with a grin.

Ty smiled for the first time since seeing them. "Yeah. I could say the same. But I won't."

"Well, I wouldn't mind staying long enough to sample whatever the blonde is offering," Rick said with a disgusting grin.

Everything inside Tyler stilled before blood came rushing through, thundering so powerfully that his ears pulsed. Those words were too damn close to words he'd heard from another man he loathed, whom he had no respect for. He refused to think about him now, though. "She's not offering you anything," he said, his voice coming out in an angry rasp, every muscle in his body coiled so tightly he felt like he was going to snap.

Rick smirked and leaned forward. "I know women. Trust me. Hot blonde, alone in a diner, tight jeans, big boobs in that tight shirt. She's advertising."

And he was done. He leaned forward to get closer to Rick. "Say another word and even your mama won't recognize what's left of you."

Rick scowled at him. "What the hell is your problem, man? Oh…I get it. You're already fucking her."

"I told you to shut your mouth, asshole. Leave. Now," he said, rage making it almost impossible to think straight. He stood up and braced his hands on the table. He hated his type. He hated his sick sense of entitlement. He'd heard this before, knew what it meant. Not while he was around.

"Enough," Luke said, holding a hand up in front of Rick. Rick shrugged him off and stood abruptly, kicking his chair back so roughly that it jostled the shelf behind him, and one of Lainey's paintings hit the floor. Shit.

Everyone was standing now. Cain shoved an arm in front of Tyler before he could take a swing at Rick, and Luke grabbed the back of Rick's shirt to yank him away from Tyler.

"Is everything okay?" Lainey said, rushing out of the kitchen and over to them.

Tyler's stomach twisted as Lainey stood there, assessing the situation. "Leave your money and tip on the table and get the hell out," he said to Rick.

"We didn't eat anything," Rick bit back.

Ty crossed his arms over his chest and stared at him. "Leave the money on the table."

"I knew from that first day you were a pussy," Rick said, throwing a twenty on the table and getting right up into his face. Luke was holding onto him, showing at least a little common sense.

"Get out of my town," Tyler said, barely holding on to his anger.

Luke hustled Rick out as Cain walked over and gave Tyler a light punch on the shoulder. "Sorry, man," he said, placing his own twenty on the table. He turned to Lainey. "Sorry for the trouble, Miss," he said.

"See you later," Tyler said to Cain.

Cain flicked his chin in his direction and walked out. The door shut, and Tyler slowly turned to face Lainey, whose face was beet red with her hands in tight fists by her sides. He searched for something to say. "Hi, Lainey, how's your day going?"

"*Hi, Lainey, how's your day going*? That's what you have to say to me, *hi*? You started a fight in my restaurant and you say hi?" She marched over to the mess and let out a small cry as she bent down.

He raised his hands in innocence. "Hey, we didn't fight."

"Close enough, Tyler. If that one guy hadn't stepped in and held the other back, I can only imagine what more would be damaged." She put her hands on her waist and jutted her chin forward. She was not happy.

He leaned down beside her, and his stomach dropped as he recognized the now-damaged canvas. "I'm sorry, sweetheart. I didn't mean… Dammit. I'm sorry," he repeated, wincing as she picked up the canvas. He hadn't meant for any of this to happen. He hated Rick. He hated everything he'd said. He would have hated him or any guy who spoke about any woman like that. But it was worse because it was Lainey. *Lainey*. He hated…the memories this had brought up about a man he'd wanted to know at one time. And that man had shattered his illusions and had inadvertently shown him what a contrast he was to the father who raised him.

Lainey paused and stared up at him, a question in her brown eyes. Up close, he could see that her eyes had little gold flecks in them. He'd missed her, and the last thing he wanted was to hurt her.

"You know, first you tell me to hang this stuff up out here, and then you damage it the first day!" she huffed.

This was bad. "It was an accident. Uh, were there any bites? Interested customers?"

She was nodding and smirking at the same time, which didn't bode too well for him. "Oh yeah, you remember old Pete Pickler?"

"Yeah?"

"He was really interested in that picture over there," she said, pointing to the one that featured the road leading out of town at dusk.

He swallowed. "Well that's good."

She did that rapid nodding thing again. "Yeah, yeah, he realized it was the place he'd stop and take a leak at during his younger days after a night at River's."

He couldn't even laugh. "I see."

"Then the church ladies said that if I'd painted the church, they'd buy that for sure—but only if it was in the fifty dollar range because they are pensioners. I find this really ironic, since those ladies spend at least fifty dollars on *pie* a week!"

He wanted to reach out and kiss the disappointment from her eyes. But he couldn't kiss Lainey—she was off-limits. Still, she was the only woman he'd wanted in a long time. She was the only woman he'd ever missed. He knew that beneath the anger and the attempt at humor was hurt. She had put a part of herself out there, and no one had even shown genuine interest in her talent. "It's just the wrong crowd. All it takes is the right person. I don't think Ol' Pete is your target audience anyway."

"What happened out here? I assumed these were your old friends?"

She was changing the subject so he wouldn't see

how hurt she really was. She was probably thinking he had major issues with people. His friends in Wishing River wanted nothing to do with him. Now these guys wanted nothing to do with him. His father wasn't speaking to him. He shrugged. "I wouldn't say they were really old friends. They were guys from my rodeoing days. Nothing more."

She frowned. "What happened? It seemed like you were going to kill that blond guy."

He took the canvas from her hands and turned it over, trying to see if there was some way it could be re-stretched. "I didn't like what he had to say," he said, avoiding eye contact with her, trying not to get all riled up again about what Rick had said.

"Oh, well, generally when my friends and I don't agree on something, we agree to disagree and not kill each other," she said in a patronizing voice.

He gave a short laugh. "Yeah, well, this was a bit more than that."

She shook her head, concern in her gaze. "Ty, you need to learn to get along with people."

He nodded and glanced down. "Okay, Lainey."

She let out a theatrical sigh then stood up and walked toward the kitchen. "Don't worry about it."

He followed her, feeling guilty. "Seriously. I'll pay you."

"Don't worry about it."

"So I guess I'll be going, then," he said, more to himself than to her. He didn't want to leave, but he knew being alone with Lainey wasn't a good idea.

She crossed her arms and pursed her lips. "You've been busy?"

Hell, she wanted him to stay. She might even be

mad that he hadn't come by sooner. Really, he should be getting some kind of award for his self-control. He'd wanted to see her every day, but he knew it wasn't right. He gave her a nod. "Yeah. Between the ranch and getting those cabins up and running, it's been pretty crazy."

Her eyes twinkled with delight, and his heart rate kicked up. "Oh, you started the cabins?"

"Making good progress. Mine is basically done."

She nodded. "Well, that's good. Speaking of the cabins, I may have a lead for you."

"A lead?"

She drummed her fingers on the island. "Yup. I'll let you know if it pans out."

"We haven't even advertised," he said, walking farther into the kitchen, getting a little worried about what kind of "lead" she had come up with.

"It's sort of a friend-of-a-friend situation," she said with a smile that made him kind of apprehensive. It was a plotter's smile. "But don't worry about that."

He rubbed the back of his neck. "Just, uh, let me pay you for that painting."

She opened her mouth and then shut it a moment later, a mischievous expression coming over her pretty face. "Not with money."

His mind went straight to the gutter, so he didn't say a word, just raised his brows.

"Let me paint you."

He coughed. "Excuse me?"

She nodded with enthusiasm. "Yes, let me paint you."

"I'm not Rose."

She frowned at him. "Who?"

"Rose. From *Titanic*."

Her eyes widened almost comically, and then she burst out laughing. At first, he smiled along with her because she had a pretty great laugh. But when she clutched the side of the island, still laughing and then taking huge gulps of air and holding her sides, his smile turned to a frown. He had no idea what was so funny. He walked over to her. She made eye contact with him and then burst out laughing again.

"I'm not finding the humor here," he said, trying to be patient when, again, he was not a patient man.

She composed herself and wiped tears from her eyes. "I wasn't, um…asking for a nude portrait."

He folded his arms across his chest, allowing a teasing tone to enter his voice again. "There's no need to be embarrassed."

She wasn't laughing now. Her face was red. "Of course there's nothing to be embarrassed about, because that's not what I was asking for. I meant I want to paint you—at the ranch. I have the exact spot in mind."

He leaned back against the counter and ran his hands through his hair. He realized Lainey somehow seemed to complicate his life with all sorts of weird ideas and requests. What was even more startling to him was that…he didn't seem to mind as much as he thought he would.

"You owe me," she said.

"You know, I was defending you out there."

"Is that right? Well, just so you know, I'm capable of defending myself. I've worked here on my own at night for almost a decade."

The unfamiliar sting of worry gripped him. "Well, that's not safe. You shouldn't."

She rolled her eyes. "Nothing happens in this town."

He didn't like it. She was way too naive to know what disgusting pigs some men could be. "All it takes is one guy."

"Grandma Tilly had an emergency plan."

"Really?"

"I can't reveal it, or I'd have to kill you. So why don't you tell me what your friends said?"

"Not really my friends," he reminded her, getting angry all over again when he replayed Rick's stupid comments in his mind.

She did a jazz-hands wave. "Okay, fine. You can shelter me from the big bad world."

He sighed roughly and ran his hand over his jaw. "What does it matter anyway?"

"Well, if someone was talking about me, I'd like to know."

"Nothing. He commented on…your attractive-ness."

"Oh, well, that happens a *lot*," she said, tucking a strand of hair behind her ear.

He stood up a little straighter. "Really?"

She narrowed her eyes on him. "Don't look so surprised."

He pinched the bridge of his nose. She had no idea what that jerk had said, which made all of this so much worse. "I'm not surprised that people find you attractive; I'm just surprised that you get picked up a lot."

She raised her eyebrows. "Really? Well, just so you

know, it happens on a weekly basis. Sometimes daily."

"You're lying," he said, fighting a smile.

She shook her head. "I'm a very attractive person. Just because you find it so hard to believe doesn't make it any less true."

She was fishing, which made this more interesting…and more dangerous. Hell, he needed some of Grandma Tilly's emergency whiskey. He wasn't supposed to be feeling this way. He had told himself nothing more could happen between them. She was too vulnerable, too sweet. Lainey needed someone else. But she was staring at him like she needed him. Wanted him. He bowed his head, rubbing the back of his neck, battling with his conscience.

"I know you probably don't get picked up a lot, Ty, and this is why you find it so hard to believe that this is a common occurrence for me."

He choked out a laugh, unable to help himself. Everything about this woman did him in. And he was tired of fighting it. "Did you lock the front door?"

"Yes. Why?"

He was going to regret this, he knew. But he'd regretted so much over the last eight years, so what was one more to add to the list?

"*Because* I've wanted to do this since the night you ran after me to kiss you," he said, bracing his arms on either side of the counter. Her heart was ready to jump out of her chest as his hard body made contact with hers. All her senses were exploding, which was what must have caused her delayed reaction to his statement. His head was bent, his mouth maybe an inch or so from hers, and one corner was slightly turned up.

She couldn't keep her hands to herself anymore, despite his comment. "That's false," she managed to whisper as she grabbed a fistful of his shirt.

A little chuckle escaped his lips before he ducked his head to kiss the soft spot beneath her ear. It was almost enough to make her knees give.

Instead, she leaned against the counter and pulled him in. "I never wanted to kiss you that night. I just felt sorry for you. I'm a sucker for the underdog."

"I'm not an underdog," he said, one of his hands settling on her hip.

She had no idea how he was still holding a conversation. She stared at his mouth, desperately wanting him to kiss her but needing to keep up with him. "You are. You're like the squirrel that got trapped in my chimney last winter. I kept trying to help him, to show him the way out, but he refused to take my help. He almost died."

"We need to stop talking," he murmured against her neck. "Especially about squirrels."

She gave a nervous laugh. "But I love talking."

"I think there are other things you might like more," he said in a gravelly voice that sent shivers down her body. His mouth was making a trail of soft kisses along her neck and up her jawline.

"You can try, but I'm not so sure," she said, her voice sounding breathy and kind of faint.

He grinned against her lips and then finally kissed her. He kissed her like he'd been as desperate as she was. His lips were hard and demanding, the softness of their first kiss replaced by the growing attraction that was impossible to ignore. She flattened her hands and ran them up his hard chest and then to the back of his head. The minute she did, his body was against hers, and she could feel all of him. His hands roamed down the sides of her body and then cupped her bottom before lifting her onto the counter. He stood between her legs, and she lost all thoughts of ever breathing again.

He was powerful and gentle, all at the same time, and he made her feel like she was the only woman he'd ever wanted. He made her feel special. He made her feel like he was what she'd been waiting for her entire life. She clung to him, to everything he was offering.

"Oh my dear, my dear."

They both stilled at the sound of Betty's voice in the kitchen. He broke off the kiss, but they were both breathing raggedly. Neither of them moved, and Lainey could feel their hearts beating. She clutched his biceps, not ready to turn to face the woman she'd known for a lifetime, her grandmother's friend, the woman who would be frying bacon tomorrow morning.

Lainey untangled herself from Ty and jumped off the counter, heat clawing its way up her cheeks. Betty was standing in the doorway to the diner, shielding her eyes as though she were looking at an eclipse. "I'm so sorry, Betty… I—"

"Just don't you mind me; I forgot my blood pressure medication—I'll need a double dose after this! I'm leaving right away. Nothing to be embarrassed about. I was young once, too. Haven't sat on a counter in ages, though, probably would need a forklift to get me on one these days," she said with a laugh. "Goodbye now. Tyler, you mind your manners."

"Yes, ma'am," Tyler said as she burst out the diner door.

Lainey covered her face. "Oh. My. God," she moaned.

Tyler leaned forward and gently kissed the top of her head. Lainey almost died then and there because she had never pictured him so endearingly sweet. This was one to add to her fantasies about him. "I guess we should be grateful she came in at this point and not ten minutes down the road."

She lowered her hands and noticed that Tyler didn't seem all that bothered. That statement made her question what she'd been thinking. What was her plan with him, exactly? She had no idea who she was anymore. Sitting on counters, making out with the cowboy of her dreams? She was breaking all her rules. She smoothed her hair and tried to appear collected. "Right. It was actually a good reminder of the time, too. I have an early day tomorrow, and I know you do, too," she said, moving away from him.

Surprise flickered across his blue eyes. She tried not to drool at the sight of him. His hair was all mussed up, and his mouth was scrumptious. Oh, she was going to regret the way this ended one way or another. "You're right. This shouldn't have happened anyway."

She shook her head and then nodded. "Right. Exactly. Because…"

"Because…"

"You have problems and stuff."

He frowned. "*I* have problems? And stuff?"

"You know," she said, desperately trying to come up with something. "Making friends."

He smiled. "I think we've 'made friends.'"

She rolled her eyes. "Oh is that how you 'make' all your friends?"

He shrugged. "You got me there."

"Hmm, yes, I didn't think so. You should probably get going now."

He didn't say anything for a moment, then he walked forward, and her heart started hammering again. "How about I wait for you to close up?"

She was taken aback and touched. "You don't have to do that. I live upstairs. I'll be fine."

He didn't say anything. "Then humor me by walking me to the door and locking up after I leave."

She shrugged but nodded. They walked to the front of the diner in silence, and when he unlocked and opened the door, she assumed he was going to leave without saying a word.

But he leaned down and gave her a quick, hard kiss. "Goodnight, Lainey."

And left her completely uncertain where they'd go from here tomorrow.

CHAPTER TWELVE

Ty knew he was in trouble when he couldn't get Lainey off his mind three days after seeing her at the diner. He was going through withdrawal.

This had never happened to him before. And he didn't like it.

Like, every time the front door of the house opened, he quickly ran to see who it was—unfortunately it was either Mrs. Busby, one of the nurses, Dean, or Cade. When a car drove down the road, he'd stop and check to see if it was her old Volkswagen. But no, it wasn't Lainey.

She'd sent dinner with Mrs. Busby, and he knew why. Their kiss in the kitchen had already confirmed what he knew the night they'd kissed in the street— their attraction was explosive.

As much as he knew they couldn't just have one night together—because he had a suspicion it wouldn't be enough—he was rethinking not getting involved with her at all. Maybe if they set up some kind of guidelines so no one would get hurt—well, so she wouldn't, really. He knew enough about himself to know that he wasn't the kind of guy to fall in love, not the kind of love she would want, anyway. He hadn't been able to feel like that since his mom died. Probably never would again.

But that didn't mean they couldn't sleep together. As long as they were very clear about expectations, because the last thing he'd want was to hurt her. The more he thought about it, the more he realized it could work.

He needed to go see her. He knew she'd be at the diner.

He stood near his truck, his muscles tightening as he spotted Cade striding toward him like he had a bone to pick. Nothing new. His house had become a battleground, and he didn't see how he'd ever become friends with the guy who had tried to take his place in his father's life.

"Tyler," he called out.

Ty leaned against his truck, folding his arms across his chest, pretending like Cade's angry stomping wasn't threatening. "Yeah?"

"I want to talk to you about Lainey," he said, slowing as he approached him.

Ty stiffened, standing a little straighter. "What do you want to talk about?"

"I noticed you've been hanging around her."

Ty shrugged, not liking where this was headed. "What is this? Middle school?"

Cade didn't like that, because his jaw muscle started ticking. "Stay away from her."

Everything inside him stilled. "What did you just say?"

Cade took a step toward him, his eyes narrowed. Growing up, Cade had always been the roughest of the three of them. But he couldn't say that anymore. Ty had been on his own for years without a dime, hanging with some not-so-reputable people. He knew how to protect himself, and he knew how to be prepared when he was threatened.

"I said stay away from Lainey because she hasn't

had an easy life. She's a good person, and she doesn't need you messing things up for her."

Ty leaned a little closer to his once–best friend. "And what? I'm a bad person? I'm going to screw up her life?"

"Something like that," he said, flicking the brim of his hat up slightly. Ty tried his damn hardest to hold on to his temper, but he saw the flash of jealousy— and he knew.

"Or is it that you want her for yourself? I'm not good enough for Lainey, but you are?" Ty crossed his arms and leaned against the truck again, as though his next words didn't matter. "You can't tell me who I can be with. If she wanted you, she wouldn't be hanging around me. You had how many years to get together with her? So either you're chickenshit or she thinks *you're* shit, just like I do."

He ducked as Cade's fist narrowly missed his jaw. Dammit. Ty barreled into him, shoving him into the mud beside the driveway. He couldn't let him get the upper hand, so he jumped on top of him. Cold, wet mud made it even harder for them to get in some good punches, but they made the best of things.

"Omigoodness, you guys are going to kill each other!" Lainey's voice over them should have been enough to make them stop, but when Tyler turned to look at her, Cade used that moment to his advantage and knocked him down. Tyler retaliated.

Lainey's cursing and yelling were like a distant warning that they should stop soon, but they didn't. They had eight years of anger pouring out of their fists. No, neither of them stopped until the sight of Lainey falling into the mud with them made them both stop moving, breathing.

She had landed on her backside, the shock on her pretty face turning to rage in half a second. "I'm going to kill you both!" she screamed.

They quickly scrambled, helping her up and out of the mud, both yammering, asking if she was okay.

She glared at Ty, and he cringed. Mud was in her hair, caked to her clothes, splotched on her face. "I'm sorry, sweetheart," he said, wincing and reaching to grasp her elbow in case she slipped again. She snatched her arm away and put her hands on her hips. He was not going to be a total ass and admire how mud had conformed enticingly to her curves.

"You've been doing a lot of apologizing lately, Tyler, and I'm thinking you should just stop doing stupid things so I wouldn't have to hear your stupid apologies."

Cade said something under his breath and backed up. Ty stole a glance at his old friend, at the beginnings of a nice shiner forming under his left eye. He probably looked just as bad.

"I don't know what the two of you are thinking, behaving like schoolboys in a playground. And in the front yard, nonetheless. What if your father had been at the window?" Lainey hissed.

Cade hung his head, kicking the toe of his boot into the dirt.

"Well?" she said, staring at Ty like she blamed him. "What do you have to say for yourself?"

He really wanted to smile at the picture she made, all bossy and angry, but he knew that wouldn't be good. He put on his best remorseful face. It had been a long time since someone gave a shit about him. He cleared his throat. "I didn't start it."

Cade swore under his breath.

"Language," Ty said with a smug smirk at his friend.

Lainey rolled her eyes at Ty. "Nothing you haven't muttered around me. Cade, are you all right?"

Cade gave a stiff nod.

"Good," she said. "I need to speak with you a minute."

Tyler tried to keep his cool as he watched Cade follow Lainey to the fence a few yards from where he was standing. He couldn't make out what they were saying, but a minute later, Lainey was charging back toward him, and Cade hung back a few paces behind her.

"Tyler, you're coming with me," she said, grabbing a hold of his hand. Maybe if he'd been in fifth grade, he'd have shot Cade a gloating smile as they walked away, but they were long past those years. And there was something in Cade's expression, in his eyes, that made him almost feel bad. Like he used to. Cade had been a brother to him once. Ty'd been the one to bring him home until he'd become part of the family. But when the going got rough, Cade hadn't stood by him.

Now he was here, trying to take everything from him. Including Lainey.

"Are you plotting my murder?" he asked as Lainey marched toward his cabin.

She spun around, a gorgeous sight all filled with mud and anger. "Really, that's what you deserve. Honestly, I don't know what you're thinking. You're supposed to be rebuilding relationships, not hitting your friends. We talked about this."

She was back to putting her hands on her hips, and her red-and-navy-plaid shirt was gaping as it stretched across her breasts. He had always been a sucker for punishment. He took a step closer, and she put her hand on his chest.

"I know that expression, and you have a helluva lot of explaining to do if you think you're going to come any closer."

"Cade hit me first, Lainey. I was just defending myself."

Surprise lit her eyes, and he wondered what the hell she thought of him. She had assumed he'd been the one to start the fight. She frowned at him and peered over his shoulder, but Cade was long gone by now. "Why would he do that? Were you fighting about your dad? The plans for the ranch?"

He put his hands in his back pockets so he wouldn't reach for her. "Not exactly."

"Well?"

There was no way he was going to tell Lainey that Cade was in love with her. He knew it. His friend might not have admitted it, exactly, but he could tell. But it wasn't his place to tell.

Cade could do it if he wanted. But Ty didn't think that would happen.

A part of him almost felt bad. Almost, but he wasn't really with Lainey himself, so he didn't have to be guilty about his friend's unrequited love. Then there was the fact that Cade was acting like a dick, so that eased his conscience as well. "Nothing you need to know about. It's personal. Cade's problem, not mine or yours."

"That sounds cold," she said. "Is he okay? Maybe

I should go talk to him."

"He's fine. I'm the underdog, remember?" he snapped, tired of talking about his traitorous best friend. "But you must be cold. Let's go inside. You can have a hot shower and get some dry clothes on. My cabin is less than a ten-minute walk."

So his mind was already in the gutter the moment he said hot shower.

Her brown eyes lit with the desire he'd seen in them the other night, and then her gaze dipped to his mouth. "Let's walk faster," he said, grabbing her hand.

"I was actually coming out here to tell you guys about the weekend I just booked."

Hell. He didn't want to talk about that, because it would lead to an argument. He had no idea what kind of people she'd booked. He didn't want to argue with Lainey. He wanted to sleep with her. "Tell me after we're not caked in mud anymore," he said, and they walked in silence until he opened the door to his cabin.

She stepped inside but didn't say anything. He turned on the lamp on the entryway table and tried to gauge her reaction.

She bit her lower lip. "This isn't one of the cabins to rent out, right?"

"Seriously? You're dripping in mud and you're criticizing my decorating?"

A hand flew to her chest, and he noticed one of the buttons had come undone. He closed his eyes and said some kind of prayer, but then thought he shouldn't be praying about wanting to have sex.

"I wasn't criticizing your decorating. You've done a fine job—for you. A bachelor. This is...wonderful," she said, doing a little clap, like he was a five-year-old.

He'd just have to show her he was a grown man. He reached for her, but she held up a hand, and his shoulders sagged.

"*N*o, let me finish. I not only rented out one cabin but two! For next weekend." She had been thrilled with her news…and thrilled with the idea of getting to see Ty to give him the news.

She had to admit she was also thrilled that she'd be getting some commission. At this rate, she would make a serious dent in her repayment. She had not been thrilled to fall into the pile of mud, though. Both guys had appeared sincerely contrite, so she managed to get over it. She was still slightly concerned with the fact that Tyler didn't seem to be making any inroads with his former friends. She spoke to Cade about trying harder with Tyler. He had agreed he'd talk to Dean and that they'd consider having a conversation with Tyler, but he wasn't making any promises.

He raised his eyebrows. "Seriously?"

She nodded, very satisfied with herself. "Yup. I told you it would happen. They'll be arriving next Friday night."

"How many?"

"Eight."

"What exactly are they expecting?"

She shifted. This was the part that made her slightly nervous. "So they're all women…. Bridesmaids. They're surprising the bride. It's a little getaway before the wedding."

He was already groaning and shaking his head. "Nope. No way, Lainey. Nightmare. That is a nightmare. I can't count all the ways that could go wrong."

"They're paying five grand for two nights."

His face turned white. "Are you kidding me?"

She grinned. "Nope! They arrive on Friday and leave Sunday."

"You mean to tell me they're going to pay five thousand dollars for three days at a cattle ranch in the middle of nowhere during our down season?"

"Precisely. We do have to feed them, but I'll take care of that. I'll talk to the cook in the canteen. We'll have to spruce up the cabins, stock the fridge with drinks and snacks. Oh and, um, you and Cade will have to take them horseback riding, cook over an open fire, and maybe sing some campfire songs."

He took a physical step away from her, and his neck and face turned beet red. "Pardon?"

She winced. "I know you're probably not a fan of, um, singing…"

"Lainey," he said, his voice sounding strangled.

"Hear me out. They're from the city; they just want a cowboy experience. Just sing up some cowboy songs, like, um, you know," she said, waving her hand around.

He gave a stiff shake of his head. "No."

"'Kumbaya.'"

"Not happening. Ever."

She crossed her arms. "Not happening as in you won't do it, or not happening as in you don't know any songs? I can help with the songs. Oh, I love that old James Taylor one, you know, about sweet baby

James?" She tried to smile even though he was staring at her like he was either going to murder her or kill himself. She stood still as he ran his hands down his face and groaned.

"Just think. It'll be worth it for five thousand dollars."

"Cade and I aren't even speaking to each other," he said through clenched teeth.

She reached out and patted him on the shoulder. "Maybe this will bring you closer together again." She tried to rub off the mud from his shoulder on a clean part of his shirt, which happened to be his stomach, but that wasn't a smart move.

His jaw tensed. "Cade and I will kill each other."

"I'll speak with him."

"You're not his mother."

"Still, we are close. I'll talk to him about getting along with you and finding a way to work together."

He muttered something under his breath as he pinched the bridge of his nose. "Don't talk to Cade. I don't need you solving my problems for me."

"Fine. I'll come up with the itinerary and then give it to you. This is going to be so great—you'll see. By the end of next weekend, when you're cashing your check, you'll be thanking me."

"I need a shower, and then I need a drink. We can talk about it once we're not soaked in mud anymore. You want to go first?"

Her cheeks burned at the thought of him in the shower. Or her in the shower. Or, inevitably, the thought of both of them in the shower. She opened her mouth but squawked. She cleared her throat and tried again. "I'll just go home."

"You're going to get your car full of mud. Why don't you just shower, and I'll throw your clothes in the washer? It's Saturday night. Oh, do you have plans?"

Too many questions, too many images floating around in her head. First things first. "Plans?" She contemplated lying for a moment.

"Yeah, plans."

She shook her head. "I had to refuse several offers."

His lips twitched. "Lucky me."

She narrowed her eyes, not sure whether or not he was being sarcastic. "You have a washing machine in here?"

He nodded. "Stacked washer-dryer in that closet beside the kitchen."

"Oh."

He was already walking to the dresser in his room. She strained her neck so she could see inside. There was a large bed and rustic dresser, plus a big picture window and a patterned quilt on the bed in between two nightstands. It was better than she'd anticipated. He came out of the room a minute later and handed her a T-shirt.

She frowned. "I...um, I'm really particular about toiletries."

"Lainey, are you uncomfortable with taking a shower here?"

Her hand flew to her chest in an attempt to feign shock. "What? Of course not. I've taken plenty of showers at plenty of different...places."

He smiled slowly. It was a darn fine smile, too, even when it held hints of mocking. It was a perfect smile, actually. Straight white teeth, a contrast to his tanned skin. "Well in that case, get going. There're clean towels on the shelf beside the shower."

Her time was up. The mud was already drying and very uncomfortable against her skin; she wouldn't be able to drive home like this. She was also freezing. "Fine. That's a very nice offer." She held out her hand, and he placed a navy T-shirt in it.

"Have fun," he said as she walked away.

She eyed him quizzically before turning to the washroom. She locked the door and looked around. It was dated, but quite clean. As promised, she found a stack of white towels on a stainless steel rack. Fifteen minutes later, she dried herself off, feeling like a new woman. She towel-dried her hair as well as possible, already knowing he wouldn't have a hair dryer. She slipped his shirt over her head, suddenly grateful for his height because the shirt ended up being modest enough, if she tugged at it.

"Lainey, you almost done in there?"

"Yes!" she said, grabbing her muddy clothes from the ground and hanging up her towel. She opened the door, and when he was standing there without a shirt on, she almost walked into him. She told herself not to let her gaze wander, but her eyes seemed to not get the memo, and she took in the gorgeous sight of Ty without a shirt. He was bronzed, his shoulders broad and his arms thick with muscle. She stopped when she got to the abs because they were too much to handle.

"I started a fire, if you're cold," he said, his voice thick and sending shivers down her body.

"Thanks," she whispered, moving aside and walking past him.

She heard the door shut and then the water running a minute later. She threw her clothes into the washing machine he'd pointed out but didn't run it, since he'd probably have to add his clothes. She noticed his shirt was already in there. She walked across the room to the fireplace to warm up, especially with her damp hair and no socks.

Being alone with Tyler in his cabin with barely any clothes on was probably not the wisest move, but it was a purely innocent situation. They were friends. Friends who were attracted to each other.

Tyler walked out of the washroom wearing a pair of clean jeans that rode low on his hips and a plain white T-shirt. Muscles rippled while he moved, and she couldn't make herself turn away. Luckily he wasn't paying her any attention. She crossed her arms under her breasts, self-conscious.

"Cold?" he asked, standing in the middle of the room.

"Uh, no, the fire is great," she said.

He shot her a glance that suggested he wasn't exactly buying what she was saying as he pulled out a bottle of whiskey and two glasses. "I think we need a drink."

She ran a hand through her hair, nerves propelling her to fidget. "Oh, are we staying awhile?"

He turned and leaned against the counter, and she found herself without words. It was him... Being alone with him like this.

"Well, I assumed you'd stay until our laundry was finished," he replied.

"Right," she said, trying to be casual, "of course. That makes sense."

"So, considering we're stuck here for a while and I have whiskey, why don't you give me more of the details about my upcoming weekend from hell?"

He was grinning when he said it, and she had to look away for a moment. His hair was still damp and mussed up, his T-shirt and jeans clung to his chiseled body, and she wanted nothing more than to walk over there and give in to the attraction and not have to worry about the consequences. The man was beautiful. Really, she had to hand it to her former teenage self—she really could pick 'em.

"Right, the bachelorette party. I really think you'll have lots of fun. I don't suppose you have any food in here, do you?"

"Let's wait until I've had my second glass for you to explain why you would ever think that sounds like something I'd find fun. Food, I actually just bought some, help yourself to anything while I add some more logs to the fire."

She opened the small bar fridge and was pleasantly surprised to see a nice selection of cheese. "Do you have crackers to go with this cheese?"

"Yup. The cupboard above the sink."

She busied herself with creating a platter with cheese and crackers and sliced up a couple of the apples she found in the fridge as well. By the time she was done, he had added another log to the fire, and it was roaring. She walked over to join him, and the distinct sensation that this was becoming a very intimate evening gripped her. An intimate evening with Tyler. She didn't know if she was prepared for this.

"That is impressive," he said as she sat on the

couch beside him but not too close. "Do you need a whiskey refill?"

"Actually, I haven't even had my first glass. It's probably better to eat something first."

"Wise," he said. "You help yourself."

She filled up her plate with an assortment of the cheddar, apple, and crackers. "Thanks."

He did the same, and pretty soon they were both eating, the fire crackling the only sound in the room.

"So, are you happier living here?" she asked after a bit, taking a drink of the smooth liquid.

He put his now empty plate down on the coffee table in front of them and sat back on the couch. She tried not to notice how small the couch seemed with him, how large his presence was.

"Did I spill something?" he asked, glancing down.

"Oh, what? Um, yeah, I thought it was whiskey… but not," she managed to choke. Really, she was not prepared for this. She wasn't calm and collected. She needed to be. *Focus, Lainey.*

He seemed to buy her explanation. "I can't say things are going really well at the main house, and I like my privacy."

Her stomach sank. "Oh, I'm sorry to hear that," she said, staring at his profile. All hard lines, not an ounce of softness in him. Outwardly. But she was beginning to know better. She tucked his shirt around her knees when she noticed it creeping up.

He shrugged. "Can't blame him, I guess."

"He'll come around. I know him…or I've gotten to know him. He wouldn't be so upset with you if he didn't care, Ty."

He turned to her, and she swallowed hard at the

intensity in his stare. "I don't need a father anymore. It doesn't matter if he comes around or not. I'm here out of duty. Out of obligation. Because it's the right thing to do. God knows I haven't done the right thing in a long time."

She drank the rest of her whiskey, wincing as it ran down her throat the wrong way. She coughed. "He'll always be your father, Ty. And you may think you don't need him, but you do. You both need each other, and you need to forgive each other."

He made a noise that didn't exactly sound like he agreed with her. "He's got Cade."

"Cade isn't his son."

"He's gotten along just fine without me. You know what? I don't want to talk about this," he said, abruptly standing and walking over to the washer. He grabbed their clothes and then threw them into the dryer and turned it on. She resisted the urge to ask him to add a dryer sheet. He didn't join her on the sofa again, and her stomach sank. He poked at the logs a few times, sparks flying out like fireworks. He couldn't deal with his pain, but she wanted to help him—and Martin—even if it meant he got mad at her.

"You don't want to talk about it because you don't like talking about your feelings. But the truth is you're hurt that he didn't welcome you home with open arms. You're hurt because your best friend is the ranch manager and a part of the family now. You're hurt—"

"Hey, Lainey?" he said, his voice harsh, his eyes flashing. "I don't need a lecture. I'm not a child you can chastise."

She stood up, her hands on her hips. "Then you should stop behaving like one, because frankly you're acting like a hurt child who doesn't want to be bothered trying to make things better because it's too difficult. I never knew my father. He didn't give a crap to get to know me or to send money. Not a birthday card, a Christmas card, nothing. So when you sit here telling me that you don't need a father, I get to say you're wrong. You need your father. Everyone needs their father. Just like you'd want your mother here right now. Just like I'd want Tilly back. You should be grateful you have any family," she said, hating that her voice cracked on that last sentence, and she reached for the bottle of whiskey. But his hand covered hers, and she held her breath, her stomach doing somersaults at his touch.

"You're right," he said gruffly.

She didn't pull back, realizing she didn't *ever* want to pull back from him. She wanted that warmth that he gave her, that security…the thrill, the rush, of being kissed by him. His gaze was on her mouth. She had one second to brace herself, and then he was there.

This time when he kissed her, it wasn't the same. It was terrifying—in the best possible way—because he was kissing her as though he desperately needed her, as much as she needed him. He captured her mouth and explored and tasted and took as much as he gave. She sank into him, the surrender feeling so good. He must have noticed, too, because he gave a low groan that had a ripple effect through her chest. His hard body covered hers. She ran her hands up his arms, his biceps, over his shoulders, until she could thread them into his thick hair, desperate to keep him close.

She ignored the warning bells in her head to not let this go too far, because she also needed him. She had never needed anyone after her grandmother died. She had gone it alone. But Ty made her want so much more—he made her want him. It was too terrifying to think about the implications, so she didn't. Instead, she just felt.

His strong body covered hers, and she let her instincts guide her; her instincts told her she needed to touch his bare skin.

"I won," she whispered when his mouth began to trail kisses along her jawline and behind her ear.

"What?" he breathed against her skin.

"I won. I was right." She groaned as he kissed the sensitive skin on the shell of her ear. "You…you admitted I was right."

He was half laughing when he kissed her again, when his hands touched her bare legs, one of them under her shirt. Laughter was gone, and it was like he was everything and everywhere. She shoved his shirt up and over his head and almost passed out at all the warm skin her fingers were itching to explore. Her hands roamed along his rippled abs, adoring the way his muscles jumped beneath her touch. She stopped when she reached the button of his jeans.

The image of her pale hands on his darker skin, the feel of his hot, taut body under her touch was so new to her that she couldn't look away. She didn't want this moment to be over. Before things became awkward, he was kissing her again, his large, callused hand now moving under her shirt, over her naked body. She should stop. Now. It wasn't fair, she wasn't playing a fair game, and she was going to regret this tomorrow.

He pulled back for a brief moment as he looked at her, his blue eyes flashing, his jaw clenching. "Nah, Lainey, I'm pretty sure I won."

She stared at the strong man towering over her, at the desire rolling like storm clouds in his eyes, at the body that was holding hers with such tenderness and passion, and knew she was in way over her head.

But she couldn't bring herself to stop.

Her hands had a mind of their own as they traveled over the hard planes of his body, and she marveled over the heavily roped muscles, the smattering of hair, the way his breath caught as she ran her fingers down his chest and to the top of his jeans. Who was she? This wasn't her. She had never gotten herself into a situation where she had no control.

She didn't have time to figure out this new side of herself, because what she'd done with her hands on his body, he proceeded to do the same but with his mouth on hers. She didn't even recognize the whimpers coming from her or the way her body moved with his mouth on it. But when he took her nipple in his mouth and she thought she was going to die from the sensation, something inside her went into self-preservation mode.

"Ty," she breathed, her voice sounding hoarse with pleasure.

He groaned something, his mouth at her breast, his hand cupping her bottom.

He didn't move, but she realized she was still

clutching him. "Ty," she said again, this time tugging at his hair gently.

He raised his head slowly, his eyes heavy, his jaw clenched. "Yeah? You okay?"

Her heart immediately squeezed at the concern in his voice, at the effort it was taking to not keep going. She shook her head, knowing what she was about to say would sound juvenile to him and that he would never in a million years understand. Tyler was a man, not a teenager.

He was everything she ever wanted, and she was going to tell him no. Her gaze was locked on his, and she shook her head.

He stilled, and the seconds felt like hours. His jaw began clenching and unclenching, and she swallowed and said the only true thing she was willing to admit.

"I'm sorry," she whispered. She wasn't going to cry, but she really wanted to, because right now she was the definition of idiot.

"What are you saying?"

She shook her head as hot tears ran down her face. "I'm sorry. I can't."

He ducked his head and slowly moved off her and to the edge of the couch. He sat there for a moment. There were no words exchanged, and the only sound in the cabin was the crackling of the fire.

He stood abruptly and then walked over to the kitchenette and straight for the whiskey. He poured himself a shot and swung it back. She was trying not to weep over the man she just rejected, since that was like the poster girl for how to never get a man.

She slowly got up but didn't know where to go.

The whiskey kind of seemed like a good coping mechanism. "Are you still sharing?" she asked, her voice sounding shaky to her own ears. He didn't answer her right away, and then he slowly turned around and leaned against the counter.

This had to go down as the most humiliating night of her life. Humiliating and stupid. She was an idiot for losing control like that, for not warning him. He stood there looking hot and frustrated.

She needed to leave. It was the only way.

He wasn't even speaking to her. He wasn't even sharing his whiskey. She stood, tugging on his shirt, finding the modesty that had clearly escaped her when his hands were roaming her naked body not five minutes ago.

How had she let herself do this? She was keeping secrets, something she'd never done before. It was like she was turning into another person. She shuddered and wrapped her arms around herself, glancing over at the dryer. "If my clothes are ready, I think I should leave."

CHAPTER THIRTEEN

$\mathcal{T}$yler didn't think himself a promiscuous sort of guy, but he'd had enough women to know that this wasn't how the night was supposed to end. He knew how to read women, he knew how to give a woman what she needed, and he had always managed to leave a woman very happy. So tonight was a complete mystery, or the woman in front of him trying to stretch his T-shirt to cover her knees was a mystery to him.

Maybe it was more than that, because Lainey wasn't just any woman. Lainey was the only woman he wanted more than just a night with. Lainey was a woman who had him dreaming about all the things he had no business dreaming about. He knew they'd be good in bed. He knew they'd have chemistry that was off the charts, and tonight had proven it.

He couldn't get enough of her.

He had forced himself to take it slow, to not rush, but the feel of her body under his, the sweet sounds she made, the way she'd clung to him, had made it painful to go slow.

And it had almost killed him to stop. Of course, he would have done anything for her, but it had come out of nowhere. He'd thought they were on the same page, that they felt the same things.

Staring at her from across the cabin now, he didn't know what to think. Her face was red, and she seemed shy and vulnerable.

He was going to have to get a grip or risk being an asshole. He poured her a glass and crossed the room to the couch, holding her glass out.

Her shoulders relaxed, and she walked over to join him. The minute her fingers grazed his hands, tears sprang into her eyes, and his frustration abated at the sight. "What it is, Lainey? What happened?"

She sniffled loudly, took the glass, and downed it. She waved a hand in front of her face and winced. "I'm sorry," she whispered.

He sighed and shrugged, falling back onto the sofa. "You don't have to apologize."

She sat down, too, but huddled into the opposite corner. "I do. I let it go too far. I don't know what I was thinking. Well, I do. I was actually thinking I'd be able to sleep with you."

He didn't know whether to laugh or be insulted, so he reached for the only friend he'd had in the last eight years and poured himself another glass. "You know, it has been done before."

The red in her cheeks deepened, and a small laugh escaped her lips. She rested her head against the sofa cushions and gave him a small smile. "I…I know, Ty. *I* just haven't done it before."

He didn't know whether she meant she hadn't done it before with him…or hadn't done it before… at all. Right now, he wasn't sure what was worse. He cleared his throat and tried to appear approachable and not like he was going to either weep or smash his fist through the wall with sexual frustration. "What exactly does that mean?"

She frowned and scooted a little farther into the corner, almost to the point that it appeared as though she was burrowing for the winter. "Do you think you could fill up my glass again?"

Uh-oh. That couldn't be good. "Are you sure you're keeping track of how many shots you've had?" he asked.

"It's fine; I grew up on whiskey." He didn't argue with her. He obliged and waited while she finished off her shot. Really, the woman's ability to slug back whiskey was pretty surprising. He propped his legs up on the coffee table, crossing one ankle over the other. He should probably settle in, because she didn't seem like she was in any hurry to talk, and quite frankly he needed to get his thoughts out of the bedroom. Hopefully the whiskey would help.

"Better?" he asked when she placed her empty glass on the coffee table.

She winced, a funny expression on her face as she stared at him. And dammit if those brown eyes of hers didn't tug at heartstrings he wasn't used to. She had eyes that could make him say yes to whatever it was she was selling. She brought out this protective side of him that he didn't know what to do with. "So, um, I really didn't expect to be in this position," she said finally.

"What position?"

She waved a hand in the empty space between them. "Like, as in, you and me. On a couch in a remote cabin with a fire and whiskey and no clothes."

He fought the urge to smile just in case she'd assume he was making fun of her. He thought she was going to continue speaking, but she didn't. She just stared at him expectantly. He quickly searched for something to say that would put her at ease.

"Would it help you to know that I've imagined us on a couch without clothes for a long time?"

She threw a pillow in his direction. He caught it, laughing, relieved to see that she was at least smiling again. "I'm not sure what to say to that," she said, still smiling.

"Take it as a compliment," he said.

"I was slightly concerned you were going to be mad at me," she whispered, that expression coming back in her eyes.

"For stopping?"

She nodded.

He sighed and ran a hand over his jaw then offered her another smile. "Not mad. Sad. Very, *very* sad."

She laughed again, and dammit if he wasn't becoming addicted to that sound and the sight of her smile. "That's dramatic."

He shook his head. "Nah," he said, turning serious. "There wasn't an ounce of me that didn't want you. Or doesn't want you right now."

She swallowed audibly, and her gaze went from his eyes to his mouth and then traveled the length of his body before meeting his eyes again. "Me too," she whispered.

"So then what's the problem, sweetheart?" he asked, the endearment slipping from his mouth effortlessly.

She tucked her knees up against her chest, somehow managing to make some kind of modest lower-half tent, and wrapped her arms around her legs. "I'm worried if I tell you, you're going to run. Or laugh at me."

Hell. He had no idea what to expect now. He made sure to keep his features neutral. "I would never laugh at you. C'mon, Lainey. Out with it," he said, leaning forward and giving her a quick kiss on the forehead. It seemed like such a natural thing to do, even though he surprised them both.

She gave a nod. "Okay. So, um, I've never actually slept with *anyone* before."

He kept staring at her, poker face on as a thousand questions barreled through his mind. He blinked and nodded slowly, like he understood, like he wasn't surprised.

"Okay, you don't have to pretend it's not a big deal. Now that I've said it, I can't take it back, so you might as well say what you're really thinking," she said, starting to appear slightly miffed.

Dangerous territory. Her statement was kind of a trap. A Lainey trap. He cleared his throat. "I think it is a big deal. Not in a bad way, but it's not what I was expecting."

Tears suddenly filled her eyes, and a jolt of panic hit him. He didn't know what to do with Lainey tears. He didn't like them. He didn't like the idea of her being upset or that he was somehow the cause of her being upset.

"Also, I should probably tell you, in case this were to ever move forward, that I'm not planning on sleeping with anyone."

Hell. This was going from bad to worse. It was like his worst nightmare.

"I knew it," she groaned. He was relieved that at least she didn't look like she was going to cry anymore. In fact, her eyes were now narrowed on him.

He walked over to the fireplace and poked it a little too harshly, judging by the sparks that almost hit his bare chest. He didn't turn around right away. "So are you going to become a nun?" he asked finally, turning around.

She rolled her eyes and crossed her arms in front of her. "No. What I mean is that I'm not going to sleep with anyone before I'm married."

Oh. Oh. He nodded slowly. "Okay."

"Okay?"

He shrugged. "I'm not sure what you want me to say. I hear there are people who do that."

"Are you kidding me?"

He shrugged again. "What?"

"I tell you that I'm not going to sleep with you—or anyone—until I get married, and you tell me that you've heard people do that?"

So, inside he was kind of reeling. He was disappointed. Really, wholeheartedly disappointed. He hadn't for one second assumed she was a virgin. Or even worse, a virgin determined to wait until she was married to have sex. It was something he didn't get, and he didn't know how to say that without insulting her. "I don't know what to say, Lainey. Other than the fact that I might cry myself to sleep for the next year."

Something flickered across her eyes—something that made him uncomfortable. Like, maybe if he were another guy, this would have ended differently, with some kind of hope they had a future. But he wasn't that guy, and they both knew it.

"Well, thanks for your honesty. I'm sorry I let things go that far without telling you. I won't let it happen again."

Shit. He hung his head. Her voice was so damn polite, and yet it sounded like she was on the brink of tears. She rose from the couch abruptly.

"Do you think my clothes are dry yet? I really need to get back to town."

He stood, and somehow they seemed miles apart in the small cabin. Her face was red, her hair was disheveled, his shirt rumpled, and he knew she was fighting to hold on to her pride.

"Lainey," he said, walking toward her slowly.

"You don't have to pretend or try and say the right thing. You've made it perfectly clear that you think I'm an idiot."

Man, he'd really screwed this up.

He didn't stop until he was right in front of her, and that reaction he had whenever she was close happened. It wasn't something he'd ever experienced with anyone; it was like the universe was telling him something, like this woman meant something a helluva lot more than he'd like to admit. "I don't think you're an idiot," he said, bending his knees so he could see her face. "I'd never think that. You have principles. Ideals. I may not share them, but I respect you for having them."

She averted her gaze. "If we had slept together tonight, what would have happened tomorrow?"

"We would have woken up really happy?"

She rolled her eyes. "No, really. Would I have meant more to you?"

He straightened up and shrugged. "That's a trick question. It's not that the sex would have made you mean more, but it would have brought us closer together."

"So the…women you've been with before have meant more to you after you slept with them? You became closer to them?"

He frowned. "Well…no, but you're not them. It'd be different with you."

"Where are those women now?"

He ran a hand through his hair. "I don't know."

Her eyes narrowed on him slightly. He shifted from one foot to the other. "Exactly," she said.

"Oh, so you're implying that I sleep with them and take off?"

She shrugged and pursed her lips.

"Well, that's not the case. None of the women I've been with have wanted commitment, either. It was a mutual understanding."

"Fine. That's wonderful. So here's the problem I have—how will I know that if I sleep with you, I won't fall madly in love with you and you'll leave me heartbroken? I'll enter into this relationship with you and give you everything of myself, and you'll walk away without ever looking back? Because here's what I'm thinking, Ty. If I sleep with you, that will be it for me. I will fall in love with you, and you'll…"

His chest grew heavy as he stared at her, at the tears in her eyes. Her words cut him down, and the reality of what she was saying gutted him. "That wouldn't happen. I'd never walk away from you without ever looking back. How do you know it wouldn't be you doing the walking?"

She let out a small laugh. "Do you remember my mother?"

He gave a nod. "Vaguely. I don't think I saw her more than once or twice."

"She was a perpetual romantic. Her entire self-worth was determined by whether or not a man loved her. I mean, she ditched me for a guy. Kids are notorious for breaking up new romances," she said with a smile that held the sting of bitterness. "It was guy after guy, and as I grew up, I realized what she was doing. I swore to myself I'd never be like her."

His heart ached for her. "You wouldn't be like that. It doesn't have to be one extreme or another."

"Well, maybe it does. For me. Maybe I only want to be with one guy for the rest of my life. Is that wrong?"

Right now, he'd say that if the guy were him, it wouldn't be wrong. But that wasn't right, because that would mean... Hell. He didn't want her to be with anyone else. "Of course that's not wrong. I just don't think it's realistic."

"That's fine."

"Did you ever meet your father?"

She shook her head. "He wanted nothing to do with us. I wasn't planned; I wasn't wanted," she whispered, and he knew he was the biggest asshole because that's exactly what he was doing to her right now. He understood her—he knew what that rejection from a biological father felt like. It carved out this hole inside that could never be filled and made you feel like less of a person.

"It was their loss, Lainey."

"Sure," she said, flipping her hair over her shoulder and avoiding eye contact with him. He stood there and he got it, he got what she was saying, more than she'd ever know, but he couldn't bring himself to tell her. He'd held on so long to his secret, he'd been alone and needed no one for so long, he was afraid that if he let her in, he'd need her more and more. He didn't want to need anyone but himself.

"I understand," he whispered, taking that last step in to her and folding her up against him. She pressed her soft body to his and wrapped her arms around his waist.

"But you should know that if I ever revoke my policy, I'll be knocking on your door first," she said, her voice muffled against his chest.

He laughed as he kissed the top of her head before leaning back slightly.

"So where does this leave us?" she said.

"Just where we are. I can drive you home," he said, stepping back. He didn't actually know where this left them. He was a man. A guy in his thirties. How could he move forward with Lainey if he couldn't go any further than kissing her? His teenage days of making out with a girl were long gone. He couldn't go back to that…

She nodded, her face red, and she walked over to the dryer and pulled out her clothes. He looked away. "I'll still do the dinners for your dad. We'll continue our business arrangement with the rentals. It'll be like nothing ever happened between us."

"Lainey," he said. He didn't like that. It didn't feel right. He didn't want to lose her.

She shoved her legs into her jeans, and he looked away, his teeth clenched. How the hell did he get himself into these situations with her? "You really should have used dryer sheets," she quipped. "Anyway, not to worry. We can be the best of friends," she said, shooting him a smile.

He swore under his breath. "We can't be friends. There's no going back to friends."

She zipped up her jeans, and the sound seemed to grate against all his nerve endings. She lifted her eyebrows. "Fine. Then enemies?"

"What? Never."

She held up her shirt, mumbling about static. She turned around and glanced over her bare shoulder after she peeled his shirt off. "Frenemies."

He shut his eyes, hoping she hurried up with getting her shirt on. He didn't even know anymore what the most frustrating part of this exchange was. "That word is right up there with BFF."

"That's because you have problems expressing your feelings," she said once dressed, turning around and patting him on the shoulder.

"Right," he managed through clenched teeth.

"We never would have worked out anyway," she said, picking up her purse and walking to the door.

He frowned and followed her. "Why not?"

She tilted her head to the side and winced. "Well, I don't really like arrogant men."

"What? Me?" He scoffed, taking a step back.

She nodded and held out her hand, examining her nails, which he knew perfectly well weren't manicured. "Also, the whole cowboy shtick was never my thing. I can't even ride a horse. I'm a city girl at heart."

"Lainey, you live in a town of one thousand. With one streetlight. That's hardly city living."

"Fine. You're probably too old for me anyway." She tapped a finger against her chin and narrowed her eyes. "Judging by the gray hair and fine lines around your eyes, I'd estimated you to be pushing forty."

He closed his eyes and racked his brain for some kind of prayer. When he came up blank, he opened his eyes and stared at the woman who was so effective at pushing all his buttons. "Lainey, you know I'm not pushing forty. I'm not even close to pushing thirty-five."

She was picking at some imaginary lint on the front of her shirt and let out a patronizing *mm-hmm*. "It's fine. We all tell ourselves things to make ourselves feel better." She put her hand on the door, and he grabbed her other one, torn between laughing and showing her his birth certificate.

She turned around slowly, and he saw it then— the hurt beneath the banter. Because they weren't just friends, and they could never go back to being friends. "Like how we're telling ourselves we can't be friends? Like how you want to blame this on me?"

"I'm embarrassed," she whispered, looking any-where but at him. "You can't have sex with me, so now you have no use for me. You're just going to discard me, like yesterday's leftovers. That's not a lie. That's the truth."

Despite all the warning bells going off in his head, despite how his actions gave him away, he pulled her into his arms and framed her gorgeous face with his hands. Hell, he didn't know why he was speaking the truth, why he'd ever go down this road, but all he knew was that hearing Lainey speak about him like that, knowing he was discarding her just like everyone else in her life, hearing the hurt in her voice, made him want to fix it all.

"Don't ever be embarrassed with me. Don't be ashamed of your ideals or your dreams, and don't ever think that your self-worth or importance hinges on whether or not you have sex. So that's my truth. Not a lie. I admire you, Lainey. Everything you've done, everything you've accomplished, and everything you believe in. One day you'll get married." He had planned on continuing, on saying that one day she'd get married to some great guy and she'd be glad she waited—but he couldn't. Because he didn't want to picture her in bed with another guy. He didn't want to picture her married. Because he wanted her. For himself.

Hell. He almost backed up a step.

She nodded. "Thanks. So, um, what do you say about getting me back to my car?"

He dropped his hands, feeling the loss of whatever had been building between them. He didn't know where to go from here. He wasn't enough of a pig to keep seeing her and hoping that their chemistry would slowly wear her down. But he wasn't enough of a good guy to ever think about marriage, either.

He stared into her eyes for a moment before looking away. "I'll just, uh, put out the fire and get you back."

And he walked away from her, hating himself, hating the man he'd become.

CHAPTER FOURTEEN

*T*y stared up at the ceiling of his cabin from his bed as the somewhat-appealing smell of frozen pizza cooking in the oven wafted into the bedroom. He'd been lying motionless just thinking about Lainey. He hated that he'd hurt her, but he didn't know what the hell he was going to do about it. He'd hurt so many people here: his father, his friends, and now Lainey.

Another week had gone by without seeing her. He had to stay away. Lainey was trying to change him—not deliberately—but it was there. She wanted him to be someone he wasn't. Part of him wanted to be that guy who could give her everything she wanted, but he wasn't capable of it. He didn't want that life. He liked being on his own. So he'd been avoiding her for a week now, to protect her.

But here was no better. His father wasn't speaking to him, even though he knew his health was improving daily. His friends still weren't talking to him. It was starting to wear him down. Everywhere he went, there was some kind of glare in his direction.

He'd been spending his nights going through his father's records, dating right back to eight years ago after he'd left. His father had never thrown anything out. He'd even found all the bills from his mom's funeral. But he'd also found out his father had lent money to a lot of people around town. Some would pay him back in little chunks, while some hadn't paid him back at all. Why the hell would his father even do that? He'd always been such a stickler when it came to money and spending.

He cursed out loud when he heard the knock. On the off chance it might be Lainey, he got up and made his way to answer it. He opened the door, and Dean and Cade were standing there, each holding a bottle of whiskey.

No one said anything—they just stared at one another, and it reminded him of the time the three of them had been smoking outside the bunkhouses and his father had found them. They'd stood there, coughing and trying to step on the butts, and not saying a word. None of them had ratted the other out, even though it had been Cade to bring the cigarettes.

"You going to let us in?" Cade asked.

"That depends," he said, gripping the edge of the door. "You sharing that?" He gestured to the bottles.

Dean grinned and slapped him on the shoulder. "I think you've suffered long enough. Also, Lainey threatened to not serve us at the diner. We hear lasagna is going to be on the menu soon, and neither of us is willing to sacrifice that."

Lainey. Dammit. Why the hell did she care about him so much?

Ty opened the door wider to let them in, trying not to look like he was happy his friends had actually decided to forgive him. Cade punched him in the shoulder—a little harder than necessary, in his opinion—and walked in. He gestured to the couches, and they all sat around the fire, Cade and Dean on one couch, while he brought three mismatched glasses over and then sat on the opposite. He tried to tell himself he was irritated that she'd meddled, but the truth was that he was pretty damn happy they were here. He may have fooled himself into thinking he didn't need them, but it felt right. They were family.

Dean poured the first round, and they held up their glasses. "To stupid choices and starting over."

He wasn't sure that was the most flattering toast, but he drank to it anyway. They all put their empty glasses down and sat there, no one saying anything.

Cade wisely decided to pour another round. This time he held up his glass to make the toast. "To old friends and starting over."

They all finished off their whiskeys and sat there awkwardly. Ty took the bottle and refilled their glasses. He held his up. "To best friends and starting over."

They paused for a moment, and he wondered if they were going to call him out for his sentimentality, but then they clinked their glasses and drank in unison, and it seemed like a heavy weight he didn't even know he was carrying lifted.

He settled back in his seat and put his feet on the coffee table. They did the same. "So, miss me?"

"Like I'd miss a burr up my ass," Cade said.

Tyler grinned.

"So are you going to share whatever it is you have baking in that oven?" Dean asked, flicking his chin toward the kitchen.

"Don't expect a home-cooked casserole. It's frozen pizza," he said as the timer rang. He stood, and Cade followed him into the small cooking area like he owned the place.

"That's fine. We're not picky. Anything else? I'm

starving," Cade said, opening his fridge.

Tyler bit back his smart-ass reply in an effort to be amenable. "I wasn't expecting company," he said as Cade shut the fridge with a disappointed huff.

He did have some pleasure in opening the oven door abruptly, which forced Cade to jump back to avoid getting burned. "Why don't you go sit down?" Tyler said. Cade got the hint and sprawled himself across the couch.

Tyler took the pizza out of the oven and slid it onto a cutting board, grabbed a knife, and placed it on the coffee table.

"Wait," he said as Cade started cutting the pizza in four giant pieces. He handed him paper plates and napkins from the handy lower shelf of the coffee table. "No crumbs. I don't have time to clean this place."

"Sure, Martha," Cade joked, taking a huge bite of the pizza.

Tyler grabbed his own slice and leaned back on the couch. They ate their food in silence for a few minutes.

"So, you been seeing a lot of Lainey?" Dean asked casually after inhaling his slice and refilling his glass. His friend had changed over the years. They all had. He was still tall and lean, in good shape, but his face looked as though it had weathered a few storms. He noticed a few strands of gray mixed in with the black.

Ty shrugged, idly watching as Cade helped himself to the remaining piece of pizza. "I guess. She's here all the time because of my dad."

"I'm sure you're not complaining about that,"

Dean said, a smile in his voice.

He didn't want to talk about Lainey because he didn't even know what their relationship was. He knew he cared about her, though. And then there was the Cade complication. "Nope." That was all he was saying. He poured them all another round. "And you actually made it through med school? You like being a doctor?"

Dean grinned and nodded. "Yeah. Yeah, I do. It's what I always wanted. It's long hours, but it's always been my dream."

"You still have the family ranch, too?"

Dean nodded. "Like I said, long hours."

Cade let out a short laugh. "Long hours, but he manages to make time for women."

Ty smiled. "Well, it's what gets you through a rough day sometimes."

Conversation was a bit awkward, as a part of him was waiting for one of them to ask where he'd been, why he'd left the way he did.

When neither seemed willing to broach the topic, Ty decided to just take the bull by the horns. He knew they'd never really get back to a true friendship if he didn't. "I, uh, I'm sorry I left town the way I did. I know neither of you saw it coming." Surprise registered across both their faces, but not anger, so he continued. "I had a lot of shit to work through, and I couldn't get my head screwed on straight after my mother died. Everything went wrong with my father. You know we didn't have the best relationship."

He paused and took the refilled drink that Dean had poured while he was talking. "The last night at home, we got into it pretty bad. Said some shit to each other that I regret. And I snapped. I left. I should have told you guys, but I just couldn't deal with any of it. And I didn't want you to convince me to stay."

That's exactly what they would have done. Maybe they'd have been right. If he had gone to them that night, maybe none of this would have happened. Maybe his dad wouldn't have had the stroke and the ranch wouldn't be on the brink of bankruptcy. Regret rendered him motionless and speechless.

"You don't owe us anything. We've all made our share of boneheaded decisions," Dean said.

Cade nodded. "I'm not one to talk. I never even had a father to fight with, so I don't know what it's like. And I don't know what it's like to lose a mother who was like yours."

He swallowed past the lump in his throat, more grateful than he'd ever have expected at their forgiveness.

"So where'd you go?"

"I rodeoed for a while, but I missed working a ranch. Found a job as a wrangler out on a Wyoming ranch. Became the foreman after a few years. And I saved my money—I knew I'd come back here. I was waiting to save a certain amount, somehow thinking that would make it better when I came home. But then I got the call and, uh, came back now."

"You think you can get this place back to profitability?" Cade asked.

"I have no choice. I feel responsible for the mess we're in. I'm working through some ideas for immediate cash flow, thanks to Lainey's help. And then I have bigger-picture plans, like going completely to grass-fed cattle, rebranding our beef so we can check off all those trendy boxes like antibiotic-free, hormone-free. Maybe we analyze our distribution and get a bigger presence in the local market. A lot of that was my focus on the ranch I worked at and man, were they profitable. We need to work this place with the future in mind. Maybe you and I can come up with a plan. Together," he said, his gaze on Cade.

Cade nodded slowly. "I like your ideas, and they are all changes I think we can implement pretty soon. The cattle here are already mostly grass-fed, but if we can make it so that it's one hundred percent and then work on branding, it'll be worth it. I don't have a lot of experience with the whole local thing, though. Just want to let you know that as foreman, I'm here to help. I'll carry through the plans you have for this place. I know you have the ranch's, the guys', and your dad's best interests. So if you need some extra help on the cabins, just let me know."

Ty had not expected that. "Thanks," he said, keeping his gaze on his friend. Tyler leaned forward, getting excited now that Cade was on board. He hadn't known how his friend was going to react — if he was going to be defensive now that he had to share the role of foreman at the ranch. He braced his forearms on his legs. "The Buy Local movement is huge. We have no presence at stores in the county, and we should. Even local restaurants. Our beef goes out there with no branding. That needs to change."

"Agreed," Cade said. "Now we just need connections."

"With the slower winter months, the timing is perfect."

"You going to tell your father?" Dean asked.

Ty rubbed the back of his neck. "I'm not exactly in his good books. Maybe Cade, you and I work out the business plan, and then we present to my dad?"

"Just watch his stress levels," Dean warned, sounding like a doctor.

"I will," he said, easing back in the pillows again, feeling encouraged for the first time since he'd been home. He knew it would work; he knew the plan was solid. Now it was a matter of details and hard work implementing everything.

"So what's Lainey's part in all this?" Cade asked.

He tried to hold back his smile. It was difficult. When he thought about her or heard her name, he smiled. This was highly unusual for him. The smiling thing. Sometimes he wondered if he'd smiled at all in the last eight years. "You ever hear of ranching vacations?"

"Shit," Cade said, refilling his glass.

Dean laughed.

"I know. That was my reaction, too, believe me. But she might be onto something. People pay big money for this. I'm not saying I want to do it forever. It's my version of hell, really. But we're talking five grand for three days on the ranch."

Cade choked on his whiskey.

Ty nodded.

"So you mean to tell me people will pay thousands to hang out with you two for the weekend?" Dean almost didn't get the question out—he was so obviously fighting a laugh at their expense.

Ty grinned and propped his feet up on the coffee table, placing one ankle on the other. "Damn straight. Basically, it's city folk. They want to experience the whole ranching life. Lainey said some of the ranches even offer people to do cattle drives and actual work."

Cade held up his hand. "There's no way in hell we're letting people come out on cattle drives."

"Details." Ty waved him off. "We don't have to do that, but it's an option. Anyway, we've got the space. We have two more cabins sitting empty. In one weekend, if we rent both out, we could make close to five thousand dollars. Minus maybe a thousand for extras like food and housekeeping. Still. It's a good way to get our cash flowing."

Cade sat up straighter, a light in his eyes.

"So would you have to do, like, campfires and sing songs?" Dean asked, still barely containing his laughter. He'd forgotten what a shit-disturber his friend was. The professional clothes and "Doctor" before his name hadn't changed him a bit. Ty was glad.

Cade swore again and grasped his throat, making gagging noises.

"I'm sure we won't," he said, partially lying. While there was no way he'd sing around a campfire for any amount of money, he would do the fire thing. That was easy.

"What about the food? We don't have a cook on the weekend?" Cade asked. "And I can't cook."

"Lainey said she'd help us out to start, until we found weekend help. We were thinking we could do baked goods in the morning, that way it's easier for her. Then something simple like stew or chili and biscuits. People think it's cowboy food anyway."

Cade nodded. Ty knew he was close to agreeing to this. He'd considered Cade even more of a stumbling block than his father. And if his father knew Cade was on board and that Lainey had come up with the plan, he'd warm to the idea even more.

"All right. I'm in. For a trial period. If this is too time-consuming and pulls us away from the new direction we want to take the ranch in, then I say we re-evaluate."

"Agreed," Ty said, leaning forward and extending his hand. "So I'll go ahead and tell you now that we have eight women coming here next weekend. A bachelorette getaway."

Cade swore and hung his head. Dean laughed. "I missed you, Tyler. You always had the most batshit crazy ideas."

He grinned. "I can't even take credit for this one, and I'm dreading it. But it's money."

Cade nodded, shaking his hand. "Fine. Done."

"I'm thinking good things are going to happen soon. I'm glad you're here."

Cade ran his hands through his hair roughly. "You should also probably know that I never set out to take your place. I could never take your place. But I had no work. I had nothing going for me, and after you left, your dad offered me a job. I took it. I worked hard to prove to him that he'd made a good choice, taking a chance on me. I worked for years before I became foreman. But I never meant to take your place."

Ty didn't say anything for a minute, so many

different emotions running through him. Everything Cade was saying reminded him of how long he'd been away. So many things had happened to all of them, but he hadn't been around. It's not like he thought time had stood still, but it gutted him. He could never get those years back with these guys. As much as he hated that they hadn't welcomed him back or tried to see things from his perspective, he was getting a glimpse into how they viewed him and why they were so angry with him. "Thanks, man. I never said it, but I'm glad you were here. I'm glad you're foreman. I know you work hard, and I'm happy that my dad hired you."

Cade shrugged. "It worked out for all of us."

"And now we get to work together every night after we finish so we can fix up the two cabins."

Cade swore and leaned back on the couch. Tyler let out a laugh, happy that his friends were here, that they were starting over. A month ago, this might have been a dream come true for him. Except he found himself thinking of Lainey and how happy she'd be if she knew the three of them were sitting there. Of course she'd probably gloat and take all the credit for it. Maybe if things hadn't ended so… painfully, he'd have gone over to the diner to tell her, to see her pretty face light up, and to hear her boast.

So maybe he would. Maybe he'd go over to the diner and see Lainey tomorrow.

Lainey knew she shouldn't be upset. It wasn't like she expected Ty to drop down on one knee and declare his undying love for her and reveal that his greatest dream was to get married and have babies with her. But she'd expected something. Something other than him looking at her sympathetically. Like she was just the poor girl who hadn't had sex yet.

Walking across the empty restaurant, she slowly started taking down the chairs from the tabletops before turning the OPEN sign. She had a full day ahead of her. A day of nosy patrons and town gossip…which would then be followed by a trip out to the ranch. Maybe she could send someone in her place. Maybe Mrs. Busby could take dinner out. But no, she didn't like driving at night.

Lainey poured herself a second cup of coffee and leaned against the counter, where her mind quickly drifted to lying almost naked on the couch with Tyler. Her cheeks warmed.

Last night, when she was in bed alone and cold and staring at the ceiling, she'd been pretty sure she was insane. She had never, ever experienced anything quite like Ty. It went far beyond the physical. Sure, he was drool-worthy. Sure, he knew exactly what he was doing. But it was beyond that. She'd been kissed before. She'd made out with a guy or two before, and she'd been able to end it without a second thought.

When she ended things with Ty, it had taken so much willpower. She wanted to feel his warm, bare skin again. She wanted to run her hands over his hard muscles, feel his rough stubble against her soft skin. She wanted him. She wanted Tyler desperately, and she couldn't have him.

She hadn't even been able to resist the pint of

chocolate chip ice cream in her freezer. And really, what was the point, anyway? It wasn't like she'd be appearing nude in front of Ty anytime soon. Just the image of his face when she told him she was waiting for marriage pretty much confirmed she would never be seeing him naked again.

"Good morning!"

Hope burst through the door, and Lainey put her coffee mug down, forcing a smile.

"Omigosh, what has happened to you?" her friend said, sitting on the stool at the bar.

Lainey groaned and automatically went to pour her friend a coffee. "Why, what's wrong with me?"

"You look like hell. A hangover?"

"Of sorts," she said, sliding her friend's mug across the counter. "A Tyler Donnelly hangover. Also dairy. A pint of dairy. I may be allergic to both."

Her friend choked on her coffee. "First, you already know those allergy tests I ran were positive for dairy, so stop pretending like you can eat dairy. Let's move on to Ty. What are you saying?"

Lainey rolled her eyes and leaned a hip against the counter. "So I for sure have to stop the illicit love affair I have with chocolate chip ice cream?"

"Lainey."

She pushed aside the embarrassment she'd pro-longed long enough, knowing she'd never be able to keep this from Hope. "Fine. Are you ready for some early-morning tales of humiliation from your BFF that might even help you feel better about your life?"

Hope rolled her eyes. "Uh, yeah. Look at my life. I'll take anything."

Lainey nodded, happy to sacrifice her pride for her best friend. "Just don't get too excited. I'm your boring friend, remember? The one who stupidly thought she should get married before having sex?"

"Oh," Hope said, wincing and plucking a muffin from the basket. "I'm sorry. You, um, told him this?"

Lainey stared into her dark cup of coffee, knowing there was no way she should be adding cream in it this morning. She drank it black. "I did."

"What did he say? And, um, was it at a moment where clothing had already been removed?"

Lainey covered her face and nodded. "It was so good, and then it became so bad."

"Omigosh, what?" Hope gasped, leaning forward and grabbing her wrist.

"All of it was so good. He was…like every fantasy I ever had. Hot, Hope. I forgot everything—I was just…like, this person who got carried away in the moment. I was like a person who has sex with a hot man."

"Wow," her friend said wistfully.

Lainey held up her index finger. "Just wait for it. But then this little voice inside me started calling out. It was like some kind of life preserver, reminding me to get out before I sank. So, nope, I did not have sex. Not this girl. This girl remembered at the very last moment that she had this plan to wait until she was married. That's a real date pleaser."

Hope slapped her hand across her mouth, her eyes wide and filled with horror. "Lainey…did he understand?"

The bells on the door jingled, and the first of the morning customers came in—Father Andy.

"It's like divine backup," Hope whispered as the priest walked toward them. "Good morning, Father," she called out before popping the rest of the muffin top into her mouth.

"Good morning, ladies," he said with a smile as he joined them at the counter.

"Good morning, Father," Lainey said, having a hard time maintaining eye contact. Thankfully, Father Andy usually took his morning coffee and croissant to go.

Lainey already had his order waiting. "Here you go, Father. Have a great day."

"God bless," he said, taking the bag, offering a wave, and leaving. He held the door open as more people started filtering through. Luckily, Charlene, one of the part-time girls, came in with them and started handing out menus and dealing with the tables.

"I should probably help out," Lainey said with a sigh.

"You should probably finish your story about how you and Ty had no clothes on," Hope demanded, leaning over the counter.

Lainey rolled her eyes. "It wasn't that dramatic. Only a few items were removed."

"Shirts?"

She gave her a nod then shook her head. "His."

"Bra?"

She sighed. "I guess."

Hope's eyes looked like they were going to fall from their sockets. "What? What is happening?"

Lainey's skin was itching just talking about this. She leaned forward. "Keep your voice down."

Hope glanced over each shoulder and then lowered her voice. "Well, I'm not following. This is the biggest news you've had in a long time. Either of us, even. Your details are all over the place."

Lainey put her head in her hands, spreading her fingers so she could see the diner. "Our clothes were wet. We fell in some mud outside the house, and I went back to his cabin. I showered, and he gave me a T-shirt to wear while my clothes got washed."

"Oh wow, this is getting really good," she said.

Lainey leaned against the counter. "One thing led to another. He's a hard guy to resist, you know."

Hope nodded enthusiastically. "Uh, yeah, who wouldn't notice? So he kissed you?"

Lainey rolled her eyes and pretended like she was comfortable with this conversation. "Yes. You're acting like we're in high school! It was no big deal. I'm sure Ty doesn't remember a thing. I'm sure it went down as one of the stupidest nights of his life. And I'm pretty sure he'll be steering clear of me for a long time."

Hope held up her hands. "Okay, listen, this isn't really as bad as you're making it out to be. What did he say when you told him?"

She was not going to cry. She was not going to cry. "It's all too embarrassing to relive. And my stomach hurts from humiliation mixed with ice cream. Not a good combo." She rubbed her belly for emphasis.

Hope frowned and fished through her purse. She put some candy things on the counter. "You need ginger, and you need to stay away from dairy—you know that. Now tell me the rest. What did he say?"

"He said he hopes I marry a great guy."

Hope's face fell. "Oh, Lainey."

"I know. It was perfect. It was like, here, I have no use for you, but I hope you marry someone else who's willing to not have sex until there's a ring on your finger."

"I think there's more to it than that. I think he probably just didn't know what to do. It was a shocker, for sure," Hope said, wincing as she drank her coffee.

"You're being nice because I look like death and because my story is so tragic."

"That's not true. He's not going to stay away from you. Just wait and see."

"Hope, I'm done with cowboys. You remember what Grandma Tilly always said about them? She was right. How many cowboys had my mother slept with? Not a single one married her." She shook her head. "Not this girl. I'm just going to plan to never see him again. Also, I've decided I really need to move ahead with my painting. I'm not waiting around. I need to leave. I knew it years ago, and now more than ever, it needs to happen. I'll just forget about Tyler when I'm in Italy."

At that news, her friend's eyes lit up with excitement, and she raised her cup to Lainey. "Here's to no cowboys and lots of Italian men!"

Lainey clinked her cup against Hope's, wishing it were that simple.

CHAPTER FIFTEEN

*I*f Tyler weren't so busy dreaming about sleeping with Lainey, he'd be dreaming about strangling her.

He and Cade stood side by side and stared at the eight women who were dressed as though they were going to a nightclub in the city on a Saturday night, not a weekend of ranching. "Welcome," he called out, feeling like an idiot as they stood by their Cadillac SUV rental. It was like he was welcoming a group of aliens to his ranch.

"Hi!" a pretty brunette said, walking forward, leading the pack. "I'm Amy, and this is Elle, the bride," she said, pulling her blond friend forward.

They exchanged small talk for a few minutes, even though it pained him dearly. It was almost as painful as pulling himself off a naked Lainey—which was something he hadn't been able to get off his mind. He felt like the world's biggest ass because of the way they'd ended things. He'd basically wished her a nice life. Like a jerk.

But as much as this weekend with these women was going to kill what was left of his already damaged soul, the money they would make was all because of her.

He'd gone over the itinerary with Cade yesterday after researching what some of the other ranches were doing, and the two of them decided they might as well make the best of it.

He handed each of the women a sheet of paper

that detailed the weekend's events. "You can, uh, read that before we get going. We'll take your bags and drive you over to your cabins and let you settle in. We'll be by in an hour or so for a tour of the ranch."

"This is so exciting!" one of the women said, almost nose-diving as her stiletto got caught in a mud puddle. Cade reached over and steadied her.

"You should also be dressed for the ranch when we come and get you. Like, jeans, sweaters, sneakers or boots—that kind of thing," Cade said. The woman smiled at Cade like he was some kind of hero. Hell, this was going to be the longest weekend of his life.

"There are some welcome snacks and drinks in your cabins. According to the email questionnaire, you are all experienced riders?" Ty asked. He needed to confirm this before selecting a horse for each one. The last thing he wanted was an inexperienced rider to be teamed up with one of their faster horses.

"Oh no," the Amy woman said. "None of us has ever ridden a horse."

Cade gave him the side-eye, the *I told you so* clear in his expression as he rolled back on his heels.

"O…kay." Ty nodded slowly. "Well, Cade and I will improvise and see how we can change up the weekend's itinerary. Let's get you settled."

Hell. The entire weekend was based on riding out, catching glimpses of wildlife, herding. This was going to leave them with nothing but…singing songs around a campfire.

He'd forced himself not to go into town to see Lainey all week, but now—now he was going with a new purpose. To kill her for talking him into this.

*T*hree hours later, Ty and Cade were standing next to each other while the women sat around the campfire they'd prepared, about a one-hour hike from their cabins. "I'm not sure I'm going to make it," he whispered to Cade.

Cade snickered. "That's because you're hung up on Lainey. I've developed a whole new attitude about this experience. These women are gorgeous, and they seem to really like *this* cowboy," he said, tapping his chest and winking at Tyler.

Tyler shut his eyes at the sight of his friend's sparkling expression. He'd lost him.

The women were a nice enough bunch, even though he'd been worried earlier. He and Cade had quickly decided that a hike to a clearing near the river with a view of the mountains might be the best thing. That way they didn't have to teach anyone how to ride a horse and they didn't have to worry about getting sued when one of them fell off.

"So you know how to make s'mores, right?" Cade asked, ripping open a bag of marshmallows. He was basking in the attention of the women, so Ty let him take the lead. At least it was somewhat funny to watch. One of the pretty brunettes helped him. He acted as though he was having the time of his life.

"Of course, here, let me help, Cade," the other brunette said, sidling up beside him.

"I think s'mores need drinks, don't you?" a red-head asked Cade.

Cade shot him a look as he and the brunettes

assembled the s'mores.

The last thing either of them needed was a bunch of drunk women around them.

"We should probably wait until you're back in your cabin," Ty said, trying to fake a smile so he came across as a pleasant man, when he realized Cade wasn't going to be the bad cop. "It's a bit of a walk back."

"Oh, right," she said, giving her friends a sort of weird glance.

He didn't know what to make of that, other than they just thought he was a tight-ass who didn't want any drinking outside. Once Cade had the first batch of s'mores going, Ty sat down on one of the boulders and stared up into the sky. This wasn't so bad. He could put up with the trivial conversation for one more night. That Elle bride woman was preoccupied with her wedding dress and that she still needed to lose five pounds to fit in it. Then the redhead started talking about something called Spanx, and hell, he had no idea what spanking and fetishes had to do with wedding dresses. He really tried to drown out as much of the conversation as possible and enjoy the cool night air.

One of the blondes approached, startling him as she touched his arm. "I think your choice of profession is really noble. And don't worry, we won't be drinking out here at all."

He frowned. "Uh, thanks. Ranchers don't really have a problem with drinking, but I just thought it would be best if you drank in your own cabin. We have a long hike back, and if you're a bit tipsy, it'd be easy to trip on the rougher terrain."

She nodded and was watching him like she…was very interested. "Can you tell me a little about the whole priest-in-training thing?"

He ignored the sound of Cade choking and frowned. He wasn't sure he'd heard her correctly. Or she was joking. He leaned forward. "Pardon me?"

She stepped a little closer and placed her hand on his arm again. He pulled back, tucking his hands in his pockets. "Aren't you entering, like, priest school or something?"

Cade cackled. Ty shot him a glare and then turned back to the woman in front of him. "I have no idea what you're talking about."

"Oh, that girl, the one who emailed us to book the trip and then dropped off the baked goods in our cabin, she told us."

Lainey. He glanced over at Cade, who appeared to be dying of s'mores and laughter.

Ty rubbed the back of his neck. He was torn between laughing and groaning with frustration. Clearly she'd felt threatened. He kind of liked that she cared enough to invent this ridiculous excuse. He coughed. "I've actually dropped out of…priest school."

Her eyes lit up, and he suddenly knew exactly why Lainey had come up with this lie. Yup, he was an idiot for thinking it was jealousy. "But, uh, I think I'll go sit over on that boulder and do a little prayin'."

The woman nodded and went to join the rest of them. Hell. What the hell was happening to him? Really, he had no idea. None of the women in this group even remotely appealed. In fact, he was almost indifferent to them. He could identify they were attractive women, but he felt nothing.

Because of Lainey. None of them laughed like Lainey did. None of them smiled like Lainey did. None of them tried to irritate him on purpose like Lainey did. None of them had eyes that sparkled like hers. No one's laughter made him smile. No one's mouth interested him. No one's body was made for his.

Dammit. He knew what this meant. He didn't get to his thirties without knowing what this meant.

He knew enough not to take advantage of their friendship, of her. As much as Lainey acted like she was tough as nails, he knew it was an act. He'd seen her vulnerable core. Even the way she stood there that night, bravely telling him she wasn't going to sleep with him, he'd already known she wasn't a girl to sleep with for just one night.

Lainey was the woman with whom you built a lifetime.

No, she was the woman with whom you built a lifetime of *dreams*.

She was the woman who got dirty, who got tired, who gave you her heart, and hell if he didn't suddenly want that. But he'd never wanted that before. After his mother died, he'd come to the conclusion that he didn't need anyone. People lied; they disappointed you. He always thought he'd be better off alone. Except now, because of Lainey, he wasn't feeling that great all alone.

He glanced over at Cade, who was looking exactly like he might have appeared a month ago—appreciatively at the women who were flirting with him.

Now, all Ty wanted was to just get back home… and see the woman who wouldn't sleep with him.

"*H*i, Aiden," Lainey said, flopping onto a barstool at River's.

"Well hello there, sweetheart," he said, taking the time to stop and chat with her for a moment even though the place was already packed.

"I'm going to need a glass or maybe a bottle of our Merlot."

He gave her a wink, and a second later, he was pouring her a glass.

"You have no idea how much this is appreciated tonight," she said, downing a big gulp and not even caring that she was wearing her heart on her sleeve.

He frowned. "You okay? Give me a second—let me serve some of these guys, and I'll be right back, okay?"

She nodded, not even bothering to pretend she didn't need someone to talk to. She glanced down at her phone as it vibrated, and her heart sank as she read a text from Hope: *The curse of first grade— Sadie is sick again. Projectile vomit. Send wine. Sorry for the last-minute cancels!*

She took another long drink of her wine and sighed. She was going to need a refill soon.

She glanced over beyond the bar, and her heart stopped as she spotted Dean, Cade, and Tyler; they were all laughing and drinking and playing pool together. The sight of the three of them almost brought a smile to her face. She was happy for Ty. Until she saw three blondes approach them and drape themselves on the pool table.

"Need a refill already?" Aiden asked.

She tore her gaze from the sight and peered into her empty glass. "Uh, please, Aiden. You know, I think I'm going to dye my hair black."

He frowned. "Yeah?"

She nodded, taking a long sip. "I am a disgrace to my hair color. I definitely do *not* have more fun."

"Ah," he said wisely, a dimple peeking out.

"Can I ask you a favor?"

"Anything, sweetheart."

"Can you pretend to be interested in me for a few minutes?" It was a desperate request, but she needed to try and save face. Tyler was getting hit on by at least one gorgeous woman who would probably love to go home with him tonight, while she was just this lonely virginal reject sitting alone at a bar.

"I wouldn't have to pretend, Lainey," he said, shooting her one of those smiles that must have scored him many women.

"Thanks," she said, glancing from the corner of her eye in the direction of the pool table.

"You know, I can give you a play-by-play if you like," he said, glancing over his shoulder.

She sighed. "Sorry, I'm not usually so…desperate."

His smile dipped. "Sometimes people can make us do things we'd never think we were capable of doing."

She stared into his blue eyes, knowing he was speaking from experience. "I feel like a fool," she whispered. "Like the whole world is operating on this different plane, one that isn't for me, and I can't compete with that, you know? I'm not a part of it, in my heart I know that, but I want to be. I want to be so badly, because it will give me what I want."

"Or who you want?"

She gazed over again at the pool area, and her heart sank as one of the women and Tyler were no longer there. She stared back at Aiden through watery eyes and nodded.

He braced his arms wide on the counter, leaning in closer, and gave her his undivided attention. "Well, here's my advice to you, Lainey."

She waited for some of the infamous River advice and tried not to cry.

"Sometimes the best thing is to go against the grain. If everyone did the same thing, there wouldn't ever be change; there wouldn't be growth. It takes a helluva lot more character to stand up for yourself and your beliefs than it does to just do what anyone else is doing. And as a guy, I know I'd want to be with a woman who's all heart, all courage."

She smiled as his words comforted her and then laughed when he playfully tugged on a piece of her hair.

"Got something in your hair?"

Lainey turned and almost fell off her chair at the sound of Ty's voice. His hands went to her shoulders and steadied her. "I'm fine," she said, shrugging.

He dropped his hands, and she tried not to notice how gorgeous he was tonight, not that she was surprised. But he had on one of those dark-blue checked shirts that seemed to make the intensity of his sky-blue eyes even more obvious, and her fingers itched to graze her nails through his stubble.

"Nice to see you, Tyler," Aiden said.

She turned back to Aiden in time to catch the smirk and the appearance of his right dimple.

Tyler gave him a nod, but he didn't seem all that friendly.

"Yes, nice to see you, Tyler," she said in a voice that she hoped sounded cool and sophisticated despite the slight slurring thanks to her almost two glasses of Merlot on an empty stomach. She surreptitiously tapped her wineglass, hoping that Aiden noticed.

Tyler flicked his chin in the direction of the glass. "I didn't even know this place had wine."

"I keep a case of Merlot for Lainey and Hope."

"I thought you were a whiskey drinker," he said, still looking stiff and not that nice.

"I'm a lady of many talents…like your other lady friends."

He frowned. "Who?"

She was aware of Aiden leaving them. "You know, the ladies who you were playing pool with"

A corner of his mouth twitched. "Ah, I see. Well, I'm too busy for them."

"Oh yeah? Busy with what?"

He leaned against the bar, close enough that if she leaned forward, she'd be able to place her head on his shoulder. "I've apparently taken a vow of chastity—you know, being in seminary training."

She inhaled sharply. Omigosh. She slapped her hand over her mouth and knew her face was turning all sorts of different shades of red. Maybe even purple. Ty, on the other hand, was leaning against the bar as though he was having the time of his life. His smile was slow, satisfied, and pure gloat.

The gloating was too much. The wine was too much. He was too much.

"I—I have no idea what you're talking about,"

she choked.

"Are you sure, sweetheart? Don't you have something to confess?"

She punched his shoulder, and he snatched her hand, laughing.

"It's not funny," she groaned, knowing she was caught.

He finally pulled back and stopped laughing. He hadn't stopped smiling, though. "Lainey, why of all the things would you tell them I was going to be a priest?"

She lifted her chin. "I was just trying to protect you."

His grin widened. "From a group of women at a bachelorette weekend?"

She clasped her hands in front of her and kept up her bravado. "Yes. You just can't be too safe when it comes to events like this."

"I see," he said, his voice turning serious. "You were just looking out for me."

"Precisely," she said.

"Or you were looking out for you?"

Humiliation scorched her body. "Of course not."

"Because you didn't want me to be with any of those women?"

She rubbed her temples, angry with herself for her acting on her crazy, impulsive idea. He was going to have a field day with this. "Ugh. I can't believe they told you. I was very clear with them that you were very private about your impending priesthood. They weren't supposed to tell you."

Tears of laughter sprang into his eyes as he choked on another laugh, and she desperately wanted the ground to open up and swallow her whole.

"Sweetheart, this would go a lot faster if you admit that you told them that because you were jealous of those women getting their hands on me."

Oh, the arrogance was going to get her riled up, but she knew he laid it on thick on purpose. She looked up at him, at that handsome face, at the man she'd come to know...the one she was falling in love with despite all her reservations, and told him the truth. "Would you accept three percent jealous and ninety-seven percent thinking of you? I mean, I know *I'm* not right for you, but that doesn't mean I want to picture you sleeping with someone else right now—especially women definitely out of my league. I...apologize for being so petty."

He didn't say anything for a long moment. It felt like several minutes. The noise from the bar receded into the background. But his smile had slowly died, and his eyes were filled with something that, if she didn't know better, she might say was tenderness. "Baby, you're in a class of your own, and you couldn't be petty if you tried. And you have everything I've ever wanted. Hell, I don't know what we are, but we *are* something."

She opened her mouth and then closed it, not knowing what to say. What she wanted was to kiss him, not really caring they were in a bar filled with half the town. It was something she'd never experienced, the need, the urge to touch someone so desperately that she didn't care what others thought of her. He pulled her off the barstool and into him.

"And why the hell do you think I'm over here right now? Do you think I didn't know the second you walked into River's tonight? Something made me turn my head. I saw you walk in; I saw you talking to Aiden. I didn't hear a thing those women were saying because I kept watching you, wanting to be with you, and hating myself for letting you go. Then when he reached out and touched you, I knew I couldn't just stand and watch. I don't know what the hell to do with you, Lainey, because I can't give you what you want, but I don't know how to let you go."

She had forgotten to breathe, but when his mouth came down on hers, she remembered how to kiss him. Tyler's mouth on hers elicited a jolt of awareness of everything that had been missing from her life—mainly him. He kissed her, explored her mouth in a way that made it difficult to stand, to remember Grandma Tilly's warning, the trouble with cowboys. She leaned into him, knowing the weakness in her knees wasn't going to get any better.

"Let me take you home," he said against her mouth.

Lainey tried to take a deep breath and regain her composure. She had no idea what was happening to her. It was like whenever Ty was in the vicinity, all her self-control vanished. The man had royally ticked her off, and now here she was, in his arms, barely able to stand up after kissing him.

It had to stop.

She knew this but still pulled back and nodded, grabbing her purse, ready to go just about anywhere with him.

She would work on stopping tomorrow.

CHAPTER SIXTEEN

*H*e didn't know what he'd been thinking. Well, he did know. He missed Lainey. He wanted Lainey. It was impossible for him to not want her. And he cared for her. He wasn't going to let her go home from the bar alone, regardless of the fact that she wouldn't sleep with him. They could be friends. Yes, that's what they would be. He was helping a friend. So here they were. All alone.

In a way, it was good she had declared some kind of life of celibacy. It would keep things platonic between them. That was good. Why didn't it feel good?

She unlocked her apartment door, and all he wanted to do was taste her again. He'd missed her so much. But he wasn't going to. He was going to leave. He was going to be the good guy.

"Ty?" she whispered.

He stood in the doorway, telling himself not to close it, not to watch her as she took off her jacket. "Yeah?"

"I missed you," she whispered, her brown eyes shining with the emotion he understood, the emotion he hated in himself.

All thoughts of celibacy and platonic relationships vanished, and he stepped forward, shutting the door with his foot and cupping her face and kissing her like she was his last breath. And just like in every dream he'd had about her, she made one of those little sounds and kissed him back, clutching his body for dear life. He backed them against the door. She was running her hands up his chest and then through his hair. He lifted her, his hands cupping her deliciously rounded butt. He turned them so that her back was against the door, her curves pressed against his chest.

He had no idea what the hell they were going to do, because there was only one way he wanted this to end, and it was out of the question. He reminded himself of that as he unbuttoned her shirt, his knuckles grazing her breasts, feeling her trembling beneath his touch.

"Oh Gosh, Ty," she breathed against his mouth.

"I know," he said, kissing her as he cupped her breasts. They filled his hands and then some, and he knew he was going to have to keep his head screwed on straight and this would have to end very soon. She clutched fistfuls of his hair as he dipped his head and brought a nipple into his mouth. He moved his hands down to the tops of her thighs, keeping her braced against the door.

She moaned his name, and he knew he had to stop. He had to stop the best thing that had ever happened to him.

He slowly raised his head, and she looked at him, dazed, her lips full and red as a whimper escaped her mouth. He clenched his teeth tightly and slowly lowered her to the ground, holding on a minute longer as they regained their composure.

"I'm sorry," he said roughly.

She shook her head. "It's my fault."

"It's not. I actually don't think we can be in the

same room together without combusting."

"I think I may need to reevaluate my position on having sex."

"Well, make sure I'm first to get the memo." He almost laughed as he handed her the shirt that he'd tossed to the ground. She held it against herself.

"Sure."

"Maybe we'll just have to stay away from each other," he said, backing up a step and watching her with a hunger he didn't know how to hide.

"Sure. That's a plan. I have to get up early tomorrow anyway," she said, turning her back and straightening her clothes. He didn't want to talk, but it was the right thing to do.

"Right. Church."

"Actually, no, it's because of Sundays at the diner."

Shit. That didn't sit right. "Right. How long are you going to be able to keep that up?"

She crossed her arms and tucked a strand of hair behind her ear. "I'm not sure. It's a good opportunity for some more business. There's next to nothing open for brunch on a Sunday."

Tilly's was always busy. He couldn't believe she needed to stay open seven days a week. Unless she needed the money for her art. "That's too many hours a week. How are you going to paint?"

She shrugged and forced a smile that was so fake he wondered if she was hiding how bad her finances really were. "Ty, I have no life. I still have evenings."

"So, like, after nine and before six a.m. when you aren't in the diner?"

"I'm young, remember? I can work long hours without it affecting me."

He wasn't buying the deflection. "Are you having problems with your roof? Can I help you? I'm not done with the books because the ranch has been keeping me so busy, but I'm sure there's some money—"

She held up her hand, and he caught the wobble of her chin. "I'm fine, thank you. I remember you and your mom at church," she said, the drastic change in subject sending off alarm bells. Or she was just too damn proud to ask for help. He was going to get that check issued for the commission off the weekend with the bachelorette party ASAP. He should have already done that.

"She'd always sit near the front," she continued.

He stared at her for a moment, trying to decide whether or not to pursue the money thing or let her deflect. But he knew what self-preservation looked like, and it was stamped on every gorgeous inch of her body. So who was he to deny her that dignity? He wasn't her boyfriend.

He cleared his throat and let her lead him down memory lane, curious to hear her stories about a past they were both a part of in different ways, from very different angles. He gave her a nod. "She was pretty faithful. She said sitting at the front was much more exciting. I didn't really find any of it exciting," he said.

She laughed. "Yeah. That's nice. My grandmother made me go, too."

He gave a nod, uncomfortable talking about this.

"I used to go with her every Sunday."

"Yeah, I went to keep my mother company, too. I always felt guilty when I tried to get out of it and then think of her standing there alone."

"Me too!" She laughed. "My grandmother would lay it on really thick."

He smiled. "It's a mom thing, I guess."

She nodded. "I stopped going for a while after my grandmother died."

"Why?"

She shrugged. "It hurt too much. I didn't like being there alone, because it just reminded me of everything I'd lost and all the people who weren't in my life anymore."

He was pretty selfish, he realized. Lainey was one of those people you just assumed had it all together all the time. She knew what she wanted out of life, and she stuck to it. But every now and then she'd throw pieces of her life into conversation, and he'd wonder how the hell she'd turned out so damn normal. No parents. Just one eccentric grandmother.

He cleared his throat and continued speaking even though he didn't really like talking about his mother. "I know what you mean. I haven't stepped foot inside a church since my mother's funeral."

"Really?"

He gave a nod. "You...started going back?"

She shrugged. "I go. Well, I guess I was until the Sunday diner thing. But it's not the same. It's lonely," she whispered, breaking eye contact with him. "It still reminds me of the people who are gone. It's like a double-edged sword. I go there and feel closer to them. I can light a candle and say a prayer, but those are just times gone by. I'll never be able to get them back. Really, I shouldn't say 'them'... because I barely knew my mother. But I knew my grandmother."

He swallowed past the lump in his throat. Maybe that's why he never went back. It was too painful to go to a place he associated with his mother without her. It hurt thinking about those days, about how everything was fine. He'd thought everything in his family was as it appeared. Hell, he'd been so wrong.

"Sorry, this is boring conversation, isn't it?"

He shook his head. "No. It's stuff we don't always put into words." He stopped talking for a moment and studied her, taking her in. "My mother would have liked you, Lainey."

Tears appeared in her eyes. "Thank you," she whispered. "I think Tilly would have liked you, too, despite her warning about cowboys."

He shoved his hands in his pockets. "Warning?"

She nodded. "She was married for a bit—not long. But she was married to her own cowboy. Said he was more handsome than anyone she'd ever met. Almost charmed the underpants off her before marriage," she said with a laugh.

He smiled. "What happened?"

"Apparently he tried to hit her."

"Man."

"Don't worry. Tilly knocked him down the stairs."

He smiled. "Good for her."

"Yeah. She kicked him out, and that was the end. She ran her restaurant and raised my mother as a single parent. But she would always warn me about trusting cowboys. She'd say, 'Lainey, I'm going to tell you something that you're not going to be able to understand until you're older, but I want you to remember this: Never fall for a cowboy, because the trouble with cowboys is that they'll rope you in with their charm and you'll forget who you are and what you stand for.'"

Well thanks, Tilly. He didn't say anything for a moment, wondering if he needed to defend himself. "I wouldn't say we're all that bad. I mean, I might have to agree with the charm, but I don't think it's a universal trait."

She burst out laughing, and he smiled at the sound, at the way her face lit up. "You know you've got it."

"Is that right?" he said, still smiling even though the mood shifted like the wind before a fast-moving storm.

Her smile dipped, and her face flushed. "Well, I'm not sure, really, because I never actually noticed any charm or anything like that."

He took a step closer, hearing the audible catch of her breath. "No, I think you just admitted that I've got it, and I think Grandma Tilly might have actually been wrong."

She frowned. "How so?"

"You managed to remember who you are and what you stand for," he said.

Her gaze darted from his eyes to his mouth, and her pulse was racing at the base of her throat, and he knew, he knew she felt the same. "Lainey," he said, raising his hand to frame the one side of her face. So when he took that final step in to her, when her soft body made contact with his, when he lowered his head to inches from hers, when their mouths hovered so close together, he promised himself he'd walk away before things went too far.

"Ty," she whispered, one of her hands clutching a fistful of his shirt. At first, he didn't know if she was going to push him away, but just as he was lowering his head, she held on tight and pulled him in. Lainey reeled him in, and he was a goner. When his mouth found hers, he knew, he knew there would never be enough Lainey for him.

"Good night, Lainey," he said, using every ounce of willpower to pull away.

She bit her lower lip and quickly smoothed her hair. "Right. Thanks for bringing me home; it was really nice of you."

They were being way too polite. Like strangers. But maybe that would be the only way for them now. "Right. I'll, uh, see you around. We're both busy anyway."

She nodded, giving him a bright smile that seemed so forced. "For sure. Oh, but I need to follow up on that portrait you promised me."

He groaned. He'd forgotten all about that silly bargain.

"See you tomorrow, Ty." And she closed the door with a soft *click*.

So much for his plan to stay away.

CHAPTER SEVENTEEN

*L*ainey waited on the porch of the main house at the ranch for Tyler to come home. She could see him walking toward her in the distance. Goose bumps scattered along her arms at the sight, the barn behind him, the mountains in the distance. She grabbed her phone and started snapping pictures before he noticed. His battered hat was hanging low, and his strong body was showcased in muddy jeans and shirt. As he came closer, he lifted his head, and his blue eyes met hers.

"I'm here for my picture."

He stopped walking and hung his head back on his shoulders. She tried to swallow her laugh. "I need a shower," he said as he rounded the corner to the porch.

"Nope, you're absolutely perfect."

He gave her a grin that made her stomach flutter.

"Seriously," she said. "I need you to walk back out there. A few yards away from me, toward the barn."

"Lainey, I'm wiped. I want to take a shower."

"A deal's a deal, Tyler. I'll be quick. Five minutes."

She might have heard him mutter something about being a ball-breaker, but she wasn't sure. He did as instructed but then turned around. "I don't get what kind of a portrait this is, if I'm not even facing the camera."

"Well, walk out a bit farther, and then I want you to turn your head and look at me," she said.

He rolled his eyes and proceeded to walk.

"Can you, like, find a piece of hay and put it in your mouth?" she yelled.

He turned around slowly. "No."

She sighed. He was very difficult. "Fine. Walk. I'll tell you when to stop and look at me."

He gave her a salute and started walking again. The sun was setting, and the sky was streaked with ribbons of purple and pink. As soon as Tyler stepped into its glow, she called out for him to stop. "Now look at me over your shoulder," she yelled.

He turned slowly, his blue eyes looking directly at her. She took her time focusing, then clicked in quick succession. Her breath caught at the beauty in his roughened, work-worn appearance, at the strong lines of his jaw. She wanted to catch the shades of blue in his eyes, the stubble on his face, the expression that she loved. She had been so right about him; he was so paintable. She stared at the stubble across the perfect jawline. Nope. Right into those stunning baby blues. Oh, she was such toast. She cleared her throat. She definitely had her inspiration and knew she'd start her sketch tonight. She put her camera down. "Okay, done," she said, her voice coming out slightly strangled.

He walked back toward her and stopped at the bottom porch step. "How are you?" he asked, his voice slightly impersonal. She tried not to take it personally. They had said they were going to steer clear of each other, that they didn't know what they were. But as she stood there, she knew she was in love with him. She had known for a long time. The night in his cabin, the night at River's, the night in her apartment. But he didn't want what she wanted.

"Good. I'm good. Just busy with the diner…and now my painting," she said, forcing a bright smile.

He gave her a nod. "That's good. Uh, that reminds me—there's an envelope on the kitchen table with your name on it. It's the commission for the bachelorette weekend."

Thank goodness. "Great. I might have another group for next month. Hopefully we can start getting more regular business," she said. The money she owed him was weighing heavily on her. She hated that she hadn't told him, but she couldn't, not until she had all the money repaid.

"Sure. Don't worry—I know you have a lot on your plate."

She nodded, fidgeting with the strap on her camera. "I think I'm going to go in and say hi to your dad before I leave. I have dinner for him…and I have some for you, too."

He nodded. "You don't have to bring me dinner, but thanks. I'll probably just eat with the guys from now on."

"Oh…oh, of course. Yeah, that's probably for the best. Make yourself one of them. Sure, that makes sense." She hated herself right now. He was turning her down in every which way.

"I, uh, I'll head out to my cabin, then, give you a chance to talk to my dad."

She kept her smile even though it ached. "Great. Have a good night."

He held her gaze for a long moment, but she couldn't figure out what he was thinking. "You too."

She turned quickly, ready to go inside, to be away

from him. She had no idea what the plan was. She needed to get to work on her own dreams. First was the picture. It was kind of unfortunate that the subject of her picture was the man she was supposed to not be thinking about. Not the brightest plan. She opened the door.

"Lainey," he said.

She glanced over her shoulder at him. His eyes were shadowed beneath his hat. "Yes?"

He opened his mouth. "Uh, just, thanks. See you around."

She nodded and walked into the house. She knew this wasn't the end for her and Tyler, but she wasn't going to force him into having a relationship with her. She had too much pride for that.

Mrs. Busby came out to greet her. She was all smiles, and her cheeks were glowing.

"Well hello, dear! Martin and I were just talking about you," she said, grabbing the takeout tray from Lainey's hands and walking into the kitchen.

"You were?" Lainey asked, following her.

She nodded. "Should I warm this up?" she asked, taking the lid off the roast beef special.

"I think it's still hot," she said.

Mrs. Busby arranged it nicely on a plate and handed it to her. "Here you go. You have a nice chat with Martin. I need to get back to town; I'm meeting my ladies for poker night."

Lainey swallowed her laugh. "Okay, you have fun."

"Will do, dear," she said and hustled out of the kitchen. Lainey walked into the living room, pleased to see Martin with a healthier glow. She noticed the curtains and window were open, and a nice breeze floated through the room. It smelled fresh and clean. The furniture was dusted, and the dark wood gleamed. It was probably closer to how it had been when his wife was alive.

"Hi, Lainey," he said, slowly enunciating the words.

"It's so great to hear your voice again," Lainey said, sitting down beside him.

He smiled at her and accepted the plate. "It's good to speak again," he said. His voice was slurred and slow, but it was wonderful progress. He started eating, carefully bringing the food to his mouth. "Maybe no more rented hospital bed soon."

She squeezed his hand gently. "You'll get there."

"Thank you for being so good to me," he said in between forkfuls of food. She smiled at him, happy that his hand was steady as he ate.

"You don't have to thank me, ever. You've been good to me for a long time. I wanted to let you know I'm really close to paying back that loan, Martin."

He shook his head. "No, you don't worry about that."

She leaned forward. "I'm not, but I know Ty has some great plans for this place, and it's not right for me to keep that money. It's not mine, and it was a loan. I haven't mentioned anything to him, but I will explain it when I give the money back."

"You're opening the diner on Sundays? Not because of the loan? You look tired."

She waved a hand. "I'm fine. I promise."

He put his fork down, and a deep frown formed on his forehead. "I saw you outside with Tyler."

Heat infused her face. So this was what Mrs. Busby was referring to. She didn't know how to answer that question. She didn't want him to worry, but she didn't want him to relay something to Tyler that would make it look like she was in love with him. She smoothed her hands on her jeans, searching for the right words. "Tyler and I have become… good friends. I'm not really sure what else I can say. I guess it's complicated. We both have different goals," she said, hoping that sounded like a real answer. It wasn't a lie, because she honestly didn't have a clear answer as to what they were.

"You deserve the best," he said, his eyes misting. "A family man."

She didn't know what to make of that statement. Was he saying that he didn't think his son would treat her well? She didn't even know if he and Tyler were on speaking terms yet or if Martin was still mad at him. "You know, Tyler has done a great job trying to restore the ranch," she said softly. "The cabin idea was mine. I hope you don't mind."

He shook his head and opened his mouth for a moment, like he wanted to say more. Lainey waited, but he closed his mouth and frowned.

"But Tyler had to restore them. He worked constantly. Nights and weekends. He's done a great job. I'm sure he can take you out there to see them if you'd like," she said, defending Tyler. She wanted Martin to see how hard he was trying. She wanted Martin to forgive him.

"Lainey, watch yourself."

"Martin, I'm fine."

He nodded slowly, handing her the now empty plate. "Thank you for dinner. Delicious." His words slurred a little on the last one. He was tired, and she needed to let him get his rest.

She held on to the plate, not moving yet, wanting to know more but deciding she didn't want to involve Martin in her issues with Tyler. She stood a moment later and forced a smile. "Well, you're welcome. I'd better head back to town. I think Michelle is in the kitchen. Mrs. Busby seemed like she was in a big rush tonight," she said, surprised when his cheeks turned ruddy.

He cleared his throat. "Poker night."

She nodded, giving him a smile. "Good night, Martin."

𝒯yler walked into the living room of the main house, hoping to speak to his father tonight. But as usual, the man was pretending he was sleeping. He knew full well his father was now capable of slow speech and his muscles were growing stronger every day. He'd heard him speak. He'd heard him laugh. With everyone but him. He shrugged off his hurt and sat in the chair beside his bed. God, how many times had he sat here since he'd been home? In total silence.

"So we've booked the cabins well into the spring. The revenue from that alone means big things for us." He watched his father's face for some kind of acknowledgment, but there was nothing. "It was Lainey's idea, you know." He thought he'd throw that in there again—even though he'd said it before, many times. But what the hell, he was running out of one-sided conversation topics, and he knew his dad adored Lainey—and spoke to her.

His father opened his eyes at the mention of Lainey.

He held his breath, like a kid waiting for approval, but dammit, he still didn't get it. Tyler didn't know what he was expecting, telling his father about the progress of the ranch, but he wasn't expecting censure. His father stared at him, still refusing to speak. He felt the weight of everything, of Lainey—wanting her, loving her, but not being able to give her what she needed—of the ranch, of this relationship that he didn't know whether it would ever get repaired.

His father's last words to him replayed again and again in his mind, and he wondered if that was it. Maybe they could never get back to where they were because—because he wasn't really his son.

Tyler's stomach churned at just thinking the words. He was just this kid his dad had been forced to raise. He fisted his hands, trying to hold on to his temper. "I don't get you. I just told you that in the winter I'm going to be able to hire again for spring. We'll slowly rebuild the cattle numbers."

His father shook his head.

Tyler stood and tried to remain cool. He didn't know what the hell he was doing anymore. He was in love with Lainey. A woman who refused to sleep with him, who wanted everything he had run away from, and yet all he could think about was being with her. He was being backed into a corner. Her faith bothered him, and he didn't know why. It shouldn't. But it did. All of it did. All these people, they wanted impossible things from him.

Then there was his father and the cold shoulder

he was still getting after being at home for more than two months. He hated to think of the real reason his father hadn't warmed up to him; it was what had made him run years ago. He waited for him, searching for a sign of softening, and then he got mad at himself. What, was he five, hoping his father wasn't angry with him? He didn't need this. He didn't need his approval anymore, and it was pretty damn pathetic that he was still trying.

"Maybe it'll never be enough, is that it?" he asked, moving away from the bed. "Speak," Tyler said softly.

"Don't hurt her."

His muscles tightened up for a moment at his father's slurred, raspy voice. This should have been a happy moment. He should have been elated that his father was speaking to him. But his father wasn't talking because it was him, his father was talking because he was protecting Lainey. He pushed aside his anger to finally get the answers he wanted. "This isn't about Lainey. This is about you and me. You tell me the real reason you can't get over me leaving."

His father's chin wobbled, and he knew he should stop, but he couldn't because his father just stared at him, refusing to give him an answer.

"What? Say it!" Tyler yelled, trying to force his hand, trying to get him to admit the truth.

His father shook his head. "No."

"Then what do you want?"

His father just turned his head and shut his eyes.

Tyler stood in the living room, the heaviness in his chest, the tightness in his muscles, making him desperate for some kind of clarity, for perspective.

He took a few steps toward the fireplace, to get closer to the family portrait hanging above it. He was probably ten years old in the picture. He and his father had both begged his mother not to make them wear suits, but as usual, she won out. They were all standing there smiling, like a real family. Life had been so much simpler then. Everything had been black and white, and there were rules and consequences for breaking the rules. But there was also a helluva lot of love. He couldn't go back there. He could never be that kid again, because that kid wasn't real. That family wasn't real. He wanted to. Right now, more than ever, he wanted to go back to being that kid, having that feeling of being loved.

He stood in that living room and wanted closure, wanted to move forward, wanted…his father's approval. His forgiveness. And his love.

Eight years was a long time to be gone. For a second, he allowed himself to remember the ranch and life before his mother had died. He'd worked that land day in and day out with his dad. He'd assumed he'd live and die on the ranch. There were some times working with his father that he didn't think he'd survive the day, but his dad would chuckle and tell him to just keep going, that the ranch would make him into a man. His mother would be there at the end of a long day, though, with a smile and a hot, comforting dinner.

After she'd been diagnosed with cancer, there had been a desperation to keep everything the same, even though it could never be the same. The changing of the season with a person who was dying meant panic. How many more seasons? Then seasons turned to weeks and then days and then gruesome, soul-stripping hours.

He'd begun measuring time in chunks…like sunsets, sunrises, dinners, breakfasts. And then the time slipped by so damn fast, and he was left wondering if their time here would ever be enough.

For people you loved with everything you had, a lifetime was never enough. His mother had clutched his hand on that last day, a brief moment of lucidity through the haze of drugs and certain death and had promised him she'd see him again. She had promised him she was right about all of it, about their faith, the afterlife, and her spirit. He'd held her hand tighter, brought it to his lips, even though he couldn't hold back his sobs, because he knew it was the end, because he knew she was wrong.

He stared at that damn picture and hated that his eyes filled with tears. The kid in the picture would have cried. But he wasn't him anymore.

He glanced over at his father one last time before he walked out of the room, hoping, like a silly kid, that his father might stop him and say that he'd been wrong. That he was happy Tyler was home. But of course he didn't.

CHAPTER EIGHTEEN

*L*ainey had spent the two weeks since she took the picture of Tyler either in her apartment sketching and painting or in the diner working. She hadn't had a burst of creativity and inspiration like that in more than a year. She worked well into the night, every night, and was running on adrenaline and coffee. Despite the exhaustion, the euphoria of creativity surged through her. She had worried that she was losing it, but this painting…she was back. She was still an artist.

She had lived and breathed the painting and now she was going to show it to Martin. She was hoping it would pull at his heartstrings to see his son out there on the family ranch, where he belonged. She was kind of nervous because she hadn't even shown Tyler yet. But she was very pleased with it. The expression she'd captured on Tyler's face was so vivid and real, the light in his eyes, the sparkle, the tilt of his mouth. The love of this land was evident in every fiber of his being, and she hoped Martin saw it, too. She even had a title for it. But she'd wait to reveal that, too.

She fidgeted with the handle on the tube her painting was rolled up in and tried not to think of the fact that she hadn't seen or heard from Tyler since she'd taken his picture.

Michelle answered the door a minute later, putting an end to Lainey's musings.

"Hi, Lainey. Come on in, sweetie. I'm glad you're

here," she said, a deep frown between her brows.

"Is everything okay?" Lainey asked, setting down the tube and holding on to the pie she'd brought.

"I think something happened. Martin just doesn't seem like himself. He seems really down. Lately he's been doing so well with his speech and his fine motor skills. He's been happier. But something is off. Mrs. Busby said the same thing."

Lainey nodded and touched the older woman's arm. "Okay, leave it to me. I'll see what I can do," she said.

"Thanks, Lainey. I'll give you two some privacy."

Lainey walked down the hall to the living room, the apple pie she'd brought still warm in the takeout container.

"Martin?" Lainey whispered, walking into the dark room. Something *was* off. He usually gave her a smile.

He made eye contact with her, but the smile she had been looking forward to seeing wasn't there. "Lainey," he managed to say in that slow, slurred speech.

"I'm sorry I haven't had much time to spend with you. I've been busy with an art piece... I think you'll really like it."

He tried to give her a small smile, but she could tell it was forced.

"How are you?" she asked, coming to sit with him. She took his hand in hers, knowing somehow that he needed comforting.

He shook his head and stared at the ceiling, his chin wobbling slightly. "Ty," he managed to say a moment later.

Alarm shot through her. "Is he okay?"

He nodded. "Gone."

Dread began swimming through her, in the way that it did when her grandmother died, when her mother left over and over again. He couldn't be gone. He wouldn't leave like that again. He wouldn't leave her.

She forced herself to concentrate. "What do you mean, gone? He can't be gone. He's working the ranch. He's here for good."

"Argued. Haven't seen him for days."

She took a deep breath. "That's okay. Sometimes you need to argue in order to repair what you had. I'm sure he left to blow off some steam. I'm sure he'll be back."

Martin squeezed his eyes shut, and tears poured from his eyes. She ached for him, watching him. He was worried he was losing his son all over again. These men were too proud, too stubborn to fix this themselves.

"Martin," she said sharply, "look at me."

He opened his eyes, and she leaned closer to him. "I know Tyler. I know he wouldn't leave you again. He vowed to help you get your health back, to bring this ranch back, no matter how difficult. He wouldn't leave you again." She wanted to add that he wouldn't leave her, too, but maybe she wasn't that confident. "What did you argue about? I don't want to pry; I just want to see if there's a way I can help. I can find him, and I can talk to him." More like smack some sense into his head and guilt him for letting his father lie here thinking he'd left again.

Martin set his jaw, and she knew that look. She

had seen that stubbornness on the much younger version of the man.

"Tell me. You need my help."

"My wife."

"You argued about her?"

"He thinks I didn't want him."

"Ah," she whispered. She knew the story. She knew how much Ty had blamed his father for the way he chose to treat her cancer. "Can't you both just agree to disagree? You both wanted the best for her. You both had the purest of intentions. That's all that needs to be said. But you both have to let it go, because nothing you can do will bring her back."

Martin shook his head and then slowly raised his stronger arm and pointed to his nightstand.

"Do you want me to get something?"

He nodded. "Envelope."

She opened the drawer and examined the contents. Extra Kleenex, medication, a bible. There was an envelope poking from the bible. She slipped it out and held it up to him. "Is this it?"

He nodded. She turned it over and saw Ty's name on the front. It had stamps on it. And then a return-to-sender stamp. She knew it was Martin's handwriting from before the stroke. So he'd written to Ty? He'd tried to make up?

"Do you want me to give this to Ty?"

Martin nodded, his eyes filled with pain.

"Okay. I'm going to find him. You're not going to lose him again, Martin," she whispered. She stood up and gave him a kiss on the cheek before walking out.

Lainey said goodbye to Michelle and left the house in search of Tyler. It was Sunday evening, her only night off, and she hoped she'd find him in his cabin. She set out for the ten-minute walk, trying not to assume the worst about him. His truck was here, she noted; that was a good sign. Lainey knocked on Tyler's door and waited. When he didn't answer after a few minutes, she knocked again and tried the door. It was unlocked. She walked in.

Tyler was standing with his back to her, staring out the kitchen window. She could see the mountains in the distance. "Tyler?"

"Hey," he said, turning to face her. He didn't give her his usual smile, and his voice sounded flat.

"Are you okay?"

"Fine."

"I was just at the house and spoke with your father."

He ran his hand over his jaw. "He shouldn't be involving you in our problems."

"Why not?"

He shrugged. "I don't know. You're not family. You shouldn't be getting in the middle of it. See, this is why I never wanted us to get involved. I warned you."

She stopped breathing for a moment, and then all the air rushed out of her, panic setting in. She'd been gambling, maybe, but this wasn't what she was expecting. She didn't know what she'd expected, exactly, but this wasn't it. "Here, he wanted me to give this to you. He was adamant."

"Just leave it on the table," he said and crossed the room and poured himself a drink.

She shook her head when he offered her a glass. "I don't think having whiskey is going to make you saying that you warned me not to get involved any easier."

His jaw was hard, and there wasn't an ounce of the sweetness she'd seen in him the last couple of months. He was hard and unreadable. He was a stranger suddenly. "I'm not trying to hurt you, Lainey. I'm just telling you what we both know. I'm not meant for family or happily-ever-afters."

She had to keep her head in the game and quell any desire to give in to her emotions. "A couple of months ago, we barely knew each other. Now things are different."

"We're at an impasse. What you want, I'll never be able to give."

An ominous chill ran through her. "What is it you think I want?"

"You want a man who's going to marry you. You want someone who's going to check off all those little boxes you've created. I'm not him."

"That's insulting. You're making me sound immature and petty."

"You want to wait until you get married to have sex. You want a man to stand there in church beside you on Sundays. You want a man to give you babies and spend the rest of your life in a single relationship, and you think you will be fulfilled. It's a sham and a lie, and I know better. You don't."

Don't cry, Lainey. Don't cry. She stood there watching the man who'd held her, who'd laughed with her, who'd shown her so much tenderness and love, and searched for some sign that he was still there and couldn't find it.

"Don't mock me," she whispered, trying to sound

strong, trying not to sound like he'd just shattered her heart and left her exposed and broken. "I never expected that from you." Lies. She had fooled herself into believing that maybe he wanted that, too, with the right woman. Of course, the right woman wasn't her.

He threw up his hands. "So then what are we doing here?"

"I don't know, I guess...I guess I thought you were different. I thought—"

"You thought you could change me, admit it. Here's something you don't know. I can't change. I am who I am. I'm a guy who wants sex, and I resent you for putting me in this position. I don't believe in your church, I don't believe in your faith, I don't believe in your ideals. I don't believe in any of it. I want something that is no-strings. That's all."

Her stomach bottomed out. Through blurred eyes, she saw the man she loved turn into someone she didn't recognize. He was humiliating her. On purpose. But she wouldn't let him see her go down. She had learned her lessons through her mother. She'd vowed to be wiser than her mother—not desperate and take love wherever she could get it. But maybe they were the same.

She had thought that not sleeping with a man would protect her from losing her heart, but she could feel it breaking. Maybe she hadn't known Ty intimately, but right now she was as naked as she could ever be. He had known her, every dream, every vulnerability, and every hope. She had loved him. Fool. She had been a complete fool. She wasn't any better than her mother, chasing after a man who didn't really want her.

She turned from him, from the harshness in his eyes. "You are such a bastard."

He smiled grimly. "Actually, you're right about that. Here's something you may or may not know after your conversation with my father—he's not actually my biological father. The night I left Wishing River, we had a huge argument, and he told me, 'Tyler, you're not even my own damn son, so just get the hell out of here.' My mom went out with a guy once and hell... God, that guy...I think he forced himself on her. She got pregnant. With me. So that's my story. I'm the kid my dad was stuck raising because he loved my mother so much. My biological father didn't want anything to do with me. Love makes people do stupid things. It changes them; it weakens them."

She swiped at the tears in her eyes. She was crying for him. She hated him, but she was crying for him because his pain, his sorrow was so palpable she could taste it in the room but she could do nothing for him. "I'm sorry," she whispered.

"Of course you're sorry, because you're Lainey, the girl with the big heart."

He wouldn't see her fall. She'd been on her own too long. She'd seen people die and she'd moved on, all on her own. She'd held it together for years. She was not going to let this man break her. She lifted her chin. "I was wrong. I thought you were someone different. It was my mistake. I was attracted to you, and I'd had this silly crush on you in high school, and I let all that influence me. It was dumb. Immature. You're right. I do want all those things. I want happily-ever-after, I want my dreams, and I won't settle for anything less. So you can stand there and throw them all back in my face, like I'm this pathetic, naive woman who doesn't know what the real world is like. But I do know. I know that people can stand by the people they love. I know people can bend and change for people they really love. I know that a real man doesn't one day tell a person that her ideals are noble and then the next mock her for them. And I know a real man would want me. I'm going to wait for him. Shame on me for thinking it could have ever been you." She grabbed her sweater, hating how badly her hands shook, how her legs trembled as she opened the door. Somewhere deep inside, she wished that he would stop her. But she knew better. This version of Ty just stood there, leaning against the counter, all cold and hard lines, indifferent to anything she'd said.

"Did you take ten thousand dollars from my father?"

Blood rushed to her ears, and she froze. *Oh no! He's found out. No, no, no! Not before I can pay him back.* She opened her mouth to answer, to try and explain, but closed it because she didn't know what to say. Her stomach churned, and she thought she might throw up. Or pass out. She reached out blindly to grab the back of the couch, to try to hold herself upright on wobbly legs. She wanted to tell him she was sorry. That she'd wanted to tell him herself. That she never meant to lie to him. But suddenly there wasn't enough oxygen in the room to push the words out. She was drowning in regrets.

He hung his head. "That's rich. So when I was telling you how the books were a mess and there was missing money, you never told me you had taken ten thousand dollars from an old man?"

She finally gulped in a breath and tried to explain. "I didn't take ten thousand dollars from an old man. He offered it. He was alone—"

"And you took advantage of him, just like the rest of the damn town. Two thousand to one person, five to another, ten to you. Congratulations, you managed to get the most out of him."

Tears stung the backs of her eyes. "Your father has a huge heart, and we confided in each other. He told me about you, your mother, and I told him about the art program. That's what the money was for. Except I had all these other problems that kept coming up," she said, riffling through her purse and pulling out her checkbook. Her hand was shaking, and she had a hard time steadying it enough to write. "I was waiting to have the full amount, but here, this is what I have for now. It's more than half."

He stood there, his jaw clenched, not saying anything.

Her hand trembled as she placed the check on the table. "You are so wrong about everyone and everything. I feel sorry for you. Somehow you got it into your head that people have been cheating your father, and it's the furthest thing from the truth. Your father was helping his friends. These people became his family, and he was helping them. And now they've rallied around him, helping *him* during his time of need. You think you can cut yourself off from all that? You're so wrong."

She opened the door and then stopped, needing to get the rest out. He was hurting as much as she was. "Here's what else I know: you're a coward. You love me. You love me, but just not enough. Because when people love each other, they do change in order to make things work, because you have to. It's called compromise. Sacrifice. It's how people stay married for fifty years. But you have to really love the person. You have to love them enough to change, enough to be uncomfortable. I know what it's like not to be loved enough. I don't need to be with a man who doesn't love me enough to believe the best in me—or in himself."

She was proud of herself for not crying, for eliciting the infamous jaw-clenching of his. She managed one last sad smile before turning and leaving. Stepping out into the cold air, she took a huge gulp, begging herself to hold it together until she got to her car. *Just keep walking, Lainey, alone. You've walked alone for so long, you can do it again.* But she was fooling herself.

The farther she walked from his cabin, the harder it became to breathe. She knew enough to know that this was something she wouldn't recover from, that she wouldn't get over. She wouldn't forgive herself for falling for a cowboy.

CHAPTER NINETEEN

$\mathcal{T}$yler stared at the empty bottle of whiskey and contemplated getting another, but that would entail him getting off his ass, and that wasn't happening. He leaned back on his couch, one ankle crossed over the other, and stared at the fire. It was a dumb fire. The last time he'd had a good fire was when Lainey had been in his cabin. Wearing his T-shirt. Then wearing nothing else. He squeezed his eyes shut as the image of her flooded his mind. But then he heard her voice, the embarrassment in it as she told him she was a virgin. God, he was an ass. He'd let her go; he'd belittled her.

He ran his hands down his face, because all her other words, all her other truths flooded his senses: Lainey yelling at him, *I know what it's like not to be loved enough. I don't need to be with a man who doesn't love me enough.* He squeezed his eyes shut and cursed himself for hurting the one person who'd reached him. She knew him better than he knew himself. She'd had faith in him when no one else in this town had. And where had it gotten her? He'd made a fool of her.

He stared at the torn-up remains of the check she'd written. He may be a bastard, but not enough to cash her check. Even in his haze of anger, he'd noticed as soon as she walked in how tired she seemed. She'd been working her ass off trying to pay that debt, and he'd shamed her for taking the money.

He'd found out about the loan, and his thoughts had gone to dark places.

He picked up his dad's letter and read it again— the one he'd refused to read five years ago, the one where he apologized, where he begged him to come home, where he said he'd wait for him until he died.

He squeezed his eyes shut against the sting of tears and ran his hands through his hair. Dammit. He didn't know what the hell he was going to do.

The knock at the door was unexpected. It was late, almost midnight. He didn't want to answer it. Hell, he hadn't been this drunk since he and Dean and Cade were nineteen and had stolen his dad's favorite whiskey.

The knocking didn't stop. What if it was Lainey? He stood and dragged himself to the door and opened it.

Cade's ugly face stared back at him.

"You look like shit," Cade said, pushing his way into the cabin. Tyler slammed the door shut behind him, knowing there would be no convincing him to leave. "You smell even worse," his friend said, heading straight for the full bottle of whiskey on top of the fridge after frowning at the empty one on the coffee table.

Tyler flopped back on the couch, not disagreeing with either statement.

Cade sat down on the opposite couch and poured himself a glass. "I'd offer you some, but since you're on the verge of alcohol poisoning or something, I won't. I wouldn't want to have to drag you to the hospital, because Dean is working the ER tonight, and he'd be really pissed if he had to waste his time on you."

"Thanks," he said grimly.

"So why don't you tell me how it is you managed to screw up your relationship with Lainey?" Cade asked, drinking his shot and then putting the empty glass back on the table.

He glowered at his friend. "How do you know that?"

"Well, first off, you haven't formed complete sentences in days. And today I went into Tilly's, and she's giving Dean and me the cold shoulder. I can't have that happening. She just added homemade lasagna to the regular menu."

Lasagna. The Italian food because she wanted to go to that Italian school. The food they'd shared that night. She'd been so embarrassed when he'd caught her scarfing down the platter. He smiled without even realizing it.

"Can you just deal with this situation and stop smiling at the air like a moron?"

"Go away." Tyler frowned again, reaching for the bottle of whiskey.

Cade poured himself a glass and removed the bottle from within Tyler's reach. "No. Not until you fix this. You wanted Lainey. You told me to back off, and I did. So what the hell happened?"

Tyler held his friend's stare, seeing the anger in his face, knowing he owed him. He threaded his fingers through his hair, tugging. "I don't know. I'm not… She's complicated."

"Oh, so it's her fault? 'Cause I know both of you, and I'd wager that you're the one with issues, not Lainey."

He wondered why he ever wanted to be friends

with Cade and Dean again. "Fine. I have issues. But I'm not complicated. I want simple things. She does not."

"I agree, yes, you're a simple man, but this doesn't make sense. You wanted her—badly. You walked around with a dumb smile for two months. You turned down gorgeous women without a second thought, and now you've messed up your relationship and you're miserable."

It was all true. "She wants…commitment."

"Oh, like you mean she wants the whole package. She wants love and marriage and kids. I'm not sure why this is a shock to you. If you knew anything about her, you'd know that. She's spent her whole life in that damn diner, doing everything for family, family who didn't even give a shit about her. She's sweet and caring." He coughed. "And very hot."

Tyler nodded, resting his hands on his forehead. He agreed with everything.

"So what's the problem? She's the whole package."

"Ever after. Commitment. Marriage. Are you kidding me? You're saying this is fine. You would do this?"

"Marry Lainey? Hell yes. I'm sure half the guys in town would, including Aiden Rivers."

Cade had never liked Aiden for some unknown reason. Tyler didn't say anything.

"Or is the problem that you don't think you're good enough for Lainey? Maybe she'll see you for the guy you really are and want out?"

Tyler leaned back against the sofa, hating that his friend knew so much about him but not wanting to admit that he was dead-on accurate. "She knows who I am. She's seen all of me."

"Well, there's your problem."

He flipped him the finger. "If you're here to help me, then help," he snapped.

Cade held up his hands. "Fine. So, just to be clear, you're the one who ended it."

"Yes."

"You, Tyler, ended a relationship with one of the hottest, sweetest, smartest women I have ever met."

He glared at Cade. "You don't know what you're talking about. Not everything is as it seems. Marriage isn't like in the movies."

"I'm not five, you idiot."

"Well, it's complicated. There's crap you don't know about. I can't promise her I'll be something and not deliver."

"Well, then deliver."

"It's not that simple."

"Why not?"

"I'm not my father's biological son." He hated saying that out loud. He'd known for eight years, so why did it make the pit in his stomach feel even bigger to say it out loud?

Cade didn't say anything, but he slowly picked up the bottle of whiskey and filled his glass, then took a sip while watching him. "Go on."

"I only found out the night before I left town. My dad…Martin…raised me as his son. My mother was pregnant with another man's baby, but they never told anyone."

"Hell," Cade said under his breath. "So that's why you really left. I, uh, I'm sorry."

Tyler shrugged and sat back on the couch. "Whatever. I'm over it."

"Your dad… Martin, he's a good guy."

"I know; he had to raise another guy's kid and pretend it was his own."

Cade didn't say anything for a few minutes. "Maybe that's not how he saw it. Maybe he saw you as his son. It wasn't pretending."

"I don't know what to think. My mother never told me. All those years."

"Did you ever find out who your biological father was?"

Tyler nodded. "Oh, I found out all right, early on. I thought I'd get some answers, some perspective. Hell, maybe I even thought I was going to have a relationship with him," he said, remembering the day he'd met his father. Martin had done him a favor by stepping in.

"And?"

"He was a lazy drunk. Didn't care that he had a son." He had walked into that bar seeking some clarity, maybe he'd even been looking for a relation-ship, but he'd gotten rejection. He'd been so damn lost for so long; his entire life had been a lie. But the worst was knowing what kind of a man his biological father was, eerily similar to that ass-wipe Rick. "I ac-tually asked him if he'd had feelings for my mother, because I was trying to figure out how she could have been with him. He smiled, like this real asshole kind of smile, and said no, that he'd just been hav-ing fun and had taken her up on what she'd offered. I knew there had to be more to it, Cade."

He ran his hands down the front of his jeans as anger washed through him at the memory, and then at the memory of Rick and his own disgusting comments about Lainey. He'd been tortured that night, that week, that month, imagining what had gone down, what his mother had suffered. And then the night at Tilly's, what Rick had insinuated had made him lose control, had made him worry for Lainey. But now, he was the asshole.

Cade swore under his breath. "Sorry, man. But I don't think it matters—who donated sperm. You don't have the whole story. Martin raised you like his own. If he didn't love you like a son, you would have known it growing up. You can't fake that. My own parents were blood, didn't give a shit about me. It was my friends. They were always more of a family than my real family," Cade said.

Tyler hung his head. "I know. I know. I just… Lainey has these ideals and these morals that I don't know if I can live up to."

"Why not? What else do you have to do with your time?"

He let out a frustrated breath. "Your advice sucks. You suck."

"Let's not lash out at the only person trying to help you, okay?"

Tyler folded his arms across his chest and waited for his friend to say something that would actually help him.

"She's the best thing that will ever happen to you. You think she's too good for you? She is. But that doesn't mean you aren't right for each other."

"I was an ass, Cade. I was a complete and total ass to her."

Cade shrugged. "Yeah, but you can apologize. Tell her it's a genetic defect from your biological father's side of the family. She'll never be able to prove it."

He almost laughed. "Doesn't it scare you to lay it all out there? To love someone so much that you'll do anything for them? Lie, cheat, steal? Anything? So you spend every day loving this woman, and then she leaves or she dies and you're just…nothing without her? Isn't it just better to be alone?" The unfamiliar sting of tears in the backs of his eyes horrified him. Damn if he knew how the hell he'd said all that aloud. Cade was looking pretty shocked, too. Sharing your feelings was very uncomfortable, and he didn't think he'd be doing it again, like, ever.

Cade didn't say anything for a full minute. "Hell no. Having that, having someone by your side, someone who has your back, who knows everything about you and loves you anyway—that's worth the risk. Because going through life alone, just fucking around without thinking about tomorrow, gets old fast, man."

He held his friend's gaze, understanding what he was saying, knowing he was speaking the truth. When did Cade become the voice of reason? Hell.

"For what it's worth, Tyler, even though you screwed up badly, you're a good guy. And if I had a woman like Lainey look at me the way she looks at you, I wouldn't think twice about putting a ring on her finger. So I suggest you get your head out of your ass sometime soon, then take a shower and go see Lainey. If you don't do it in within the next week, I call dibs."

"*W*here's Lainey?"

Tyler paused in the doorway to the living room as his father's slowly spoken words drifted to him. His muscles tensed, and he contemplated lying, but that wasn't really his style. He had nothing to hide. He had…nothing.

He walked into the semi-dark room and stood at the foot of his father's bed. The light from the kitchen was just enough that he could see the deep frown in his father's forehead—and the accusation in his eyes. He'd decided at some point during his drunken sleep after Cade left that life without Lainey wasn't an option. His days without her were miserable. But the biggest thing he'd been trying to deny was that he loved her. Regardless of what happened here with his father, regardless of whether or not his father ever forgave him for leaving, he was going to fix things with Lainey. He was going to grovel if he had to.

"I said, where's Lainey?" His dad bit each word out.

Lainey. What the hell was he supposed to say? He'd treated the only woman he'd loved like garbage? He'd stood there and watched her heart break—he'd caused her heart to break—and let her walk out. No, he couldn't say that exactly.

This morning, he'd woken up with the worst hangover of his life. He'd dragged his ass out of bed and showered, deciding he needed to fix things with his father. He took a sip of the strong black coffee, hoping it would cure his throbbing head. "I don't know where she is."

"Why? What have you done?" His words weren't clear yet, but they were clear enough that Ty knew exactly what he'd said.

"She never told me about the money."

"Don't take it back. Don't take money from Lainey. She needs it," he choked, his voice thick and strained.

Shame washed through him, because his father actually believed that he'd take money from Lainey. "I know that. Of course I wouldn't take anything from her."

His father closed his eyes and gave a stiff nod.

Tyler stood at the end of his bed, not exactly ready to absolve his father of the fact that he'd basically told him he wasn't good enough for Lainey. "I let her go."

His father clenched the blanket with his strong hand. "It's too late for that. Too late to let her go. She loves you."

Just hearing that out loud, knowing that even his father recognized it, made his gut churn. "Lainey believes in the whole white-picket-fence thing. She believes in marriage and happily-ever-after."

They sat there glaring at each other until Ty felt too stifled to stand still any longer. He didn't owe him any explanations anyway. It was his own life.

"You're an idiot." His dad struggled to get the next words out, but finally he found his voice again. "Women like that don't come along more than once in a lifetime, Tyler."

He already knew how great she was. "Like Mom?"

His father nodded. "Yes."

"Then why didn't either of you tell me the truth

growing up? What the hell happened?"

His father shook his head, wincing. "She was young. Eighteen. He…coerced her."

Tyler hung his head and rubbed the back of his neck. So it was true. "Mom told you?"

His father raised his good hand. "That's all she'd say. She was young and inexperienced. He was older, a wrangler on one of the ranches. He took her out on a date, and she was in over her head. She didn't talk about it. I met her a month later. I knew she was for me the second I laid eyes on her. I never touched her beyond a kiss on the doorstep. She…she found out she was pregnant a month after we started courtin'. She told me what happened, scared out of her mind, thinking I'd leave her."

Ty blinked, trying to focus, seeing this man who'd raised him, really seeing him for the first time.

"I'd never leave her. I knew enough, even back then, to know she was above me, that I was the one getting the better end of the deal."

Tyler nodded, finding it hard to breathe against the heaviness in his chest. He knew his mother was the best; he'd just wanted to get his father to finally give him details. He clenched his hand around his mug. He wished he'd known when she was still alive. He wished he could have talked to her once more. But maybe it was better like this. Maybe this version was the better version for him. Maybe it was the way it was supposed to be.

"I didn't want her parents to know. Bad enough they thought I got her pregnant before we were married. She loved me, Tyler. And she loved you."

He stared at his father, the rough, slurred words

preventing him from moving another step. Something happened inside. Maybe a place that had been shut down eight years ago when he found out the truth slowly came back to life. He needed to turn away for a moment, from the emotion in his father's eyes. "Why didn't you ever tell me? When I was growing up, why didn't you tell me I wasn't yours?"

His father let out a huge sigh and raised his gaze toward the ceiling for a moment. "Your mother and I didn't want you growing up thinking you weren't wanted. Your mother lived with a lot of shame for what she perceived was her mistake, and she didn't want you to bear any of it. She loved you and always said you were the greatest gift she ever received."

His throat ached as he stared at the man he'd always thought of as his father. His chin wobbled, but there was steel behind those blue eyes. He didn't have words to describe the pain of everything. He didn't want to admit how much his father's final words had gutted him that night.

"I went looking for him," Tyler said. In some ways, he wished he'd never gone searching for his biological father, even though he knew he'd need to for closure.

"Thought you might."

Tyler ran a sweaty palm down the front of his jeans. "Didn't really give a shit about me."

"Don't matter, Ty. You are your mother's son. You're my boy." He took a deep breath. "I regretted every day what I said to you. I...I was lost without her. I swore to your mother I'd never tell you."

"She was wrong. Mom may have been pretty much perfect, but she was wrong about not telling me. I, uh…" He searched the right words to convey his emotions and struggled and stumbled trying to articulate what this man meant to him. Lainey would have known what to say, because she didn't hide from feelings. "I don't know how you could love another man's baby like your own. But I know you did. I know you must have done it because you loved Mom so much—I understand that now. I know you loved me like I was yours. I… Thank you."

His father ran his hand over his face, but not before Ty saw the tears. He glanced away, biting down hard on his back teeth, holding back his own emotions, before declaring, "You're my boy."

And that said it all. Tyler knew that the man in this bed was his father in all the ways that mattered. He knew it because it was *his* damn approval he sought, even after all these years.

He couldn't breathe for a moment as those words found all the places inside that had been closed off. For a second, he was a kid again, his father fixing his entire world for him. He needed to do the same for his father now. "I shouldn't have left for that long. I just let the hurt build. I tried to make sense of it. I thought I had been this burden to you your entire life."

His father held out his hand, and Tyler stared at it for a moment, that motion, that arm extending, offering him solace and safety as it had done his entire life. He slowly rounded the corner of the bed and took his father's hand in his. He knew he wouldn't always be able to do this. He stared into his eyes, blue eyes like his, and knew this time with him, however long was left, was time that he was going to savor. It would all slip away so fast. A lifetime in a season.

Ty pinched the bridge of his nose and fought the urge to cry like a damn baby. He took a deep breath as the weight lifted. "But I've got my head on right again. And, uh, I hate talking about this stuff."

His father laughed. "Me too. Let's stop this crying and shit."

"Agreed."

Neither of them said anything for a few minutes, but the silence was warm, like home. For the first time since he'd come back, it felt like home again.

"So what about Lainey?"

Ty gave a short laugh and sat on the chair beside the bed, stretching his legs out, suddenly more... optimistic. "I screwed up, Dad."

"I know. Why don't you want to marry that girl?"

Ty ran his hands down the front of his jeans, searching for the right words. Hell, he hadn't done this much talking with anyone besides Lainey. "I want to marry her. I just…"

"You're scared. You're afraid to need people again. After your mother."

Tyler groaned and ran his hands down his face. He had no idea his father knew him this well. "Thanks."

"You're no quitter and no chickenshit cowboy. You're made of steel, Tyler, just like I raised you." His dad's eyes begged him to understand. "And you do need people. You need all of us."

He nodded slowly.

His father's speech was a little less slurred, like the inability to get their past out in the open was a huge weight he had been carrying. "What the hell are you going to do without her? Just work here and go drinking with your two stupid friends?"

He smiled. "Well, when you put it like that…"

"Now see that tube over there?" he asked, pointing to a black tube leaning against the wall in the corner.

"Yeah."

"Open it."

"What is it?"

"Just open it."

He stared at it a moment and then knew, before he twisted off the cap, that it was from Lainey. He carefully pulled out the rolled-up paper. He paused for a second before unraveling it.

His stomach dropped as he stared at the painting. It was that day…when she'd forced him to pose for the camera…when he'd blown her off. But the man in the painting, him…that guy…the expression on his face, in his eyes…he had been staring at her with love and adoration. He hadn't even known it. But she had, she'd captured it, she'd painted him looking at her like she was his whole world. Not just her. The ranch, his home, too. Everything he loved was in that painting. She knew better than he did.

It had only taken him two weeks to figure out what she'd known all along.

He cleared his throat and slowly rolled it back up.

"She's very talented. She made you look pretty damn good."

Tyler let out a laugh. "Yeah."

"And the barn, the sway of the grass, the sky with those clouds moving through."

Tyler was having trouble concentrating on the conversation because the wheels in his head were turning. He knew what he needed to do. She had done everything for him without ever knowing it. He needed to do this for her. Before he went to ask her to take his sorry ass back, he needed to earn back Lainey's trust.

CHAPTER TWENTY

Lainey gazed out at her crowded diner, forcing herself to concentrate on feeding the customers and not on the tall, dark, handsome cowboy who had robbed her of her pride and her heart. Damn Tyler Donnelly. She had been in over her head with him. What had she been thinking? It was her fault, she realized, right from day one. She'd made him out to be this big, tough, but vulnerable cowboy who just needed someone to love him. She'd been the one approaching him, all the time. She'd allowed herself to get hurt.

She was a total idiot. She had painted a portrait of the man; could she get any more fangirl than that? He was out of her league. Next time she dated, she was going to find some nice church boy or something. Yes, a church boy, maybe one who went to bible study—not a badass cowboy.

She resisted the urge to get some of Tilly's emergency whiskey from the kitchen. The diner was too full for that. She followed her grandmother's advice and said a prayer as she took in the packed restaurant. The church ladies were here. Cade and Dean were deep in conversation at the counter. Pete was staring at the infamous "Leak" picture, as he now affectionately referred to it.

The doors burst open and Hope stormed through. Thank goodness. She hadn't seen her at all, between work and Sadie catching every bug at school. Hope paused for a second as she spotted Dean and then walked to the opposite end. Lainey met her, coffee carafe ready to serve. "I think you could use this," she said, handing her friend a mug.

"I could say the same about you," Hope said. "Any Tyler sightings?"

Lainey shook her head. "Nope, but then I'm not surprised."

Hope frowned. "Really? He hasn't been by at all?"

Lainey drummed her fingers against the counter. "Why would he? He's not coming around here. Ever, Hope. I told you—it's over."

Her friend gave a little shrug. "Never give up."

"I'm not going to waste any more time on him. I'm moving on with my life, remember?"

Hope nodded. "Of course, of course. I'm just saying to keep the faith."

Lainey glanced around the diner, not wanting to keep talking about Tyler and her friend's unwavering faith in the man.

Her mouth dropped open as Pete took the "Leak" painting off the wall along with the tag and walked toward her.

"Omigosh," Hope whispered as he approached.

"Well, Lainey, you sold your first paintin'," Pete said, handing her the tag.

She searched for something that wouldn't sound insulting and decided to just stick with, "Thanks, Pete."

He pulled out his wallet and counted from a large stack of bills. "You managed to remind this old cowboy about some of my better years. Well done, little miss."

Her heart squeezed as she caught the sheen in his eyes as he carefully picked up the canvas and walked out of her diner like he was carrying precious cargo. Her art had touched someone. It had meant something to someone. That was what she'd always wanted.

"Congratulations, little miss," Hope said, laughing and lifting her mug.

They watched Pete leave and smiled as he put the canvas in the back of his truck and drove away. "I can't believe it," Lainey whispered to Hope.

Hope smiled, her eyes sparkling. "I can. I'm not surprised one bit."

She was forced to get back to work as Father Andy signaled for a coffee refill. "I need to get back to work. Sit tight."

She crossed the diner and gave Father Andy a refill. She even had a little spring in her step as she walked across the diner. See, she didn't need Tyler. Better to stay busy and focused and not think of cowboys. Unfortunately, half the diner was filled with cowboy hats. And Ty's two best friends were sitting at her counter. She was trying to ignore them most of all.

"Lainey, you can't be mad at us because Tyler did something stupid," Cade said as she walked by.

She sighed and stopped, looking at the two handsome men. Why couldn't she have fallen for one of them? "I'm not mad at you. But…seeing you guys reminds me of him. I don't want to be reminded of him. In fact, I never want to see him again," she said, rounding the corner of the bar.

"I'd buy one of your paintings, but I don't really

have room for them," Cade said.

Lainey laughed. "You're sweet, despite the rumors, Cade. You don't have to buy one of my pictures."

"If you ever do one of the hospital, I'll buy it for my office," Dean said.

Cade scoffed. "Why would she want to paint a hospital?"

She left them to their arguing and popped into the kitchen to see if Betty was almost ready with Dean's and Cade's order so she wouldn't have to listen to them all day. She came out of the kitchen a moment later holding two large plates of lasagna, which had now made it onto the regular menu. She paused at the little commotion at the doorway.

She almost dropped the plates as she recognized the very fine butt in the low-slung jeans. Tyler's back was to her, and he was propping open the double doors and then slowly pulling his father's wheelchair up the two steps. *Move; just keep serving tables; don't just stand there.*

But she couldn't move, because when he turned the chair around and stood in her doorway, the softness in those blue eyes made her incapable of budging. The doors remained open, and the chatter in the restaurant slowly died down, everyone turning to stare at the two cowboys in her doorway. She hadn't seen him in weeks, and she thought that now that she had decided she despised him, he'd get less appealing. But he didn't. It wasn't fair. He was more appealing because he looked…tired and just as sad as she was.

"Lainey, pass the lasagna," Cade called out.

When she didn't move, he came over and took

the plates from her hands.

Martin sat tall and proud in his chair as he removed his hat and placed it on his lap. Ty took his off, slowly walking forward, running a hand through his hair. She forgot to breathe as he approached. "Hi."

She crossed her arms. "Sorry, we don't have any empty tables."

"I'm sorry, sweetheart," he said, his voice laced with tenderness, his handsome face serious. He stole all her smart comebacks, he stole all her defenses, he stole her heart, just like he'd done so many years ago inside this diner.

Her heart pounded painfully as she stood there, wishing and dreaming that he would somehow make this all right, that he had come to his senses. The crowded restaurant receded, and it was just her and Ty.

"I was an ass, Lainey."

He paused when someone clinked a glass and then a male voice said, "Hear, hear."

Judging by his frown and the direction of his gaze, it was Dean or Cade.

"I love you more than anything. I screwed up badly."

She couldn't cave this quickly. It wasn't enough. She deserved more. "You pushed me away. You told me hands off."

"For the record, I'd never say hands off to you, Lainey," Cade called out, his mouth full of lasagna. She shook her head.

Tyler flipped him the finger before turning his attention back to her. "I was wrong. Never again, I will never shut you out again. I love you. I knew it the first morning I came back to Wishing River and saw you here. You were right about everything. I am capable of change; you are worth it. If I could go back, I'd start over again. I'd make it right. I'd make it so I never shut you down, and I'd take away that last conversation we had."

"If you like it, then as the wise Beyoncé has said, you'd better put a ring on it!" one of the church ladies yelled out.

Tyler shook his head. Lainey was torn between laughing and crying.

She fidgeted with the string on her apron, trying to look cool and collected as he took another step closer to her. She could practically feel everyone in the place lean forward. Betty had come out from the back and was standing in the doorway of the kitchen. Lainey realized then just who they all were to her; as alone as she'd felt, complaining she didn't have a family, they were…they were all here, watching out for her, wanting the best for her.

"Lainey," he said, his voice thick and tender and making her toes curl. He raised his hand to cup her cheek, his callused thumb gently caressing her cheekbone. "I'm sorry I dismissed what you believe in and that I made you feel like you were wrong. You were right about everything; I was wrong. Your ideals, your morals, I admire them. It was me all along. I was too afraid of what I felt for you, what that would mean. I admire you for sticking to your principles and for holding out."

"Good boy, Tyler," Father Andy called out.

Tyler ducked his head, his jaw clenching. He looked up a moment later. "I want to be that man, the only man in your life. I want babies, I want a white picket fence, but more than anything, I want you."

"Tyler," she whispered, wondering if she'd held out long enough.

"I need you to hear me out because once I start, I know you're going to interrupt and yell at me."

She raised an eyebrow and tried not to let her worry show. "Why would I need to yell at you? What have you done, Ty?"

His grin widened, and he glanced over her shoulder and winked in Hope's direction. She twisted around to see her friend's expression, but Hope was blowing her nose in a napkin. What was going on?

Lainey turned back to Tyler. She had never seen him like this. He was a man who was usually pretty in control of his emotions—but she could honestly say the man appeared giddy right now. "Promise you'll hear me out and let me finish."

Then he up and ran out of the restaurant.

"Did you know he was into all this drama?" she heard Dean whisper to Cade.

"Do you know what he's up to?" she whispered to Martin.

He gave her a lopsided smile and a wink.

Tyler came back in, carrying the art tube she'd dropped off for his father.

Worry bubbled inside her chest. "Okay, go ahead."

"Last week, with the help of Hope, I contacted the art school in Italy."

She opened her mouth, but he held up his hand. She closed her eyes and counted to five.

"We sent them a copy of the painting."

"What painting?" she choked.

"*The Prodigal Cowboy*."

She ignored the snickers from his friends.

"Ty..."

He nodded. "They still want you."

"What?" she whispered. How could he have done this? "Even if I—"

His hand went up again. "Let me finish, remember?"

"Fine."

"You do the one-year program. They want you. You can start in January. That gives you enough time to prepare. You can set Betty up to manage the restaurant—you know she'll be able to run it for you. I'm here, too. I can check in a couple of times a week."

"You go girl!" Betty yelled.

She blinked back tears as a dozen or so questions and problems popped into her mind. What did that mean for them? He was okay with her leaving for a year? Did that mean he wanted to break up with her? Had she misread him this whole time?

"I can see the wheels turning at a crazy high speed over there, so let me finish," he said, his smile dipping and all humor leaving his eyes. He cleared his throat. "I did the math. I went over it with my dad, and we have the money. We have enough for flights and the school."

Tears flooded her eyes until he was blurry. "I can't take that," she said. "There's no way I can take that." It was the money again. It was ending their relationship. She had imagined the life she wanted existed outside Wishing River, but falling in love with Ty made her realize everything she ever wanted was right here. As long as he was here.

"Well, that's what people do for the people they love. For family. It's not about money—it never was."

She was shaking her head as he walked toward her. "Ty."

"Still not finished talking," he said, raising his arms and cupping the sides of her face with his hands. She sighed and closed her eyes, loving the feel of his strong, warm hands on her. "I want us to be a family."

Her eyes sprang open just in time to see him bending down on one knee.

"I was thinking we get married. Maybe we have our honeymoon in Italy. I'll fly out there at Christmas or you come back home. It's one year. I've waited a lifetime for you. We can get through one year." Before she could say anything, he signalled with his index finger to wait. He pulled something out of his pocket and held up a white-gold ring with filigree detailing and a diamond in the center.

"Before my mother died, she gave me her ring. She would have loved you. And I love you. I love you so much. Will you marry me, Lainey?"

She had no words; she just stared at him through blurred, watering eyes, not believing any of it. He'd planned this? He'd thought it through? He'd met with his father. He knew…he knew how much her art meant to her. In the beginning, she didn't think she'd ever get over how handsome of a man he was. But it was his heart that made her feel warm and safe and cherished. He was her family, the family she'd always wanted. And as much as they hadn't talked about the future, she knew they were meant to be together.

"I don't know what to say," she finally blurted out.

He lifted a brow. "Yes?" She watched in disbelief as he slipped the ring on her left hand, and it fit perfectly. He'd made all her dreams come true—even the ones she'd given up on.

She let out a surprised laugh. "Yes! Of course yes!"

He jumped up and grabbed her, lifting her against him. She buried her face in his neck, breathing him in, letting the moment fill her, wishing it would never end. She held on tighter as the cheers and hollers from the diner patrons surrounded them.

She didn't even care that they all watched. Tyler slowly lowered his head, and his lips found hers. He kissed her slowly, softly at first, almost reverently, as though he was a dream, as though all of it was a dream. When her hands scrunched a fistful of his shirt, he deepened the kiss, her head tilting back and her knees threatening to buckle. He applied a delicious pressure, a claim of sorts. She let go of his shirt and slid her hands up the hard contours of his chest, and his body filled in the gap, wrapping her up close. "I love you," she whispered against him.

"I love you, too. We can make this work. I'd do anything for you, Lainey. I know how talented you are, how you gave up your dreams for everyone else. I'm not going to be another person you give up your dreams for. I want to give you your dreams. I want to give you everything," he whispered, bending down to kiss her again. She kissed him back, tasting the truth of his words, the promises of their future.

"The only thing is that I say we don't wait too long till the wedding," he said, pulling back slightly to speak.

"Really? You don't want to wait until the summer and then go on our honeymoon right after?"

"Of course not. I'm not a fan of self-imposed torture."

She burst out laughing. "Fine. I agree with you," she whispered.

"Seriously?"

"I think it's a mutually beneficial arrangement."

"I'll make sure it is." He smiled against her lips before kissing her quickly again. "So, like, maybe next week?"

"I'm available!" Father Andy yelled out.

She smiled up at Tyler. "I think that's perfect."

EPILOGUE

Tyler stood at the altar of the church and tried to ignore his idiot best men as he gazed at the crowded room. He didn't even know this many people lived in Wishing River. He straightened his tie and cleared his throat, making sure everything was in working order.

He wasn't nervous about marrying Lainey—that was the one thing he *was* sure of. He just wanted everything to be perfect for her. The church was filled with white roses and candles. His gaze scanned the pews, taking in the usual suspects, and he knew:.All these people were here for Lainey. They were her family. His soon-to-be wife was a beloved member of the community. She was everyone's daughter, and they were all here to celebrate her big day.

He looked over at his father, who had insisted on sitting in a pew and not in a wheelchair for the service. He and Dean and Cade had made sure it happened. Mrs. Busby was sitting beside his dad, taking very good care of him, in between waving at Tyler and dabbing the corners of her eyes.

He knew they still had a few minutes, and he glanced over to where the candles were. A sensation washed over him, maybe a memory, maybe a sign. But he saw his mother standing there, holding his hand, telling him to put the quarter through the slot. He heard the flicker of the candle; he heard his voice begging her to let him light it. She did let him—after warning not to burn down the church.

He'd lit the candle, and she'd whispered that he say a prayer for whoever it was they were praying for that day. Ty swallowed hard and resisted the urge to go over there. She was gone. Lighting a candle wouldn't make her appear in the pew beside his father. It wouldn't bring her here to enjoy his wedding day.

He took a deep breath and tried to shake the feeling, the voice, the pull. He couldn't turn away from it, though. Even if there was the slightest chance she was calling to him, in whatever form, he knew he could never deny her. He surrendered to the instincts that pulled him and slowly walked over to the grouping of candles. He knew he didn't have a quarter in his suit but searched for one anyway. He stopped breathing for a moment as his fingers touched the coin in his pocket. He slowly pulled it out, not wanting to think about it, and placed it in the tin. He picked up the long match and lit it, knowing he'd light the white candle. He held his breath, and the candle lit immediately. It glowed strong and bright, and he talked to her…for the first time in years, prayed for her, his mother. He asked her to watch over them today, to be there with them today. A part of him felt foolish, almost childish for wishing those things, but he knew that his mother would have believed, and he knew Lainey believed, too. Maybe that was enough. He blinked back tears.

A hand touched his shoulder, and he turned to see Father Andy standing there. "She would have been very proud of you today."

Tyler shoved his hands in his pockets. "I think she would have been very happy to have Lainey in our family."

Father Andy smiled. "Very similar women. She would have loved her."

"I'm a lucky man."

Father Andy nodded, gripping his shoulder a little tighter. "You're a good man, too, and your mother knew that. I knew her very well, and she always spoke of you, always prayed for you, and as much as I remember that about her, I remember you, too. I remember the little boy who turned into a big boy and then a teenager and then a young man—I remember you bringing your mother to church, standing beside her, holding her hand, doing everything you could for her that last year. You made her so proud, Tyler."

He cleared his throat, surprised how deeply those words affected him. "Thank you."

"It's too late for confession," Dean called out from behind him. "Go wait for Lainey. It's time."

He took a deep breath, a calm peace settling over him as he walked back to the altar with Father Andy and Dean. Maybe he'd waited for this day his entire life. Maybe everything had led him here, to her, to Lainey.

He blinked, and suddenly she was there, at the back of the church, and he couldn't breathe because the reality of her, that she would be his wife, that they would be together for the rest of their lives, took it all away. She was smiling at him, the most beautiful woman he'd ever seen. Her hair fell around her shoulders, and her white dress clung to her curves, and despite the fact that he was standing in a church, he did allow himself to imagine taking that dress off later today.

Little Sadie appeared in front of Lainey, followed by Hope. Sadie started walking down the aisle. She was grinning at everyone in the pews as she sprinkled pink rose petals. Not that he really knew much about kids—or anything at all—but he had to say she was pretty adorable.

Hope started down the aisle behind her daughter, and Tyler happened to glance over at Dean and did a double take as he read the longing in his eyes, his gaze fixed on Hope. Dean caught him staring and then scowled at him.

Tyler gave him a slow grin, making a mental note to torture him later with his newfound knowledge.

After they took their places at the altar, everyone stood and turned to the back of the church. Lainey made her way down the aisle gracefully, her eyes on him only.

The faith shining in them, the faith in him, was humbling.

He knew this would be the last time she'd ever have to walk alone. He would be her family, her husband, her lover, and he would make sure that she knew she was loved and wanted every day they had together.

When she reached his side, he took her hands in his and leaned down to whisper in her ear. "You are so beautiful, Lainey. I love you. And I'm so glad I dropped out of the seminary."

Her eyes widened, and she laughed softly.

Father Andy took over the service, and pretty soon they were exchanging vows in front of their family and friends. He took a step closer to Lainey, framing her beautiful face with his hands, and gazed into her tear-filled eyes, right before he kissed her for the first time as her husband.

Tyler leaned down and whispered against her lips. "Thank you. Thank you for rescuing me." Then he kissed her with everything he had, all his promises, his hopes, his dreams for their future.

ACKNOWLEDGMENTS

I am overwhelmed as I try and write the acknowledgments for this book... I am deeply grateful to everyone at Entangled Publishing for bringing this book to life.

A special thank-you to Hang Le for creating not only a stunning cover but for capturing the very mood of this book and the heart and soul of these characters.

To Jessica Turner for your marketing expertise and for your patience and generosity in explaining and guiding me in this process. You are awesome to work with!

To Stacy Abrams for your thoughtful and insightful editing and comments... If we ever have the pleasure of meeting in person, I'll be buying you an umbrella. :)

To Jaime Bode and everyone else at Macmillan for your support and enthusiasm for this book.

To Curtis Svehlak, who I've had the privilege of working with on my last few books...thank you for always being on top of things but also for your cheerfulness! Every time you end your emails with, "Thank you SO much," it brings a smile to my face and makes me feel like I've accomplished something great. :)

To Heather Howland, who I know is a force at Entangled but I have never had the pleasure of directly working with, thank you for your tireless work, and I hope to meet you one day!

To Louise Fury at The Bent Agency, thank you for championing this book and for making my dreams come true.

To Liz Pelletier, thank you...for everything. It was always my dream to work with you, and despite some cringe-worthy edits that had me swinging back whiskey like the cowboys in this story, it has been an absolutely insightful journey. Thank you for managing to draw out the passion and the hearts of these characters with your incisive editing. I "look" forward to our next book together. ;)

To my husband, thank you for being my forever hero...thank you for driving through a snowstorm to print out my galleys and drive them back to the hospital with a coffee. You don't need a Stetson and a horse to steal this girl's heart.

As always, to my dear readers and hardworking book bloggers, thank you for your support, your reviews, and your emails. I treasure each and every one of them and try my best to give you the stories and the emotion you ask for. We are all kindred spirits, and I'm truly blessed to have your loyalty.

Thank you to the countless other people I have missed but who have had a role in making this book possible.

— Victoria xo

Fans of *Two Weeks Notice* will fall
in love with *Nothing But Trouble*,
the hilarious and romantic first in
USA Today bestselling author
Amy Andrews's new Credence series!

Read on for an excerpt...

CHAPTER ONE

*T*here were some days Cecelia Morgan would gladly shove her boss off the top of Mile High Stadium in downtown Denver. This was one of them. Wade "The Catapult" Carter may be QB royalty, but he was lousy at relationships. *Allergic* to them, actually. And today, like so many days, that was a giant pain in *her* ass.

"But I thought he really liked me," came the forlorn voice of another jilted Wade Carter conquest.

"Of course he did."

CC straightened her pen and her drink coaster as she sipped on her Red Bull. Comforting slightly hysterical women was all part of her job description, and she'd become a pro. This one's name was Annabel. CC knew that, because Annabel had called her frequently the last few weeks chasing Wade. God forbid he should ever give out *his* cell number.

Plus, she'd supplied it to the florist this morning. The florist who had a standing order for a letting-her-down-gently floral arrangement. And a drawer full of cards that all said the same thing.

I've enjoyed our time together. Unfortunately, I can't commit to further dates. Thanks for your company. —WC

For crying out loud—the man didn't even personalize it with his full damn name!

"He took me to that flashy new restaurant three

nights ago. You don't take just *anyone* there, CC. *There's a waiting list.*"

CC stifled a sigh. Waiting lists didn't matter when you were more famous than God *and* John Denver in Broncos country. Celebrity opened doors. Wade didn't use his obnoxiously, but he didn't have to.

People knew who he was.

Restaurants ushered him to tables, fancy watch companies sent him *exclusive timepieces*, car salesmen handed over keys.

And women opened their legs.

"Oh God." There was a long groan on the other end of the line. "He was just using me for sex, wasn't he?"

CC blinked at Annabel's candor. She drew in a deep breath and thought about a warm SoCal beach. The Pacific Ocean. Blond surfer dudes with tans and abs.

Six months. Just six more months.

No more twenty-four seven availability. No more midnight runs to the nearest gas station for Wonka Nerds. No more phone calls from emotional women she barely knew.

Technically, after the call from her broker this morning, she could walk her ass out of his apartment right now. She had all the money she needed—she didn't need any more of his. But she'd signed a contract, and Wade's lawyers did not screw around. She'd seen them in action too often. "Wade doesn't discuss his dates with me."

CC stuck to the company line instead of saying what she wanted to say, which was, *Ya think?* And also, *Weren't you using him, too? Bagging a famous jock for some social capital?*

Bragging rights with the gal pals?

Because she knew Wade would have given Annabel the usual spiel up-front. He didn't go out with any woman unless he had.

He wasn't interested in anything more than a few dates.

He wasn't interested in anything long-term.

He wasn't interested in a wife.

How many times had she heard Wade say that either over the phone or face-to-face? "Don't fall for me, darlin'. I don't do past next week."

And as much as CC really hated this part of her job and she thought Wade needed to stop treating the women of the world like he was in a candy shop and they were the buffet, he was always up-front with them.

Always.

But…as usual, there were some who thought they'd be different.

They'd be the one.

"Don't get me wrong—it was really freaking awesome sex. I mean…holy cow, CC, that man knows things about a woman's body. Like, *knows* things."

Oh God! Palm trees. Seagulls. The sound of the surf.

"He does this thing with his tongue—"

"Ooookay!" CC was quick to interrupt.

Too. Much. Information. CC might pretty much run Wade Carter's life, but there were some things she just didn't want to know about the man. Some things you just couldn't *un*hear.

"I'm telling you, that man has *stamina*."

Well, yes. He'd been the star quarterback of the Broncos for thirteen years. There were three Super Bowl rings in his safe to prove it. He had stamina.

Throw the man a parade.

"Okay, well, thank you for calling."

"No. Wait! *CC?*"

CC sighed. She'd never perfected the art of the polite hang-up. Wade was excellent at it, but these women broke her heart.

"*You* know the man. What did I do wrong? What could I have done differently?"

A humorless laugh rose in CC's throat, and she quashed it ruthlessly. What could she have done differently?

How about not putting out?

It was that simple. Her boss was a man—one with stamina and apparently crazy-good skills with his tongue she *did not want to know about*. One who used sex for recreation with absolutely no intention of follow-through.

In other words, he was a total, unashamed, card-carrying horn dog.

What did a woman do differently with such a man? How did she get *that* guy's attention? She said the one thing Mr. Hotshot Quarterback wasn't used to hearing. The one word women just didn't say to His Royal Sexiness.

No.

Sure. He might walk away without doing *that thing he did*. But it might just make him work a little harder, too.

Seriously, what was wrong with these women?

She'd known treat-them-mean, keep-them-keen

since she was six years old. But maybe that was just a result of having five older, very protective brothers.

Not that she'd had a chance to treat anyone mean since she'd taken up this job. Being Wade Carter's PA-cum-*slave* for the last five and a half years had pretty much decimated her social life and killed her sex life dead.

Not only did Wade always know where she was, thanks to that annoying app he insisted she install on her cell, he was also uncannily attuned to when she was about to get lucky in her rare moments of free time. It was like he'd shoved an estrogen monitor under her skin one day when she'd been too exhausted to protest and rang her when it hit the red zone.

"CC?"

CC dragged her attention back to the woman waiting on the other end of the phone. She should have pulled out her usual line about not discussing Wade with anybody. But she didn't. There was something in the pitch of Annabel's voice that tugged at CC's heartstrings.

She sighed as she fingered the neat stack of Post-its sitting at an exact right angle to her pen. "Annabel, you're perfect just the way you are. Don't change for any man, okay?"

And she hung up the phone, thunking her forehead against the desk. That was it. She was done. She couldn't do it anymore. Deal with Wade's women. She *wouldn't*. And, thanks to her windfall, she didn't *have* to anymore. Yesterday, she hadn't had quite enough money to leave. Today—she did.

It was as simple as that.

It was time. Time to go. Not in six months, not at the end of her contract. *Now*.

CC pulled her head off the desk, cheered by the thought. She was…free. She smiled and then she grinned. She could just…walk away. A laugh pressed itself against her vocal chords and she gave it voice.

Of course, Wade *could* be an asshole about it, and the thought of his lawyers sobered her laughter. She had to be smart about this, *really* smart. So, as tempting as it was to walk in there and tell him to shove his job and his women up his ass—and it was *sooo* tempting—it was *not* the way to approach the situation.

She had to pick her moment. She had to be composed and reasonable. State her intentions with clarity and sincerity and calmly hand in her notice. Appeal to him for understanding. Assure him she'd find him a top-notch replacement.

Hold his damn man-baby hand a little bit longer…

But it *had* to be today because her mind was made up and frankly, one more weepy phone call was going to see her spiking her Red Bull with vodka. And CC had no intentions of making a side trip to rehab on her way to California.

*W*ade glared at the blinking cursor on the blank screen. It'd been doing that for the last three hours. Sitting there. Blinking. Defying him. Calm.

Not too many things defied Wade Carter. Mostly, they just saw him coming and got out of his way. Everything from a three-hundred-pound linebacker to a three-hundred-pound hog.

Well…everything except his mother. His PA. And this fucking annoying cursor.

When he'd been approached by a publishing house immediately after his retirement three years ago to write a book about his life, he'd dismissed it out of hand. But so many people had asked for his memoir since—fans and sports commentators and NFL execs—that he'd started to think about it seriously. The publishing house, who had coughed up a million-dollar advance, had offered to get a ghostwriter, but Wade had refused.

He might not have graduated summa cum laude, but he was capable of writing his own story. He'd read all the great American classics and could get his head around algebra. He'd actually been a reasonable student—he just hadn't seen the point wasting time inside the classroom when he could be out on the field, where his true vocation lay.

And now, here he was. Just him and the cursor.

Wade had no idea why it was taking him so long to write the first word. He and CC had prepared copious, detailed notes about his life and career to be included in the book.

But he didn't know where to start.

Where was he *supposed* to start? At the beginning? Back on the hog farm in Credence? Or when he started playing college ball for the CU Buffs? Or when he was drafted by the Denver Broncos? He'd had a long and illustrious career in the NFL before his knee had blown out for the last time a few years back.

And yet he couldn't figure out where to start.

He glanced up from his screen, seeking inspiration through the floor-to-ceiling windows throwing summer light into his office. From his penthouse vantage point, he could see the gleaming curves of the horse-shoe-shaped bowl belonging to Mile High—or whatever the hell it was called these days—and, even now, he could still hear the roar of the crowd inside his head.

Behind the stadium, in the distance, stood the jagged outline of the Rocky Mountains. They rose majestically—strong and indomitable. As strong and indomitable as the spirit within Mile High on game night.

It was a view that always awed him. The juxtaposition of the modern and the ancient, the man-made and the natural. These two great megaliths had shaped him, and the sight of them both humbled and strengthened him.

It was inspirational stuff. Except today. Today he had nothin'.

He groaned as he plonked his head on the desk, disturbing one of the many piles of neatly stacked papers CC had meticulously printed out and compiled, each marked with Post-its and labeled clearly in her legible, no-nonsense handwriting.

That handwriting irritated him more than usual right now.

"You should have gotten a ghostwriter."

Wade lifted his head off the desk and shot an annoyed look at his PA lounging in his open doorway. She was in her regulation blue jeans. She always wore jeans, whether it was cold enough for them or not. It'd been one of the few things she'd insisted on when she'd agreed to be his PA almost six years ago—no more ridiculous corporate wear.

Today, she'd teamed it with a red stripy T-shirt. She thought it made her look Parisian. He thought it made her look like a tiny, female version of *Where's Waldo*.

"There is nobody more equipped than *me* to write about *me*."

Wade tried and failed to keep the exasperation out of his voice. It was the same argument he'd had with the publisher. And won. And he was in no mood to have it with CC—again.

"Yes. But." A slice of her mahogany bangs fell across one eye, and she brushed it away. She wore it longer than the rest of her hair, which was super short and choppy all over. "Writing is a different skill than throwing a ball."

Leave it to CC to point out the fucking obvious. But still, Wade hated how this was already kicking his ass. He succeeded at everything he did. Nothing defeated The Catapult.

Not even the blinking cursor of doom.

"So I should spend weeks talking to someone else so they can tell my story?"

"Sure, why not?" She shrugged. "You do like talking about yourself."

Wade grunted as he returned his attention to the screen. "Why do I pay you so much money, again?"

"Because I'm the only PA on the face of the planet who doesn't quit after you wake me at three in the morning to go and buy you Nerds and condoms."

He grinned at the memory. Yeah, she'd been *really* pissed about that. But it'd been the deal they'd made. Six years of twenty-four seven. He paid her a shitload of money—because he could afford it and a good PA was worth their weight in gold—and her time was his. *All* of it.

"That was an emergency."

She folded her arms. "Your apartment burning down is an emergency."

Wade laughed. He loved how CC didn't try to flatter him *or* pussyfoot around. And he appreciated it. She was like a cranky, bossy older sister—except at thirty-two, she was six years younger than him. His mother always said men needed someone to call them on their horseshit.

Well, his mother never said "horseshit" because not even forty-plus years in rural Colorado could coax the southern Texas lady out of her. But when she said balooey, they all knew what she meant.

CC wandered into his office. "I also don't complain when I have to provide regular phone counseling to distraught women."

Wade flicked his gaze up from the damn blinking cursor. "It sounds like you're about to, though."

"Seriously, Wade." She sighed as she pulled to a stop on the opposite side of his desk, crossing her arms under her breasts.

She totally wasn't his type. He was the full jock cliché—into tall, busty blondes. And CC was his PA, and he'd promised her all those years ago, when he'd seen her knee her then-boss in the balls for making a pass, that he would *never, ever* go there with her.

But you couldn't beat biology. He was a man; he was genetically wired to notice boobs.

"Just give them your damn cell number already."

CC seemed testier than usual, but she was hardly a ray of sunshine at the best of times. He shook his head. *Hell no.* Being able to abdicate all the unpleasant things was one of the perks of being seriously fucking rich. "Annabel?"

"Yes. Annabel. And before that, it was Chrissie. And before that, Shondra."

Yeah. He'd been picking some doozies lately. It didn't seem to matter how many times he told the women he took to his bed that he wasn't looking for a wife—they were getting more determined. It had taken a lot of fun out of dating. And frankly, he was wondering if dating was more trouble than it was worth.

For him *and* CC.

Between women and this book, he was going a little stir-crazy. Maybe he was losing his mojo?

"Can't you be a little more…discerning?"

He propped his feet up on his desk and raised his arms to tuck his hands behind his head, the back of his chair reclining slightly. "What can I say? Women like me." Then he smiled that smile he knew would make her roll her eyes.

She didn't disappoint. He half expected her to mimic a gag reflex, but she opened her mouth to speak, instead, her face suddenly intent and serious as she took a step closer to his desk. "Do you have a moment to discuss something, Wade?"

Wade didn't like the sound of that. The last time she'd been this serious, there'd been a major Nerd shortage two Christmases ago. Thankfully his cell rang, cutting her off, and he grabbed it quickly, holding up his hand, indicating for her to hold her thought. He couldn't cope with a Nerd shortage and the blink, blink, blink of the cursor taunting him from the screen. Noticing the word "Mom" displayed on the screen, he pushed back in his chair again. Few people had this number. His parents, his brother, some old NFL buddies, and CC.

He put her on speaker. "Hey, Mom."

"Wade." The soft lilt of her southern accent was as soothing as it'd always been. "How's my baby?"

CC rolled her eyes again, and Wade stifled a laugh. He was thirty-eight years old, filthy rich, and about as close to sporting royalty as was possible for an ex-quarterback to be, but he'd always be her baby.

"Same old, same old."

"Staying outta trouble?"

"Always," he said and ignored CC's not-so-quiet snort.

"You're going to church?"

"Every Sunday."

CC mouthed, *You're going to hell*, and Wade grinned.

His mother laughed, obviously not fooled. "Well, now listen, darlin', don't go getting all worked up, just calling to let you know your dad had a bit of a... funny turn, and he's in the hospital."

Wade sat up abruptly, his feet hitting the floor with a *thud*. "What kind of a funny turn?"

His father was as strong as an ox, but he was almost seventy. Sure, Wyatt, his older brother, did most of the heavy lifting on the farm these days, but his dad was still in the thick of it.

Why in hell hadn't Wyatt contacted him?

CC took two steps closer to the desk, her forehead furrowed, her cell already out of her pocket.

"He went all dizzy and short of breath yesterday. He had some kind of arrhythmia or something. But Doc McNally sent him to Denver to be sure, and the heart specialist here says he needs a pacemaker."

"A pacemaker?"

Wade felt a little dizzy himself. And maybe like throwing up. His father had something wrong with his *heart*. His father, who'd first tossed a ball to Wade when he'd been three years old.

"You're at St. Luke's?"

"Now, darlin', there's no need to rush over; your father's right as rain. Cussin' up a storm."

"I'll be there in twenty."

Wade hung up, pushing to his feet, meeting CC's gaze. "Fuck."

She nodded. CC's father had walked out on her mother when she was three, and she'd made damn sure Wade had kept in close contact with his since she'd been in his employ. Three days ago, a Post-it on his desk in the morning had reminded Wade it was his father's birthday. And he'd gotten distracted and forgotten to call.

Fuck.

"Just ordered an Uber. It'll be here in five."

He shook his head. "I'll drive." It'd give him something to do. Something to concentrate on.

"Okay. I'll cancel." Her thumbs got busy on her cell. She glanced up from the screen. "Go."

Her urging sliced into his inertia. Right. Yes. *Go.* And he was moving. "Send me some info on pacemakers."

"Already on it."

Of course she was. "I'll call from the hospital."

"Yep," she said, not looking up from her cell.

He was at the door when CC called his name. He turned back in time to intercept a packet of Nerds she'd just pulled from her pocket and tossed in his direction. He caught them in his right hand, out of pure instinct, the packet rattling with familiar, sugary goodness.

"Thanks."

She nodded dismissively, but she was all intent again as she watched him, which put an unpleasant itch up his spine. He had a feeling whatever she wanted to talk about was way more serious than a Nerd shortage, and he could only cope with one crisis at a time.

Wade did not multitask. That's why he had CC.

Thank God.

IF YOU ENJOYED THIS EXCERPT, LOOK FOR
NOTHING BUT TROUBLE
WHEREVER BOOKS AND EBOOKS ARE SOLD.

An emotional, touching story for fans of Nicholas Sparks...

"A stunning, emotional romance."

—Jill Shalvis, *NYT* bestselling author

"Yarros' novel is a deeply felt and emotionally nuanced contemporary romance…"

—*Kirkus* starred review

"*The Last Letter* is a haunting, heartbreaking and ultimately inspirational love story."

—*InTouch Weekly*

"I cannot imagine a world without this story."

—Hypable

She's just one of the guys…until she's not in USA Today *bestselling author Cindi Madsen's unique take on weddings, small towns, and friends falling in love.*

JUST ONE OF THE GROOMSMEN

by Cindi Madsen

Addison Murphy is the funny friend, the girl you grab a beer with, and the girl voted most likely to start her own sweatshirt line. She's perfectly fine answering to the nickname "Murph," given to her by the tight-knit circle of guy friends she's grown up with. Time has pulled them all in different directions, like Tucker Crawford, who left their small town to become some big-city lawyer, and Reid, who's now getting hitched.

Naturally the guys are all going to be groomsmen, and it wouldn't be the same without "Murph" in the mix. The fact that ever since Tucker's return to town, she can't stop looking at him and wondering when he got so hot is proof that she needs to mix things up. She'd never want to ruin a friendship she's barely gotten back, but the more Addie comes out of her tomboy shell, the more both she and Tucker wonder if there's something more there…

Don't miss one of NPR's "Perfect Sweater-Weather Romances"...

WHAT WERE YOU THINKING, PAIGE TAYLOR?

by Amanda Ashby

After her carefully ordered world imploded, Paige Taylor cracks up. On her tenth self-help book, it seemed like a good idea at the time to reinvent herself—move from Manhattan to the tiny beachside town of St. Clair—and take over the local bookstore.

But instead of discovering her spiritual Nirvana, she's neck-deep in a floundering business, the locals treat her like a plague victim, and her mom's suddenly decided to visit—with no end in sight— and keeps coming home with one surprise after the next.

Added to that pot of crazy, the one guy who sets her pulse racing has sworn off women forever. He's got a Samsonite filled with baggage, but damn he looks good hauling it down the street. And giving her those sexy half-smiles. And tempting her to take him for a test ride.

Soon Paige discovers that reinventing herself takes more than just a change of address and a pithy quote on Instagram. She needs to face the truth about her life, and that's something she can't do alone.

THE HONEYMOON TRAP

by Christina Hovland

How to Survive Your Next
Relationship Disaster 101

Step 1: Get pumped. Your new house, in your new town, comes with a sexy and shirtless man next door. Score!

Step 2: Don't let your freak-out show when Mr. OMG Shirtless turns around—and it's your old crush.

Step 3: Hold your head high when you run into him again on the first day of your new job—literally— and spill coffee all over yourself.

Step 4: Stay calm when he introduces himself as your new boss…and then announces that your first assignment is to go on a fake honeymoon together.

Step 5: Keep your $h*t locked tight when the new boss/old crush and you are forced to sleep in the same room…with one bed.

Step 6: Try to ignore just how freaking hot he is, and how much you want to touch him…

AMARA
an imprint of Entangled Publishing LLC